'What a thoroughly entertaining read! A classic and hugely satisfying story of a family in all its rights and wrongs, sins and quirks, bickering and love. *Good Good Loving* is emotional, thoughtful, profoundly human, wise and good good fun'
Bidisha

'This is a story steeped in displacement, in the ache of leaving family and land behind, and it doesn't flinch from the heartbreak of internalized misogyny and pain that cuts across generations. The characters are flawed, stubborn, and absolutely *infuriating*, but you feel such tenderness towards them. And just when the story guts you, it turns around and makes you laugh'
Ishi Robinson, author of *Sweetness in the Skin*

'A comic masterpiece, as funny as it is heartbreaking. Brilliantly structured, the narrative twists backwards through time like a corkscrew. A large cast of exuberant characters burst out of the pages and into your heart. Original, warm, compassionate, angry, and unforgettable, this is Yvvette Edwards' best book yet'
Sally-Anne Lomas, author of
Live Like Your Head's on Fire

Good Good Loving

Yvvette Edwards

Virago

VIRAGO

First published in Great Britain in 2026 by Virago Press

1 3 5 7 9 10 8 6 4 2

Copyright © Yvvette Edwards 2026

The moral right of the author has been asserted.

All characters and events in this publication, other than those clearly in the public domain, are fictitious and any resemblance to real persons, living or dead, is purely coincidental.

All rights reserved.
No part of this publication may be reproduced, stored in a retrieval system, or transmitted, in any form, or by any means, without the prior permission in writing of the publisher, nor be otherwise circulated in any form of binding or cover other than that in which it is published and without a similar condition including this condition being imposed on the subsequent purchaser.

A CIP catalogue record for this book
is available from the British Library.

Hardback ISBN 978-0-349-01969-7
Trade paperback 978-0-349-01970-3

Typeset in Garamond by M Rules
Printed and bound in Great Britain by
Clays Ltd, Elcograf S.p.A.

Papers used by Virago Press are from well-managed forests
and other responsible sources.

Virago Press
An imprint of
Little, Brown Book Group
Carmelite House
50 Victoria Embankment
London EC4Y 0DZ

The authorised representative
in the EEA is
Hachette Ireland
8 Castlecourt Centre
Dublin 15, D15 XTP3, Ireland
(email: info@hbgi.ie)

An Hachette UK Company
www.hachette.co.uk

www.littlebrown.co.uk

*In memory of my much-loved great-aunts,
Windrush sisters*

*Helen Josephine Molyneux
Susanna Elizabeth Molyneux
Virgie Rosalind Skerritt*

For Ashton, Hugo and Ayla, other much-loved peeps

The End

January 2020

Ellen didn't have the energy to open her eyes, but wasn't worried about that, because she didn't want to. What she did mind was not being able to close her ears. It felt very unfair to be so completely mentally alert while she was lying there on her hospital bed trying to await a peaceful passing. Her hearing was perfectly intact, and as a consequence she was forced to endure the never-ending discussions about the mass of her failings – which felt very unfair indeed. Even Miss Gloria, who she hadn't seen for – what, eighteen years? – had passed by that morning, her mouth full-up of lies, telling the nurses she'd come to say a private goodbye, then as soon as they'd left the room, letting Ellen know exactly how high she'd held her up in her stomach all that time, like anything that happened to her had been down to Ellen.

She was sure that listening to everyone's grudges before

she went wasn't supposed to be part of the process. Didn't people normally have to die first in order to discover the truth about what people really thought of them? Come back as jumbies and hover invisibly about the place eavesdropping? And that's not even to mention how fed up of waiting she'd become. There wasn't long to go, of that she was certain, but she'd had enough and was ready, boy was she ready, Lord she was ready, and had been for what felt like an unreasonably long time.

She wasn't concerned about where she was headed, if she really was headed anywhere at all, Up or Down, though it seemed to her that most of her life had already been spent in hell and as a consequence, she should be headed upwards by default. If that was the case, she'd be quite content, not about eating honey and ambrosia pudding for the rest of eternity – she wasn't sure that would sit well with her diabetes, whether dying wiped out all pre-existing conditions including the ones that had ultimately finished her off. No, it wasn't the food she was interested in, it was the opportunity to finally get a few things off her chest around a number of unanswered prayers, quite a number in fact, though to be fair, most were related to the same subject. She was looking forward to that very much. And to finally being reunited with Clay.

Someone cleared their throat, then said, 'Bad-mind.'

It was CJ's voice, impossible not to recognise, because he had his father's voice, had always had Clyde's voice. Even before CJ's voice had broken, it had that same mellow tone and gravelly bass as his father's. It always astonished Ellen that both her husband and her son were musically tone deaf, neither able to sing a note in tune if their lives depended on it, because, when you heard them speak, you just imagined they'd be incredible singers, Barry Whites. In fact, Clyde's voice had been the first thing that had attracted her to him.

'What she did to dad, man.' It was Claudette's voice, Ellen's first born.

'No one can forget that,' said Joycelyn, the daughter who had arrived next.

'I can't stop thinking about him crying ...' said Claudette.

'Saying *Ellen, Ellen, Ellen*,' said Joycelyn.

'He loved her hard,' said Claudette.

'Even though she done him bad,' said Joycelyn.

There was a pause, then, 'Proper bad-mind,' CJ said.

Ellen was happy CJ had spoken, because like his father, he always had to have the last word and now he had, everyone was quiet and with any luck, might stay that way. When she thought about all she'd done for the hard-back adults in the room about her, all of whom she still thought of as kids and would probably always think of as kids till the day she died – literally any moment – the sacrifices she'd made for every last ungrateful one of them, it was hard to believe she'd raised such a pack of backbiters, though this was hardly breaking news, as they'd betrayed her many times before, and though today's words hurt, they were nothing in comparison with hurts from the past, some of which stood out very sharply in her mind, times they'd sided with the enemy and cut her too deep for it to ever entirely heal over. But then they were their father's children, the three of them, always had been, always would be.

And of course they were their father's children. How could they not be? All born in November, Claudette first, then Joycelyn a year and a day later, then CJ close behind, a week short of one year after his sisters, three kids in three years, all born in Montserrat and all conceived in February when Valentine's Day and Clyde's birthday were separated by seven days, though Valentine's Day had nothing to do with all that February nookie. Back home, Valentine's Day arrived and departed like any other passing day. Clyde hadn't ever bought her flowers or chocolates – *or champagne!* – to celebrate it and that had been okay because even if Ellen had been aware of the existence of Valentine's Day, she'd never been much of a romantic. She had her mother to thank for that, Mrs Silcott, the person who'd left her behind with a neighbour for eight years after she left Montserrat and went to work in Curaçao, then returned and when she came to collect her, stared at Ellen and said, 'That's not what I was expecting.' Yes, that same Mrs Silcott had helped Ellen to cast off any romantic notions she might have somehow managed to cling on to despite the complete lack of fantasy in her childhood.

No, Valentine's hadn't been the cause of her and Clyde having all that good-good loving in February; it was Clyde's birthday one week earlier, and it was all birthday nookie. Even though Ellen had always been the kids' main carer, the person who'd fed and clothed, sent for and raised them, who'd nursed them through their illnesses, attended their parents' evenings and checked they'd done their homework; even though she had always been the one who, for the most part, had kept the roof over their heads and their bellies full, they were their father's children – and how could they not be when their very beginnings, their actual conception, had been for his pleasure?

'I went to the house this morning. It's like it's dead. There's no heart there any more.' That was Dumpling's voice, the fifth and final child, born after Clay. Now those two had more in common than anyone could have guessed and not just because they were the *English kids*, the only siblings to arrive after she and Clyde had left Montserrat and were settled in the UK. Dumpling was a genuine Valentine's baby, red-skinned and the prettiest, the only one of the girls she had spoiled. She was born in the early hours of Valentine's Day, not even a full day old when the family were gathered in the kitchen, staring down at her where she lay in Ellen's arms, wrapped up in her baby blanket like a bunch of flowers.

'Her cheeks,' Claudette had said. 'Just like little dumplings.' And that was it; everyone called her Dumpling from that moment. Even after Clyde had decided on an official name – Francesca, which Ellen hated, though she'd done her duty and gone with Clyde to the Registry Office to enter it onto the birth certificate – everyone carried on calling her Dumpling, and still did now though she was forty and pregnant with her third child; heavily pregnant, and when Ellen said *heavily* pregnant, she meant that Dumpling was far advanced into her pregnancy and also that she was a lot heavier.

Ellen doubted Dumpling was suddenly being careful about what she ate, because Dumpling had always done and eaten whatever she fancied, and as a consequence she'd always been a little on the weighty side and each of her pregnancies had permanently added to an already heavy frame, which wasn't a good start to keeping a husband happy. In fact, scratch the 'happy', it wasn't a good start to keeping a husband full stop. And then perhaps because this was a very-very near-death experience which meant, Ellen realised, that she had a very-very limited amount of time left to be truthful, she allowed herself to acknowledge that in reality she knew precisely jack shit either about keeping husbands happy or keeping them full stop. Forty-nine years of marriage hadn't qualified her to give advice to anyone on either of those subjects. Really, she should simply say *Dumpling should mind what she's eating* and leave it at that.

All the family already knew the baby was going to be a girl, which was a little disappointing because there were already plenty of girls in the family, but you had to be grateful for what you got, Ellen supposed, and just hope they were healthy and had the right number of bits in all the right places. She couldn't imagine her newest granddaughter would be named after her, despite the fact she would clearly arrive around the time of Ellen's departure, and she was heartily glad of it. She hoped for a luckier life for all her grandchildren than the duff hand she'd been dealt.

'I just wanna sell it and move on,' CJ said.

'You not gonna extend the kitchen first?' Claudette asked.

'You did say you were gonna do an extension,' Joycelyn said.

'I am,' CJ said. 'S'gonna cost twelve grand, but'll add forty to the value. I'm gonna take out the wall the back door's on and extend the kitchen out. Then put folding doors across the whole back so all you see's garden.'

'That's the one thing you've gotta give her,' said Claudette. 'Eden.'

'She always kept a nice garden,' Joycelyn said.

Ellen allowed herself the indulgence of picturing her garden which, other than Clay, was the only thing in her life that had ever responded positively in direct proportion to the love and attention she'd lavished upon it. If it did turn out that she was headed Up, she'd be very interested to see how that garden compared with her own – assuming there was an actual garden up there and not just a great hall with a magnificent floor covered wall to wall in white shagpile. Eden had been plainly laid to lawn for decades up until 1986, the year Clyde moved out of the family home and in with Icylda, who subsequently chucked him out six months later after he cheated on her with another woman – like after the way Icylda stole Clyde from Ellen, she thought she could then teach the old dog to sit *and* stay! On the night of the day he'd packed his case and left, after Ellen had gone to bed, she'd thought two things: one, that she would never fall asleep and two, that she might just remain in bed and never get up out of it again. However, not only did she fall asleep, but she woke with a yearning from nowhere that demanded satisfaction, a craving to create, to nurture something simple, so she got up, went downstairs, made herself a cup of tea, then somehow ended up in the garden where she stood, mug in hand, taking in the large bland space. She finished the tea, went shopping, and on her return dug up an oval-shaped piece of lawn across the back and planted the six rosebushes that were still the pride of her garden today, in a mixture of colours; red, peach, orange, salmon, pink and yellow, a near full palette of the colours of the early-evening sunset she'd viewed so many times from the beach at Montserrat's Carr's Bay. Many days she'd carried a cushion outside into the garden for comfort while she sat on her bench and simply lost herself in them, filled her eyes and mind and chest with their beauty and lush heady fragrance. For a time she was obsessed with colour in the garden, adding those plants that flowered most prolifically or for the longest period or bore the biggest blooms, but Clay helped her discover green, to find peace in it, beauty in the breadth of its hues.

That had been the beginning and her garden had evolved over the years to what it was now – assuming someone had been looking after it while she'd been in the hospital – a block of paradise outside the back of her home that was so beautiful the family had named it Eden. Though it was the height of bad taste for her son and daughters to be discussing the remodelling of her home in her hearing, before she'd actually died and they'd inherited it, Ellen couldn't believe it had never occurred to her to put glass across the back wall herself. She imagined what it would have looked and felt like sitting in her kitchen and having a panoramic view directly onto the garden. It would have been like sitting in her beloved garden itself.

Then Dumpling said, 'I'd dig all them plants up. Concrete over 'em. Too much work. S'a full-time job.'

Ellen felt her heartbeat quickening, heard that quickening echoed in the sudden escalation of the monitor's bleeping and wondered if this was it, her final moment, her death precipitated by words from the mouth of the child she had nurtured best wanting to murder the thing she'd loved most. It felt like she was hearing everything at a distance: Claudette calling for help, the room door being thrown open, the medical people entering, asking the family to step outside, checking her, pulling her eyelids open to expose her pupils one after the other to what should have been an unbearable light. She felt the cool air of the room against her chest as the doctor pulled her gown apart and the cooler disc of the stethoscope placed at the edge of a breast and a soft but even cooler alcohol wipe preparing a space on the inside of her right arm, then the injection needle's prick. Almost immediately she began to feel calmer and heard that calm echoed in the slowing of the bleeping as the drugs took effect. She knew she was DNR but she also knew they would do everything to ensure she was comfortable when she passed and she hoped that was what was happening now, that this was it, the End, and the possibility overwhelmed her with relief. She hadn't heard her mother's voice in years and though she listened intently for it, mercifully, she heard nothing. Had they been open, she would have closed her eyes. Consciously, she said goodbye. Her final thought was *Clay!*

When she awoke, she knew she was still alive because she could clearly remember the dream she'd had, so vivid she'd been convinced she really had died. In the dream, Clay had been painting her fingernails green, a brilliant emerald green that reminded her of him and Montserrat and all its wonderful greens everywhere about you wherever you rested an eye, and it had filled her with an enormous happiness that now matched her sadness at realising it hadn't been real, that she was still alive. She also knew she had not died because of the blipping monitors and the fact she still didn't have the energy to open her eyes.

She knew there were at least two people in the room, one of whom was CJ, because she could smell the sweet and acrid aroma of marijuana that lingered about him whenever he'd had a puff, a smell not entirely buried beneath the fresh burst of aftershave applied to mask it and the Wrigley's Spearmint gum he chomped on afterwards to prettify his breath, a combination she'd smelt on Clyde so frequently it had become his signature smell. If she was able to speak she would've told CJ the same thing she used to tell his father, that instead of cancelling the weed smell, the gum and the aftershave merely added to it, creating a new, more complex aroma that she thought of as minty-spliff cologne. She also knew CC was with him, her grandson, CJ's youngest child, aged three, because in addition to the constant pip-pip-pipping of the machinery she was rigged up to, she could hear the frantic non-stop tinkling and dinging sound effects which accompanied the games he enjoyed playing on his father's phone, interspersed with his occasional *yesss!* or *noooo!* depending on his performance.

To be perfectly honest, Ellen found the repetitive electronic sounds irritating and she knew that CC's wotless mother – had she been in the room – would have asked CC to turn it down, because she had little patience for the demands or noises of any child, especially her own. There was no chance however of her being in the room, because the first thing she had done after giving birth to CC was to instruct the midwife to hand him to CJ, who had taken his new-born son into his arms, instantaneously becoming the equivalent of a full-time single-parent dad, despite living in the same house as the wotless mother. In fact, Ellen would go further and say her son had been turned into a single-parent dad living with *two* kids.

She knew CJ and CC were in the room, but she wasn't sure if anyone else was there till she heard a raucous snort which was cut off mid-flow because it had been loud enough to wake the sleeper, and even before Dumpling spoke Ellen knew who it was, because all Dumpling's pregnancies had been the same. During the last three months she'd appear to be lively and fully awake, then you'd hear a roar and when you looked, she'd be passed out like a drunk, head floppy on the neck, mouth wide open, snoring her head off, which is how Clyde always slept, and when Clyde did, there was no relatedness at all between that sound and the melodious baritone voice that had attracted her to him in the first place.

'Sorry,' Dumpling said.

'S'fine, sis. You ain't missing nothing. She's sleeping anyway,' CJ said.

'Was never this bad with the other two,' Dumpling said. 'Can hardly keep me eyes open. This is definitely the last one.'

CJ laughed. 'You'll be drawing your pension *and* the Child Benefit at the same time if it ain't.'

'You're a fine one to talk,' Dumpling said, then laughed. 'I don't even know how this one happened.'

'It's your third,' said Claudette.

'You must have some idea,' said Joycelyn.

'Next time their dad passes looking for some, just say no,' Claudette said.

'Tell him to go look some from his wife,' Joycelyn said.

'I do,' said Dumpling. Her voice was small and sounded hurt, which was typical of the way she spoke when she felt even the teeniest bit sad, and which Ellen had always put down to her being the youngest amongst her siblings and as a consequence, the forever baby.

'Well he ain't forcing himself on you,' Claudette said, 'I know that much.'

'Being as he can't even stand without his stick,' Joycelyn said.

Ellen wasn't able to see Dumpling's face, but if she

could, she knew her eyes would've been full of tears, her lips pursed up like the lips of a spoilt child, and Ellen's mind turned once again to the fact none of the children were married, none of them even in anything resembling a normal long-term relationship. She conceded that CJ's relationship with the wotless mother had been a long-term one, but it was far from normal for a man to be conducting his life like a single parent when he was actually in a relationship and living with the mother of his child. All those years and wasted efforts. The trouble she'd gone to ensuring CJ never cooked a thing in her kitchen, never washed a spoon or cup, all so that when he became a man no woman could take liberties with him. Yet here he was, in a relationship with a woman who could not cook and did not clean. She really couldn't understand how it had happened.

Every time Ellen thought about it, it puzzled her no end that she and Clyde had been married nearly fifty years when he died, yet not one of the children raised inside their union had ended up in a normal relationship. Not one. Forty-nine years they'd been married, but they'd been together four years before that, the years during which Claudette then Joycelyn then CJ had been born outside of wedlock, because the only advice her mother had given on the subject of relationships and sex was 'make sure you walk the straight road.' Despite the fact Mrs Silcott had delivered that advice to her daughter the first time she noticed the two germinal nubs on the formerly flat expanse of Ellen's adolescent chest, and had then continued to deliver it with increased frequency till it was being said every time the two of them parted company, despite all of that, Ellen had absolutely no idea what her mother had been alluding to till after she'd given birth three times. Yes, nothing useful had she got from her mother, except a small pot of money and the old house back in Montserrat that she'd gone out to have a look at in 1963 and returned from four years later, a married woman and mother of three.

The first time she'd laid eyes on Clyde, she'd been tidying up the front yard of her mother's place in Cudjoe Head, collecting up the coconuts that had fallen from the overhanging palms over the few days previous. The trees were so plentiful everywhere you went in Montserrat, in so much abundance, that coconut water was drunk more than any other juice on the island; so refreshing in the hot sun, cool and delicious, with a sweetness sometimes so delicate the taste was almost savoury. In England, where she had spent the last eight years, a person had to take out a second mortgage to drink coconut water, whereas back here it was not only plentiful, but free. After eight years without it, when she returned in 1963 she couldn't get enough of it.

Ellen's preferences around coconuts kept shifting. There were days when she was obsessed with the jelly, cracking open the young coconuts and using her fingers or a shard of the shell to pry loose the thin translucent coating on the nut's interior, which always took her back to eating them as a child, experiencing the same thrill she did back then, the sheer joy of every child eating jelly. On the day she first met Clyde however, she'd been feasting on the crisp white flesh of mature coconuts for about a week, breaking them open, and instead of using a shard of the shell as a spoon, using its edge as a wedge, inserting it between the shell and the firm white flesh, breaking bite-sized pieces off and mashing them between her teeth to extract every last drop of flavour, before spitting the chaff out onto the ground where the free-ranging chickens were poised to promptly devour it. Older people used to warn the youngers, including the girls – especially the girls – about the aphrodisiac effects of eating too much coconut, warned about the ways it could change a person's nature, drive them insane with the need. Up until then, Ellen hadn't given the matter hard thought, hardly even recalled any of those warnings as she'd overindulged in the eating.

She had been in Montserrat for nearly a month now, and she'd been concentrating her efforts on the inside of the small three-roomed house she'd recently inherited. She'd lived in the house with her mother after her return from Curaçao, before they travelled to England, but it had been left vacant while they were abroad. She'd been intending to whitewash all the interior walls, beginning with the largest room. Both the front and back doors were open, and because of the elevation of the land, high up, some 500 feet above sea level, the house was exposed to the fresh western breezes that entered the front of the building then funnelled their way through the living room before exiting the back door.

She'd just finished her fourth wall and gone out into the front yard for a break. Parched, she'd brought her cutlass outdoors with her. Although she collected the fallen coconuts every day or two, there were four new ones on the ground. She selected one of the large green fruits, holding the weighty pod steady on her palm, then, with a series of practiced swipes, cleanly removed enough of the top to reveal a hole the size of a small coin. The tall thin palms provided little shade and she was aware only of the brilliant sunshine and the intense heat as she put the cutlass down and raised the heavy coconut to her mouth, tipping back her head to drink from it. The water was always best in young coconuts, before the flavour had been drawn out and into the flesh, at its most satisfying, and that was what she was focused on while she was drinking, slowly savouring the cool and delicious water as she swallowed, till her concentration was interrupted by the prickling sensation of being observed. When she opened her eyes, he was standing directly in her line of vision.

There was no fence that defined the boundary of her property and he could simply have walked up to the house, but he hadn't. He had stopped just outside the perimeter of her land and, as she watched him, he took off his hat, swiped the length of his forearm across the perspiration on his forehead, then looked at the coconut she was holding between her two hands and asked, 'Y'ave any going spare?' It was the first time she heard his mellow, bassy voice.

He was, by a clear margin, the most attractive man Ellen had ever seen. He was so handsome she found it difficult to look at him directly, had to keep snatching glances, like a person trying to stare at the sun during a solar eclipse. Moreover, she couldn't speak to him. Instead, she put down the coconut she was holding, picked up another and handed it to him, then in six or seven swipes of her cutlass sliced the top from it cleanly as his palms cupped the base, unflinching.

Clyde was twenty-one then, already used to being admired, and had the relaxed confidence of a man who knew exactly how attractive he was, already knew that for some women, like Ellen, his beauty could be overwhelming. He was still only just learning how to successfully navigate his relationships with women. He'd learned that, for some, toning his charisma down, acting like he had no idea how attractive he was, was a turn-on. He'd also discovered that the slippery sex with women like Ellen was always good, that it made him feel like a god, invincible, so instead of toning it down, he did the opposite and turned it up, blasting his full attention onto Ellen like a floodlight, before raising the coconut and tilting his head back to drain it.

Only then was Ellen able to properly take him in, when his gaze was averted and she could watch without being watched back, her eyes raking over his strong legs and arms and more slowly, the part of his hard belly exposed by the T-shirt whose hemline had risen with the raising of his arms; his sturdy neck and sensuous Adam's apple that rose and fell to the rhythm of each swallow. She took in all of that. And his skin.

Ellen's father had been one of the darkest coloured men Ellen had ever heard of, so dark it had become his pet name; Black Joe. Before she was old enough to attend school, she was referred to as Ellen for Black Joe which, like everything else in her life, she'd accepted without murmur, despite Black Joe being a virtual myth. She knew he was real because *everyone* had a dad apparently, and she knew he existed somewhere, but she couldn't remember ever seeing or meeting him and as a consequence was always rapt with attention whenever he was spoken about, gathering the details and stories of his life to fill in and flesh out the montage of him she'd been constructing in her imagination forever. But even if she'd wanted to, it was impossible to put distance between her real self and the myth that for her was all that existed of Black Joe. The moment she started attending the island's only junior school, where there were already two other pupils named Ellen, because she was the darkest of the three she immediately became known as Black Ellen.

She'd spent her entire childhood in Montserrat, so had no animosity towards skin as dark as that which covered her bones. She had never, for example, tried to bleach it hoping to become lighter, but she did know – had somehow always known – that she'd need both sense and luck to navigate the world successfully, that the privileges the world had to offer had not been set aside for the taking of girls who looked like her. Ellen hadn't been thinking about colour when she went to the bank with Mrs Skerritt as a young child, hadn't even realised she'd observed and filed away in her subconscious the fact that most of the staff there were men and the handful of women were all light, one of them near-white, like she'd never thought about the fact that there was no breadfruit season because the breadfruit tree produced fruit all year round. These were just facts of life, natural occurrences she understood without any conscious awareness.

Clyde's skin was the colour of sand on the beach after rainfall, the colour of the warm fresh honey in Mrs Skerritt's hives, and she wanted to be against it, to touch and taste it, and some fifteen minutes later, that's exactly what she was doing, and as a matter of fact it had nothing to do with his voice at all. Lying on what was surely her imminent deathbed, it occurred to Ellen that there was no one to hear her thoughts and pass judgement, nothing to prevent her being completely honest and if she wasn't, the only person she'd be deceiving at this point was herself. She'd told everyone that Clyde's voice had been the thing that had attracted her to him because it was more romantic than the truth, and because she'd always been known for the high standards she maintained and because she'd expected those same standards from the kids and none of that sat well alongside her being irresistibly attracted to Clyde's skin, its lightness; or as they called it back home, his red skin.

Clyde lowered the smooth green fruit in his hands and looked at her. A moment ago, Ellen couldn't meet his gaze and now she couldn't look away. For years after, she would wonder if someone had put a hex on her, whether a jumbie had possessed her, or if she really had consumed too many coconuts, drunk so much of the juice it had drugged her, made her high, because she had no explanation involving free will in which she could understand how she had allowed a man whose name she did not yet know to lead her back into her mother's house and undress her, then lay her down and undress himself. Worse, she could hardly bear to recall her response, *undignified* being the diplomatic term she'd always used in her mind, a euphemism that fell very short in explaining what she considered to be out and out coarseness. The desire unleashed inside her that took fuel from seeing his skin beside against on top of hers. The contrast between them like the flesh of coconut against its hardwood inner shell. The roaring pleasure that began on her insides and made its way outward to encompass every living inch of her surface, making even the fine hairs that covered her body rise up and stiffen. She couldn't recollect where they began, just remembered herself licking his miraculous skin about his neck, the ridges of his belly, the rumbling sexiness of the sound of his moans as first he gently pushed her head downwards, then urgently pulled her away before everything was prematurely over.

Never in her wildest dreams had Ellen imagined her unremarkable body contained the capacity for such immense joy inside it, and even now, facing death – surely! – it was a matter of astonishment to her. She couldn't imagine her mother had ever experienced the like. If she had, it would surely have softened some of the bitterness, the hardness that had defined her. Even though she hadn't heard her mother's voice inside her head since 2015, Ellen still couldn't stop thinking about her. Now she was wondering whether the reason she hadn't heard her mother's voice earlier when she thought she was dying was because she hadn't truly been dying then. It was clear she didn't have time to waste on her mind going around this foolishness in circles again, so she did what she had become so adept at during her lifetime and parked those thoughts. If she could have she would have sighed, and her inability to sigh brought her back to her previous line of thought and the fact she had submitted to all that pleasure so quickly, and the fact she had used the word *submitted* brought her face to face with the enormity of her capacity for self-deception, which seemed to have expanded during her lifetime, though it felt like something she should have grown out of. But maybe that was the ultimate deathbed experience, the inability to recall the past in any terms other than true? The truth was, she hadn't so much submitted to that pleasure as revelled and wallowed in it. She'd lost her mind in it from that first time, and whatever had happened between them, however Clyde had behaved, despite the hurts and pain he had inflicted on her, she had lost her mind every single time they did it and nothing else she ever did in her lifetime had made her feel more alive, ever.

She heard her room door open and Leah's voice.

'Is Granny still ...?'

'Yes,' said CJ.

'Don't think she's got long,' said Claudette to whoever else was present.

Ellen heard the door quietly close and a moment later, Leah leaned onto her and into the closest approximation of a hug that could be carried out with someone who was lying on their back and unresponsive, and she felt the wetness on her cheeks as Leah kissed her several times.

'Hi Granny,' she said, then sat on the bed beside her, taking hold of one of her hands. 'Your nails look beautiful.'

Ellen realised her granddaughter must have painted her nails while she was asleep, or somewhere between sleeping and waking, that the dream she'd had of Clay painting her nails had been a merging of her dream with the real world and she sincerely wished she could talk because she would have loved to know what colour they really were. She felt her granddaughter running her hand slowly and gently up and down the length of the same arm, and Ellen knew from the sounds she was making that she was crying.

It occurred to her that she'd been a silly woman as far as this grandchild was concerned, that while Leah had her faults – God Almighty Himself knew the girl had her faults! – despite the fact she was likely to argue about anything with anyone and seemed to have no notion of respect for her elders, she was probably the only family member who would genuinely miss her. Only one other person who had visited had cried, not that Ellen was swayed much by tears. Some people were able to turn them on as easy as running tap water while others were careful to never let anyone see them cry but that didn't mean they had no feelings, just that every emotion they had was not a piece of theatre for the whole world to notice and partake of. Only one other person had cried at her deathbedside, Wilhelmina, the only friend she'd ever trusted and had trusted as much as she would've trusted an older sister, who had snuck in at the crack of dawn one morning so early even the nurses must have been surprised to see her. She had firstly apologised and then let loose a continuous wave of eyewater which poured for some time, before she pulled herself together and said before leaving, 'It wasn't as long as you think,' which Ellen was certain was a barefaced lie. Yes, apart from Wilhelmina, whose tears were likely to have been shed as much for herself as they were for her dying friend, apart from her, whose tears didn't even count, Leah had been the only visitor to cry while visiting her during this time it seemed would never end. The difference was that Wilhelmina's tears had made Ellen exhausted, whereas her granddaughter's tears were having a very different and entirely uncharacteristic impact, causing an ache deep inside herself, something that was powerful, like grief, and she had to consciously remind herself that you could never trust women, especially the ones you really thought you could, most of whom were as bad as the men, worse even, a familiar line of thought that helped her regain perspective and emotional control.

'I can't do this,' Leah said, then leaned against Ellen again in a hug and her hot breath whispered in Ellen's ear, 'I love you, Granny. I'm sorry you had to deal with so much shit...'

'Leah! Language!' said Claudette.

'... If you see Grandad, tell him off. Kiss Clay for me. Rest in peace old lady.' Leah rose from the bed. 'I'm going,' she said.

'Wait for me,' said Linus and immediately Ellen felt buoyed by lightness. She hadn't realised Linus was present, Leah's older brother and her favourite grandchild, such a lovely boy, so caring and kind, singularly the family member who reminded her most of Clay. She felt her spirits rise despite her fatigue and suddenly it was clear to her that he was the reason she was still alive, the reason she hadn't yet departed; that she'd been waiting for this blessed boy to arrive and say his goodbyes. Once he did, she was ready and could go.

Linus leaned over her and kissed her forehead. 'Bye Grams. Love you.'

Then Linus and his sister were saying their goodbyes to everyone else and the space around her was flooded with voices. Ellen felt herself getting lighter as her thoughts began slipping further away and her worries dissipated, and none of it mattered because a young boy had materialised before her eyes and she knew who he was even before her eyes were able to adjust to the bright light surrounding him: her beloved son, Clay. He had one hand raised and swaying as if saying hi and he was smiling his sweetest smile. Though she wasn't moving, somehow she was getting closer to him and because of that she realised he wasn't saying hi. He was holding up a small toy car, showing it to her, and the fingernails on the hand holding it had been painted the emerald green of her dream. She had thought that car lost forever and she was so happy he'd had it with him all these years, that he'd had something he loved to play with while he'd been waiting so patiently so long for her to come. And as her chest began to fill with love and her body became weightless as air, she stretched both arms out ready to embrace her boy, and the knowledge they would never be parted again caused the joy inside her to expand till it was everything.

Settling Clyde

2017

(Three Years Earlier)

Clyde was too upset to eat the breakfast his daughter had prepared for him: scrambled eggs and tinned tomatoes, with soft white bread cut into small cubes with the crusty edges removed so they were like fluffy croutons, food you would never serve to a grown man who was still in possession of a few of his own teeth and for whom you still had respect. In his opinion, Claudette had prepared him a platter of baby food and even though he was too ill to get up and cook himself anything different – and he didn't really have the skill to do so even if he wasn't feeling so poorly – he'd made his mind up to die rather than eat it.

Claudette sat near his knees on the edge of the narrow bed with her head oddly angled because the height between the bottom and top bunks was not quite sufficient for an adult to sit fully upright, though there was enough room for Clyde to lay on his back with his shoulders and head propped up by the pile of pillows beneath them. Claudette was holding a bowl in one hand and a spoon in the other, trying to encourage him to try a mouthful, but he wouldn't open his mouth. Clyde watched her raising and lowering the spoon in front of his mouth as if he was a baby, the way Ellen had fed Claudette when she was a baby, the way he'd seen Claudette feed Linus and Leah when they were babies. He was sure he'd even seen Claudette feeding Linus's daughters, Iffy and Ibbs, the same way.

'Come on, Dad, you have to eat something,' Claudette said.

'You need to keep your strength up,' said Joycelyn, who was sitting on a chair she'd dragged in from the kitchen, with his two-year-old great-grandson, Kimani, on her lap. It further embarrassed Clyde that he was being fed baby food in front of Kimani, who was little more than an actual baby and whose gaze Clyde could not meet as he sat on his grandmother's lap sucking away on his dummy and staring at Clyde with eyes wide and unblinking. Clyde kept his mouth clammed closed as hard as he could.

'Please,' Claudette said, pressing the rim of the spoon against his unyielding lips.

'Just try, Dad,' Joycelyn said, as he turned his face to the wall and away from them.

Claudette sighed. 'He's just not eating anything.'

'You tried your best,' Joycelyn replied.

'He's upset about the accident,' Claudette said.

Clyde wondered whether they believed he'd gone deaf, or just thought that because he wasn't looking their way he could no longer hear them.

'Everyone has accidents,' Claudette added.

'It's part of life,' Joycelyn said, and he wondered what her life was like that she could talk about cleaning a grown man's shit off the bedroom carpet as if it was just one of those things. He'd known for years that she was taking care of her ex's mother who lived around the corner from her and whom the ex himself had abandoned the same way he'd abandoned Joycelyn as soon as she fell pregnant with Candice, Kimani's mum. He'd always wondered why she'd taken up that burden of responsibility. After all, it wasn't as if the relationship had been ongoing for years; they'd not been together a year by the time the ex had split. There was something demeaning about it all, ingratiating, but then it always felt to him like there was something ingratiating about Joycelyn, the way she followed Claudette around parroting everything she said and every view she held. Maybe she was at her ex's mum's every day cheerfully scraping shit off the carpet and scrubbing Zoflora disinfectant into the patch to mask the stink. He wouldn't put it past her.

'Dad, I'm gonna leave the tea here . . .' Claudette said. Clyde felt the mattress bounce back as she stood. 'On the chair where you can reach it.'

Clyde knew the tea would be hot and sweetened with three sugars, just the way he liked it. Now that he did fancy. He turned his head back around and looked at the mug on the chair Joycelyn had been sitting on, which she had moved closer to the bed as if it was a side table.

'Just stretch out your arm when you're ready,' said Joycelyn. She lifted Kimani off her lap as she stood. 'Say ta ta to pappy.'

Kimani said, 'Ta ta. Ta ta.'

'Give pappy a bye-bye kiss,' Joycelyn said and held Kimani's body as he leaned forwards so that his face was above his great-grandfather's. Despite how rough he felt, Clyde forced a smiled for Kimani's sake. As he did so, Kimani pulled the dummy out of his mouth, then leaned forwards as if to kiss Clyde. Clyde puckered up the lips Claudette had moisturised twenty minutes ago (before rubbing the rest of the Vaseline on her hands into his cleaned cheeks and the crack of his backside), then out of the blue, before anyone could stop him, Kimani jammed the dummy in his hand into Clyde's off-guard mouth, and as both Claudette and Joycelyn burst out laughing, Kimani bared his collection of six tiny teeth, grinning his head off and laughing as well. For Clyde, it was the final straw. He could no longer contain his feelings. The tears brimmed and spilled over.

'Daddy, don't upset yourself,' Claudette said, as if he had stuck the dummy in his own mouth and, having humiliated himself, was now making a fuss about it.

'You're gonna make yourself ill,' said Joycelyn, as if he didn't already have stage-four cancer and wasn't being passed around like a homeless vagrant with his commode in tow.

'Just get out,' he said, and when neither of his daughters

moved, he shouted again, 'Get out!', this time with all the volume he could muster.

'You need to calm down,' Claudette said.

'*Please*,' Joycelyn said, keeping firm hold of Kimani on her hip as the two women left the room, quietly pulling the door up behind themselves.

Clyde didn't try to stop the tears. Not since the terrible incident with Clay could he remember feeling this wretched. He'd always thought of himself as upbeat, an optimist, a man whose glass was half full, which to be fair it genuinely had been much of the time, mostly with Hennessy. He was a decent person, a family man, a loving father and grandfather and great-grandfather. He just couldn't understand why he was experiencing such sufferation, why his old age had become burdened with so much tribulation. How, at the age of seventy-five, had he gone from being a man widely respected to a geriatric in a nappy, sleeping on the bottom bunk of a children's bed, with his commode between a pile of video games and two stacked crates of Action Men, and even his great-grandson making sport of him like the two of them were size?

There was no logic to explain this, no science or reason. For the first time in his life, he wondered whether someone had put obeah on him. Yes, it was a far reach, but nothing else made sense. He just couldn't understand who could be bad-mind enough to do such a thing? He knew for a fact he'd been loved by the vast majority of people he'd known. His crying turned to sniffles as Clyde started thinking about them, so many people stretching back over seven decades; neighbours, his family, friends at work, down the pub and in the bookies, all those people he'd loved who he'd made feel so welcome at parties in his home. It couldn't be any of them, surely? And it couldn't have been his brother, Cassius, because he was dead now, had died four years ago and he couldn't imagine it had been his brother's widow, Janet, who he was sure would have been glad Clyde hadn't done the nine-hour flight to Tallahassee for the funeral. One name kept recurring but he kept rejecting it, continuing to plough through the long list of everyone he'd ever known. Finally, because there was no other name in the running alongside it, Clyde had to accept that he knew who it was who'd used obeah on him and the unfairness of all that life had saddled him with made his eyes well up again. For some reason he didn't understand, he needed to expel the name from his insides in order to confirm that what was happening was real.

'Ellen.'

Just the thought of being the victim of such wickedness made him cry anew and this time, he could not stop. Sobbing, he repeated the name aloud over and over again. *'Ellen. Ellen. Ellen!'*

Claudette entered her living room carrying a tray heavy with the mugs of tea and coffee she'd made to the specifications of the family members convened there. Her daughter, Leah, followed behind holding two plates bearing a variety of biscuits. Because Leah was carrying the biscuit plates, Joycelyn followed behind her sister and her niece empty-handed. Ordinarily she would have been following her sister and carrying the biscuit plates. She had been preparing to do exactly that, had just finished arranging the custard creams, ginger nuts, Rich Tea and the bourbons in orderly lines across the two plates and was twisting the packets closed to return them to the cupboard when Leah picked up both plates and said, 'Let me give you a hand, Auntie,' and by the time Joycelyn had said it was fine, she could manage, both Claudette and Leah had left the kitchen.

Joycelyn followed them both because she'd been following her sister for almost her entire life, ever since she was two and her mother and father had travelled to England, leaving her and Claudette behind in Montserrat with her father's mother, old Mistress Fenton, and her tiny world had been transformed from one in which she was secure, happy and settled, to a different home in a strange part of town, with a new adult in charge and the terrifying absence of anyone she'd known or lived with till then, apart from her older sister. Back then, she had followed her sister around in mortal fear that Claudette would disappear too, becoming distraught whenever her sister was out of her sight, so distressed and inconsolable that it was impossible for her to function. It got so bad that arrangements had to be made for her to start school a year early, as Joycelyn became increasingly more hysterical by the day when Claudette got to five and started attending. The conscious fear had vanished now, had vanished decades ago, so completely that she couldn't even recall that terrifying time, and since then the act of following her sister had become an ingrained instinct.

Clyde was propped up in the TV chair, heavily wedged into position with cushions and pillows to ensure he didn't tip out of it. Ellen was also there, sitting at the end of the sofa on the opposite side of the room, facing him but looking only at her great-grandson Kimani on her lap, and cooing as he played with the bangles on her wrist. Dumpling was there, but had left Frank Junior and Fiona at home finishing off their homework. CJ had come, giving them a heads-up on arrival that he would have to leave if Shani went into labour.

When the teas and biscuits had been distributed, Claudette, Joycelyn and Leah took their seats, then Claudette took a sip of her cuppa, cleared her throat and began.

'We are gathered here today to talk about Daddy and where he should live. As you know, he's staying with me at the moment, but he's not happy,' she said.

'It can't go on,' said Joycelyn.

'I don't get it,' CJ said. 'We agreed we'd all have him for two weeks at a time so it was fair to everyone.'

'Two years ago! Is that fair to Dad?' asked Claudette.

'No siree,' Joycelyn said.

'I can't have him full time,' said Dumpling. 'I've got three bedrooms for me, Frank Junior and Fiona, and Frank Junior's got his GCSEs next year.'

Joycelyn said, 'Well don't look at me. You know Kimani's sharing with his mum. I'm already on the sofabed when Daddy's at mine.'

'I've got Iffy and Ibbs at the weekends and in the school holidays, and Linus is back every time he has an argument with their mum. You might as well say he lives here. So yeah, I've got an extra room, but it's not empty,' Claudette said.

'But it is spare,' Dumpling said, recognising her mistake before she'd even finished speaking and closed her mouth.

'Should Claudette not let her son and granddaughters visit?' asked Joycelyn.

'I wasn't saying that,' said Dumpling, despite knowing any attempted appeasement was now useless.

'Cos I don't see you inconveniencing *your* kids to make space,' Joycelyn said.

Dumpling didn't reply. She always felt hyper-emotional in disagreements with her sisters, which made it impossible to judge clearly whether she was in the right or wrong, though it felt like she was always in the wrong, whatever she did or said, and like she was always being ganged up on. Ever since that time she'd told on them when she was really young, never imagining the traumatic outcome it would lead to, she had been careful, very careful, not to enter a heated war of words with either of them if it was possible.

'Anyway, what about CJ?' asked Claudette. 'He's got a spare room that's actually spare.'

'Hang on, hang on,' said CJ. 'Till the baby arrives. Which is basically any second.'

'Well why can't the baby stay in your room? It'd be much easier in the night-time anyway,' Dumpling said, backing her sister up.

'Shani doesn't want the baby in the same room as us.'

'But is it Shani's house though?' asked Claudette.

'I don't think so,' said Joycelyn.

'But it is her home,' Leah said.

'Anyway,' CJ said, 'why ain't we talking 'bout the fact mum's got four bedrooms and it's just her and Leah living there?'

'Exactly,' said Claudette.

'Not one but two spare rooms,' said Joycelyn.

'Two actual doubles, too,' said Dumpling, happy to see both her sisters nodding in agreement. 'I say we all vote as to where Daddy goes so he doesn't have to keep moving around like this. It's not fair on him and it's not right.'

CJ said, 'Agreed. I vote Daddy moves back home and the rest of us take it in turns to go every day and help mum out.'

For the first time, Ellen spoke. 'No.'

'You must know this isn't right, mum!' said Claudette. 'Look at him.'

'Have mercy,' said Joycelyn. 'He's dying!'

'I said, *no*!'

Clyde began to make a keening sound, rasping and loud. His legs and arms shook from exertion as he began trying to push himself up and out of the chair, glaring at Ellen as though he was on his way over to finish her off. CJ, Claudette and Joycelyn surrounded him, reasoning with him, encouraging their father to take his seat again and calm down. Ellen put Kimani on the settee beside her and stood up, pushing the sleeves of her shirt up above the elbows, clenching then raising her fists.

'Stand him up,' she said. 'Let me box down that expressive face.'

Leah stood and said, 'Stop it, Granny,' and Ellen didn't resist as her granddaughter settled her back down into her seat, then sat down beside her, lifting an astonished Kimani up onto her lap again.

Claudette said, 'It's where he belongs.'

'Till death do them part,' Joycelyn said.

Leah said, 'You can't force Granny to live with him if she doesn't want to.'

Claudette was giving her daughter *the look*. It was the look that said, *you better not*, or sometimes *stop it*. In this instance, it was clearly saying *shut up*, but Leah wasn't looking at her mother. Claudette loved her daughter very much, but she didn't understand her, had never understood her. Even when Leah had been a toddler, she'd been nothing like her older brother, Linus, who for the most part, when he was asked to do something, did it, unlike Leah who had never obeyed, never known her place and in response to almost any request, would ask, *why*? It wasn't how Claudette had been raised, and each and every time the question felt like a challenge to her authority.

Although she'd been three when her mum and dad left Montserrat and went off to the Motherland to make their fortune, Claudette had no memory of those first three years. Her earliest memory was of her sister crying, she didn't know what for, just that they were sitting together on the steps outside the front door of old Mistress Fenton's house. The memory was a brief one, only a second or two long, but in it the day was bright and the sun was shining and it was probably early morning, because Darg was on the ground at the bottom of the steps sitting upright on his haunches looking up at them, and normally, as the day progressed and the heat intensified, he would find himself a shady spot to lie in, usually under the house, and when they looked under there and called *Darg!* he would blatantly open one eye so they would know he'd heard them, then close it again as though he'd given the idea of responding some thought but it was just too damn hot. In Claudette's memory, they were sitting on the top step and Joycelyn was turned towards her, both arms wrapped tightly around her older sister's waist, bawling loudly.

As well as that memory, she could recall being asked to do things: to collect water, tidy the yard, kitchen, house. She remembered taking clothes to river to wash. She remembered being asked to collect eggs, carry message, pick peas, peel hard food, pluck chicken. She remembered looking after her sister, plaiting her hair, plaiting old Mistress Fenton's. In all of her memories, she did what she was told. It never crossed her mind to ask *why?* Because her grandmother was an adult, that's why. Because she was a child. That's why. Because a child and an adult weren't equals, they weren't size. Her answer to her daughter's question had always been the same; because I said so. But Leah had never accepted that answer. Now at twenty-four, with no kids and no partner in her life or on the horizon, she still talked about Claudette saying 'because I said so' as if it had been a form of child abuse. Claudette was giving her daughter the look that said *shut up*, and although Leah wasn't looking at her, if she had looked at her mum and noticed, it was entirely possible her daughter would ask why she was looking at her like that instead of simply obeying the implied command. Yes, Leah had been, still was, very difficult.

CJ said, 'What's supposed to happen with him mum? Tell me that. Where's he supposed to go?'

Leah said, 'Uncle, Granny doesn't wanna live with him. She said no.'

Claudette said, 'Leah, stop.'

'Why should I stop? It's Granny's decision.'

'Listen when your mother speak,' said Joycelyn.

'I'm not a child, Auntie. And neither is Granny.'

'What about Carlton and Sue and Headly?' asked Dumpling. 'Couldn't Daddy stay with one of them?'

Carlton, Sue and Headly were also Clyde's children, all born around the same time as Claudette, in Montserrat, Curaçao and St Thomas in the Virgin Islands. All had since moved to different parts of the world. Carlton lived in New York, Sue in Florida and Headly was living in Antigua, where his wife originated from, all of them in much more frequent contact with their father and siblings since the advent of free international calls via WhatsApp. For a moment there was silence in the room as everyone contemplated this suggestion. It would involve getting Clyde across the globe in his sick state. Someone would have to travel with him – he wouldn't be able to manage the journey alone – but it wasn't impossible.

'Let me guess; you all gonna take a vote on this too?' Leah asked.

'Well, they're his children as well,' Dumpling said.

'But why's Dad got to move to another country when he's got family here?' asked CJ.

'And a wife!' Clyde said.

'Stop it Grandad,' Leah said.

'*You* stop it,' said Claudette, embarrassed at her lack of control over her outspoken daughter.

'It must be possible for us to sort this out. For God's sake, Daddy's got seven kids,' said Dumpling.

'And a wife!' said Clyde.

'Grandad!' said Leah.

'Well, it's true, isn't it?' asked Claudette.

Joycelyn opened her mouth to agree with her sister, but before she could do so, Ellen spoke again. 'I said no and I mean *no*.'

For the life of him, Clyde could not believe what was happening. He understood what Ellen had been saying since the fireworks party, that she was refusing to have him back, but he'd been anticipating that they would at some point move beyond that – hadn't they always? – that eventually he would be returning to the marital home. From his perspective, the only thing that needed to be overcome was his upset at the realisation the woman he'd devoted the bulk of his life to was doing obeah on him, and that was no small ask. It was Ellen who should be seeking forgiveness from him, not the other way round. Now he was having to reassess what he wanted, because as astonishing as it was, it really did seem that she wasn't going to change her mind, and he could no longer tolerate being looked after by the daughters who had looked up to and admired him their whole lives, who he had sneaked sweets to on the quiet in the evenings after they'd brushed their teeth, who he'd taken on secret trips to Kentucky in the years before Ellen had developed a taste for it herself, back in the early years when she was still insisting the chicken hadn't been washed and seasoned properly and it wasn't cooked right through; he couldn't believe those same daughters he had spoiled like little princesses were now giving him bedbaths, washing and drying and powdering his cock, wiping his backside, changing his pissy bedclothes when his nappies leaked and emptying and cleaning out his commode. Of every person gathered in this room (he didn't include Carlton, Sue and Headly who he'd hardly even seen during their lifetimes apart from a couple of holidays now and then, and whose homes he could not imagine arriving at with his commode in tow; truly could not imagine it), of everyone here, the person he would be least embarrassed to have carry out those tasks was Ellen, his wife, who already had experience of nursing him through illness and cleaning up behind him, who was very familiar with his body and had masses of experience handling his cock, but the blasted woman was refusing. His options had narrowed down to one person and one person only, and of all the people in the room, it was the person he respected most and would have least wished – had he more choices – to impose himself upon. But he was out of choices. The knowledge made his eyes fill with tears, but his voice was still strong when he spoke.

'CJ, I want to stay with you,' he said. Then, because CJ didn't answer straight away and because he was afraid his son might refuse him in front of everyone, he added, 'Please,' and this time, as he spoke, his voice broke.

CJ had never imagined a scenario like this and though it was blatantly happening in front of him, in real life, he couldn't believe it. Up to this moment, he had considered his life charmed, like his father's life had been charmed. Becoming a full-time carer, the possibility of such a thing was so remote it had never crossed his mind.

'At the end of the day,' said Dumpling, 'what Daddy wants takes priority over Shani.'

As Leah leaned forward to reply, CJ raised his hand, quieting her. Dumpling seemed to think that the reason CJ had not yet responded was because he was weighing how Shani would feel about it. In reality, however, he was trying to avoid having his father move into the spare room at all. It was his house, not Shani's. She got her own way with most things, but him putting a roof over his terminally ill father's head was not her decision, it was his. It wasn't Shani he was thinking about, it was himself, his life, the instantaneous and previously unthinkable evaporation of all his freedoms. Before he surrendered, he decided to have one last push on the battlefront.

'Are you sure, Dad? It's gonna be pretty noisy round the clock for months, with the baby waking up screaming all times of the day and night and vomiting down the house. You might rest better somewhere else.' When he said *somewhere else*, what he meant specifically was *in one of his sisters' homes*.

Clyde said, 'I'm sure.'

'We'll come around,' Claudette said, 'One of us, every day.'

'You won't be on your own,' Joycelyn said.

'Sounds like a done deal to me,' said Leah.

Clyde hadn't realised how tense he was till he sighed with relief and felt his stomach muscles unclench. He smiled at CJ, who he should've known would never let him down.

'I'll come back and get you later,' his blessed son said. 'Just gimme a chance to sort out your room.'

CJ's charmed life had begun with being the only boy-child born into a family full of girls. Had he been an only child, he might have had to pull a little of his weight. As it turned out, there were enough girls, alongside Ellen, to cover the entire household's shopping, cooking, laundry, cleaning, ironing and washing up, which left only the hoovering and putting the bins out and even those two meagre chores, twice a week – if that – were divvied up between CJ and his dad. Once the school day was finished – then the working day, when he got to that stage – that left him plenty of time to enjoy a life of leisure and pleasure, and filling that time for CJ had been effortless. He liked his reggae. He enjoyed his weed. He loved his Hennessy and he lived for his women.

At the age of fifty-one he had six kids who ranged in age from nine to thirty-three and he had thought he was done with having children till he met Shani, thirty years his junior, who had been a challenge, a laugh and great in bed, who, like him, enjoyed music and drinking and burning – which had been great fun for the short number of months they were together before they discovered she was pregnant, but had since become quite a contentious issue as he thought she should stop drinking and burning while she was carrying his child, and she thought they should stop drinking and smoking weed together, and, as he had not, she hadn't either.

When he got home she was facetiming one of her girlfriends on their bed, and waved to him as he entered the room, without pausing in her conversation, so he withdrew and went to the nursery – *Dad's room!* – and stood in the doorway looking around inside it. He had already painted it blue, which was handy, and he thanked God he hadn't listened to Shani and thrown out the double bed when he had put up the cot. He'd been conscious that his current youngest child, Jayden, came up for weekend visits and slept over regularly during the school holidays. He went over to the cot, took hold of it and began to pull, sliding it over the carpet towards the bedroom door. There he discovered it was just a fraction too large to pass through it, so went to get his toolbox. When he returned, he began taking out the screws.

Though he tried, it was quite impossible not to think about the extent to which his life had suddenly changed. Despite his age, he considered himself a playboy, and he had lived as such. Even though he was a father and a grandfather, it was very rare that he'd found himself or his time limited. Yes, he had six kids, but he provided and their mothers took care of them. With the exception of work – mostly part-time, he was self-employed now, a plumber, good money, no need to kill himself – the rest of the time, he was able to choose how he passed his life. His father coming to live with him was life-changing, and whatever his sisters said about coming every day to support him – which would be a massive help – it was still fundamentally his life that would be impacted.

He felt no anger towards his father. None of this was his fault. He had always been a great father, the coolest of dads. Now he was terminally ill, of course CJ would step up to the task and do everything he could, even if the road ahead terrified the shit out of him. He also didn't feel anger towards his sisters, who already had very full lives with kids and grandkids of their own and who really didn't have the space to accommodate Dad. Each of them would have taken their father in if they could because that was what family did. They, like him, had been put into an impossible position, and it really was a fact he was the only member of his sibling group who had the space and the time to take care of Dad. No, he wasn't angry with his sisters at all. But he was furious with his mother. At a time like this it was beyond him to understand how she could withhold her help. His mother had taken an oath when she married, for better or worse, in sickness and in health, till death do them part. Those were not just words; they meant something. It was a contract between them and they'd both signed it. Taking care of Dad was her actual duty. Whatever differences they'd had in the past were exactly that: in the past. Terminal illness wiped the slate clean. He could not, would not, ever forgive her for abandoning her husband like this. It was pure bad-mind. Evil.

By the time Shani came off her call, he was unscrewing the final two pieces of the cot frame. She came into the baby's room – *Dad's room!* – leaned her back against the wall and looked down at him sitting on the corner of the bed. She was wearing jogging bottoms. They weren't maternity ones that covered her tummy decorously. The waistband of these jogging bottoms had settled underneath her bump and she wore a crop top above it, so between both items of clothing, her thirty-nine-week pregnant stomach protruded like a life-affirming statement. She was tiny, five foot four, with a slight frame and perfect ample breasts which had virtually doubled in size; in fact she had virtually doubled in size during her pregnancy and was heavy, heavy and full of curves he found incredibly sexy. She handed him one of the glasses in her hand, Hennessy over ice, just the way he liked it. She had a glass in her own hand with a drink inside it that looked the same. He hoped it was the mocktail version.

'Why you taking the cot down?' she asked.

'The baby's gonna have to sleep in our room.'

'Why?'

'My mum's not taking my dad back and he's too sick to be sofa surfing. I said he could stay with me.'

Shani raised an eyebrow. 'With *you*?'

'*Us*. Is that okay?'

'Do what you like. It's your house,' Shani said with

the absence of emotion he was coming to recognise as her MO.

'Sorry. I should've asked . . .'

'I don't own you. You don't own me. You don't need to ask me anything.'

CJ felt his stress levels rising. Shani was always telling him that neither of them owned the other, which obviously he knew, but it was something he was unaccustomed to hearing from the women he dated. For some reason, though Shani was saying they were both equals, neither beholden to the other, somehow what he heard each time was that she was free to do what she wanted and if he pissed her off sufficiently, she'd simply leave. Maybe it was to do with the age difference between them. Maybe this time, he'd bitten off more than he could chew. One evening soon after they'd first started seeing each other, Shani had been scrolling through her messages on her phone when she'd suddenly burst out laughing. When he asked what was so funny, she explained that a friend of hers had messaged to say she'd just packed up her baby's father by text, which was some next-level communication, the idea of which made his blood run cold and for some reason he couldn't shake, it was something he frequently recalled whenever a text message from Shani popped up on the screen of his phone.

'I'm sorry,' he said. 'I should've checked with you first.' All he wanted in his life was peace. And right then, some comfort. He reached out and took her free hand, pulled her closer to him so she stood between his splayed knees, her breasts on eye level, finely detailed through the stretched fabric of the sheer top. Soon, these would be the baby's. His window of opportunity had already shrunk to the size of a spyhole. It was now or it might not be for a very long time. He opened his mouth and latched onto one of her nipples, then closed his eyes. Things were going to be okay. He was overthinking everything. He wasn't on his own, he had Shani to depend on. She'd basically take care of the baby anyway, and when she had time would help with his dad. He began to feel calmer. His eyes opened as Shani stepped back, looked down at the tools on the bed and then at him.

'You've forgotten the cot, lover boy. I think you've already got enough on your plate.'

CJ finished taking the cot down, then put it back up again in their bedroom, on Shani's side of the bed to make it as convenient as possible for her to sort the baby out in the night-time. Then he left and drove to his sister's to pick up his dad, fortunately picking up Claudette as well, who returned with him to finish making up the bed and sorting out the room before giving Clyde his first dinner in what was now his permanent home. Almost immediately, Shani's contractions started. Twenty-two hours later, Cian Clay Fenton – CC – arrived in the world, five pounds three ounces, perfect, with a strong and healthy pair of lungs. Claudette stayed behind with Clyde till the proud parents returned and while CJ went back out to pick up some baby milk, bottles and a steriliser, as Shani wasn't sure she was producing enough milk. When CJ returned, he took his sleeping newest son from Claudette's arms and put CC into his cot, smiling fondly when he realised Shani was so worn out she'd fallen asleep on the side furthest from the cot, on what was technically his side of the bed. He was about to wake her and shift her over to her side when he heard Clyde calling, so he turned off the bedroom light and left the door slightly ajar as he headed to Clyde's room.

He found his father sitting on the edge of the bed trying to get up so he could use the commode, and, berating his father for not calling him earlier, he helped Clyde to his feet. As he was lowering his father onto the commode, he heard the low sounds of CC awakening and beginning to fuss and cry. Although he could hear the sounds, he wasn't consciously paying attention to it, had mentally blocked it out in a way he'd perfected decades ago, after all CC was in the same room as his mother. But once Clyde was settled, he went out of the room to give his dad some privacy and as he pulled the door closed, he registered the fact that CC was still crying.

In the bedroom, Shani was fast asleep on CJ's side, completely oblivious to the baby's screams. He was about to wake her when he remembered she'd just been in labour for twenty-two hours giving birth. In fairness that did qualify as a good reason to need sleep, so he left her and picked up CC. He carried his son into the kitchen and found him a ready-mixed bottle of feed. He went into the bedroom, where his father had finished his business, put CC down and helped his dad back into bed as the level of CC's screams built up to enraged. He picked CC up, put the bottle in his mouth and passed him to his dad, leaving his father to feed him while he emptied the commode. He'd had no sleep for the last thirty-six hours, so as soon as CC had finished his feed and fallen back asleep, CJ took him from Clyde's arms and returned him to the cot. Shani continued to snore. He made himself a cup of tea and sat in the quiet of the kitchen, internally patting himself on the back for having successfully navigated the most stressful forty-eight hours of his life, and enjoying the fact the worst was now behind him, a state of oblivion he remained in for another ninety minutes. Then CC woke up again and Shani continued to snore.

When CJ opened the door to his bedroom a few months later, Leah had CC in her arms, pacing the floor and jiggling him gently. She raised her fingers to her lips to indicate he was almost there, nearly but not quite asleep. CJ entered quietly and sneaked some clean clothing out of his drawers then carefully tiptoed back out and into the bathroom to shower off the mess and dirt of the job he'd been called out to that afternoon, a bastard burst pipe that had been hard to get to and awkward to repair, that had, to the homeowner's dismay, involved taking up large areas of their parquet flooring and had kept him on his belly for more than six hours, torch in mouth, head and neck stuck down a hole struggling to fix it.

As he showered, he thought about Shani. He knew she'd be somewhere where bashment was being played, music he felt emphasised the age gap between them, more like beats for energetic kids to jump around to, which took him down a slightly depressing line of thought he'd been on many times; had he ended up with a partner his age, like any of the four other women he'd had children with for example, who'd all been roughly the same age as him, or at least only a little younger instead of three decades, who all knew how to cook and keep house and were actively interested in playing mum, had that happened, maybe at this time of the evening he would be able to smell the aroma of a homecooked meal coming from the kitchen instead of returning in time to release Leah from the evening care shift, so his shift could begin. By the time he came out of the bathroom, his niece was on the sofa in the living room, phone in hand, scrolling.

'Was everything okay?'

'Yeah. I gave Grandad his meds. Shani said don't wait up for her.' As CJ rolled his eyes, she said, 'You picked this.'

'You hear me complaining?' CJ asked.

'Anyways, I ordered you some Chinese. It's in the kitchen. I don't mind how you pay me back.'

'Oh my days. Thank you.'

When she told him how much she'd spent, he overrepaid her, forcing the extra cash on her despite her protests. 'Just take it,' he said.

He saw her to the door then went into the bedroom and discovered the laundry basket was too full to put the lid on even without adding the clothes he'd taken off, so he pulled a wash together, then put the remainder of the dirty clothing back inside. He sneaked over to the cot and looked down at CC, who'd turned three months old that morning. He was zonked out cold. CJ leaned over and kissed him, being careful not to wake him. CC smelt of formula and talcum powder and, close up, CJ could hear he was a little snuffly. He made a mental note to keep an eye on that.

Then he went to check on Clyde. He'd been provided with a hospital bed after falling out of the double bed three weeks ago. CJ blamed himself. A couple of times when he'd gone into the room his father had been perilously close to the edge. All the clues were there. He should have anticipated that a fall would eventually occur. Months back, the nurses had given CJ a diet sheet that recommended adding high-calorie and nutritional ingredients to his meals, because Clyde ate like a bird now, tiny mouthfuls of dishes enriched with cream and butter and mashed avocado and arrowroot. Even so, Clyde was so slight of frame that there was nothing to cushion him when he fell and even now, weeks later, the bruises were still evident. CJ adjusted his father's pillows behind his head and lowered the top of the bed so that the incline was reduced and looked more comfortable. He pulled the blankets up over his father's chest, pulled in the opened window, then checked the battery life on the baby monitor on the bedside table and, satisfied, left the room.

CJ heated up a plate of Chinese takeaway and ate it like a starving man. When he finished, he piled it up again, with only slightly less food, and took it to the living room. He turned on the TV and settled in front of it to watch something-whatever till he finished. He'd poured himself a glass of Hennessy over ice, one and no more, mindful he was the only person home and responsible for both CC and Clyde, a status which would not alter with Shani's return. Not only did Shani yearn for the easy life of the child-free, not only was she fairly hands-off when it came to CC, but she also had little inclination to clean, was entirely content to live on fast-food deliveries from Deliveroo or Uber Eats, and although she was nice to Clyde, often sitting with him and chatting, showing him TikTok videos and Insta photos, she was not involved in his care at all, not even feeding him. She occupied the space in their relationship that he had always inhabited in his relationships up to now, and just like the women he'd been in relationships with, despite the fact he felt like he was not centre in the focus of her attentions, he was head over heels in love with her.

He awoke to the sound of CC crying. He turned off the TV, picked up his plate and glass and took them to the kitchen. He collected a bottle from the fridge and stuck it in the microwave to take the chill off. He went into his room, took CC out of the cot, fed, winded and changed him, then settled back against his pillows on what was now his side of the bed, nearest the cot, with CC lying on his chest. He was still snuffling, so CJ dripped a little Olbas Oil on the pillows around them and continued to hold CC on his chest, intending to keep him there only till CC fell asleep.

He awoke to the sensation of CC being lifted from his

chest and, when he opened his eyes, Shani was lowering him into the cot. She smelled of spicy rum and fragrant weed and the after-linger of expensive perfume he'd bought her. He pulled himself over to sit on the edge of his side of the bed, feet on the floor, removing the T-shirt and joggers he'd fallen asleep in. Shani walked over and stood in front of him, a life-sized silhouette in the darkness.

She whispered, 'So, did you miss me?'

She pulled off her dress and underwear and dropped them on the floor, and CJ had the fleeting thought that he would have to pick them up tomorrow, probably wash and dry them and put them away. He answered, 'Yes.'

She placed the flat palms of her hands against his cheeks, pulled his head towards her and kissed him. She pushed his head away and said, 'Prove it.'

He did.

CJ slowly lowered Clyde into the warm water, resting him on top of the inflatable wedge that supported the top half of his body so he could lie in the bathtub in comfort, his bony body cushioned against the hard surface of the bath. Clyde lay there warm, relaxed and weightless. The only parts of his father that were visible were his head, shoulders and his arms lying along the top of the bath's edge. The rest of him was submerged beneath the bubble mountain CJ had learned to maximise for the pleasure of both his dad and his son, using a squirt of baby bath, a whisk and plenty of elbow grease.

Clyde's head bobbed along to the music that came

from the speaker CJ had bluetoothed his phone to, old-skool ska, the musical backdrop to his youth, reminiscent of raves back home and here, the parties, good good parties, the food and drink and weed, the moves, the joy. He smiled and raised his hand to take hold of the glass CJ handed him, half filled with Baileys over ice, the tipple he'd always enjoyed at Christmas which had now become the drink that accompanied the ceremony of his Sunday bath, cool and sweet and delicious and easier on the way down than the Hennessy he had devoted his life to. He sipped it, closed his eyes and swallowed. He held the glass up and CJ took it, put it down, and, using the edge of the bath towel, dabbed at the moisture around his mouth. Clyde's eyes were still closed when he heard the flick and rush of flame, a long drag, then the small steamy room was filled with the sweet smell of marijuana and he felt the tip of the butt of the spliff pressed against his lips. He took a small drag, held it in a moment before exhaling, then continued bobbing his head.

CJ sat on a stool beside the bathtub sipping his Hennessey, amazed as usual to find himself entirely content. As he always did now, he reflected that although he had no doubt his father had always loved him, they had never shared time together in this way. He couldn't recall his dad ever bathing or shaving him, or spending time curating outfits for him to wear as CJ did daily now, involving Clyde in his careful attempts to replicate outfits his dad would have put together himself, so that even though he now spent most of his time indoors, he was as smartly turned out as he'd been when he had dressed himself. It was a new experience for CJ, his discovery of the giver's joy, and he was grateful for the counterbalance it provided to the heartache of watching the man he loved slowly die. He knew his father could not have enjoyed this time in this way with anyone else. His sisters, the Macmillan nurses, none of them could have curated this perfect space; they wouldn't have known how to. Had Clyde returned to the marital home with Mum, she would never have rolled and fed him spliffs. He acknowledged his father was in the best place for him and he acknowledged again that it hadn't happened because of his mother, but in spite of her.

They were completely different people, his mum and dad. He'd questioned his father's love for his mother when he was younger, but he had never questioned his mother's love for his father. Even now, CJ could feel his father's sadness that the true love of his life had abandoned him and he struggled to understand. It was heartless. Merciless. He would be the first to admit Dad had made mistakes, but that's what they were, mistakes. He was not fundamentally a bad person, unlike Ellen, whose actions had made her bad. What she'd done was cruel and he couldn't forgive her.

Rising steam had covered Clyde's face in moisture and CJ used the towel to pat around his dad's lips, then fed him another puff. Desmond Dekker and the Aces' anthem '007 (Shanty Town)' began playing. CJ's head began bobbing as he turned the volume up a fraction more and handed his father his glass.

The Bonfire Night Party

November 2015

(Two Years Earlier)

'You been on your feet all day, Mum,' said Claudette, holding Ellen's coat open in front of her.

'From early this morning,' said Joycelyn, who was waiting with a cup of soup in her hand to give to Ellen once she'd put her coat on.

'I only just put in the patties ...' Ellen said, looking towards the oven.

'We'll sort them,' said Claudette.

'You're gonna miss the fireworks,' Joycelyn said.

'But ...'

'No buts,' said CJ, moving his mobile phone away from his mouth, interrupting the conversation he was having. He put the phone back to his ear and turned to rest his gaze on his youngest son, Jayden, who was weaving through the groups of people standing around the kitchen chatting and drinking, in a high-speed hurtle towards the back door. As he passed close by his father, CJ reached out and caught him by the arm. 'Slow down before you cause an accident.'

'Sorry,' Jayden said, and his father released him.

'Take Grandma to the garden and make sure she gets a chair to sit on.'

'Okay.' Reluctantly, Jayden held his hand out to take Ellen's.

'And fix your face,' Dumpling said.

Immediately Jayden grinned up at Ellen and she smiled back as she shrugged her coat into place and took the soup from Joycelyn. 'Come on Grandma,' he said, tugging. Ellen allowed him to lead her to the back door. As he opened it, he began to shout, 'Grandma needs a chair! Grandma needs a chair!'

The adults all laughed, including CJ who put the phone back to his ear. 'That was my youngest, tearing round the house like a madman.'

'Did you see how he smiled at Mum though?' Claudette asked as she began opening the packets on the counter in front of her, separating batches and putting buns down individually onto a tray.

'How he smiles at *all* women; proper flirting already,' said Joycelyn, picking the buns up and slitting them open to accommodate the burgers.

Dumpling closed the cupboard door and paused with the serviettes in her hand. She raised her eyebrows, pursed her lips and lifted her chin towards CJ who was laughing into his mobile and saying, 'Hear me out, babes, hear me out.'

'Chip off the old block,' she said, then as Clyde entered the kitchen with his friend Franklin, smiling in the direction of his daughters and raising his glass so they could see it was empty, she added, 'Chip off the older blocks too.'

'You just reach?' Claudette asked Franklin as Dumpling put down the serviettes, stepped towards the two men and relieved Clyde of his glass.

'Couple minutes ago,' said Franklin. 'You all right?' he asked, wrapping his arm around Dumpling who smiled at him.

'We're fine,' Claudette said.

'Nice to see you,' said Joycelyn.

'You want whiskey or a Tennent's?' asked Dumpling.

'I'll 'ava Tennent's,' Franklin said.

'Let me get your drinks,' said Dumpling to Clyde and Franklin. Then as she passed CJ she said, 'I'll fill you up,' and swiped CJ's nearly empty glass from his hand as he was raising it to his lips, taking it with her to the other side of the kitchen where the countertop resembled a busy bar.

'How's Miss Gloria doing?' Claudette asked.

'She's fine,' said Franklin. 'I tried to get her to come, but . . .' he shrugged and held his palms up helplessly.

'Tell her we said howdy,' said Joycelyn.

'I will,' he said.

Clyde was looking around the kitchen for Ellen, disappointed she wasn't with the girls and that he couldn't see her anywhere else in the room. He was fresh from the barbers, immaculately dressed and on a charm offensive.

So far this evening, he'd seen her twice and he'd turned up the charisma full force both times, but she hadn't responded. The second time, she'd blatantly cut him dead mid-sentence and walked away. He was worried, but not about Ellen's responses. He considered himself a veteran when it came to navigating his present terrain. There were tactical manoeuvres that needed to be carried out and that was fine. Now wasn't the time anyway, with the house packed with people and the party in full swing. However, before their talk began, he needed to commandeer every opportunity to sweet-talk her, needed – as he had done so many times over the years – to coax free that part of her that loved him no matter what he did, that yearned for him in his absence and forgave all his misdemeanours. Because this time was different. Serious. He was using the same tactics that had worked for him in the past, but the truth was that before he'd always been playing a part. He'd said he had changed when he knew damn well he hadn't. He'd said he had learned from his mistakes when he hadn't really considered his actions to be mistakes at all. He would never forget the time he'd been distracted – Lord have mercy! – in the middle of promising to be faithful to Ellen, by the bounce of Wilhelmina's shapely bottom as she danced. But that was the old him. This time, he had genuinely, one-hundred-percentedly changed. As Dumpling handed Clyde and Franklin their drinks, Clyde intentionally bumped CJ with his other elbow.

'Hold on a sec,' CJ said into the phone before muting it. 'She's in the garden, Dad. I've not forgot.'

'Not forgot what?' Claudette asked as Leah's voice said, 'Hi everyone, hi Mummy,' and Claudette was swallowed up in a hug. As a chorus of hellos and interrogations began, Claudette took hold of Leah's shoulders, forcing her to step back, and swiftly examined her from head to toe and back up again.

'Now's not the time to start discussing my boobs and backside, mum,' said Leah, 'I've got a friend with me, so can we just try be normal for once? Everyone, this is Shani, my mate from uni. This is my mum, my aunties, my grandad, my Uncle CJ – who's gonna be doing the fireworks display. You're not gonna remember who's who, but it's polite to introduce you anyway.'

Leah watched as everyone said variations of hello and welcome, as CJ hurriedly ended his phone call and Clyde took advantage of the delay to get in there first and introduce himself to her friend. Leah would be the first to admit that Shani was good-looking, really good-looking, and she was used to the guys at uni losing their shit when they were in Shani's orbit, but they didn't bother her because they were young and inexperienced and not Leah's actual relatives. She had higher expectations of her grandfather and her mother's brother, though she didn't know why she expected more from them. Neither had ever given her reason to believe they were capable of doing better. Whilst Shani was saying hello and shaking CJ's hand, he was staring directly at her cleavage.

'Nice to meet you,' he said to both breasts.

Shani paused the length of time it took CJ to register

she hadn't responded and drag his gaze upwards to her face.

'If you're in charge of the fireworks, I suppose I should give these to you,' Shani said, handing him a carrier bag wrapped around two large fireworks, which he took out and examined.

'*Burning Bush* and *Erupting Cannon*? Oh my days! We're soulmates,' he said.

As everyone around them erupted in laughter, Leah said, 'Good grief!'

'Soulmates? First off, you'd have to be my type,' Shani said, smiling as sweetly as if she'd delivered a compliment.

'On that note, we're just gonna get some drinks and find Granny,' Leah said, and, waving away the protests, led her friend over to the other side of the kitchen, where she began pouring two drinks.

'I'm really sorry my uncle and my grandad were speaking directly to your breasts. They can't help it. They have a disability,' Leah said, and Shani laughed.

'Your grandad's cute and your uncle's funny.'

'Surface stuff. They're misogynists. Most of the men in my family are. It's my great-great-grandfather's fault.' Leah handed Shani her drink. 'He had forty-nine kids . . .'

'No way,' said Shani.

'Yes way. And he died at thirty.'

'You're lying!'

'I wish I was. It's really the family curse, but some of the men in my family treat it like a bar.' Leah opened the back door and stepped out. 'C'mon,' she said, 'I want you to meet my brother and my nieces.'

Ellen heard the chorus of hellos begin around the barbecue area where Linus was flipping burgers and looked across to the back door to see her granddaughter had arrived with a friend. The girl had no proper respect for her elders, with her facety self, always speaking to everyone like she and them were size, but despite that, or maybe because of it, the young kids in the family loved her, especially the girls. Ellen thought it was typical that the girls would most like the person she would least have chosen for them to look up to. She watched her great-granddaughters, Iffy and Ibbs, jostling with each other and protesting, each vying to be closest to Leah, and Leah reminding her nieces they were sisters and that sisters have to take care of each other. She lifted up both nieces and kissed them before introducing Linus and them to her friend.

Ellen studied the friend, noticing how firmly her feet were planted on the ground, like a man's, very confident of herself, and the thought went through Ellen's head that the friend was a whistler, she was positive of it. She could tell just looking at her. A whistling woman and a crowing hen were an abomination unto the Lord. She watched as the friend smiled at Linus, her poor grandson, run ragged as a headless chicken by Iffy and Ibbs's mother, the vex-faced girlfriend who was with him one minute and broken up with him the next till the poor boy hardly knew if he was coming or going. She watched

Leah's friend smile at Linus, the kind of smile a woman like her would have, big, full, irresistible, and she was happy to see that Linus's smile back was just friendly, nothing more. It was one of the things she loved about her grandson, that he was able to interact with the opposite sex in a way that was just like one person responding to another and nothing to do with whether they were a woman or a man, just that they were people, something she didn't see much of from her husband or CJ. It was how Clay would've been as a man, she was sure of it.

'Look at me, Nanny, look at me,' shrieked Fiona, and Ellen turned her head to look at Dumpling's youngest, who would be seven next month and was holding a sparkler in her hand, moving her arm around in circles as fast as she could so that it created a spiralling light at the top end that was fading at the exact same rate at the bottom. Ellen smiled and said, 'Beautiful,' as the sight transported her to fireflies back home and her fascination with them when she'd been a young girl of the same age, to innocent years and the times she'd chased and caught them and created her own twinkling stars at night in cloth-covered jars. 'Very beautiful,' she said as Fiona skipped away.

'Hello Granny,' said Leah and bent over to kiss Ellen on the cheek.

'You've put on weight,' said Ellen.

'I was about to say the same to you,' said Leah.

Ellen was confident she hadn't put on even an ounce and was offended to be falsely accused. 'Not me. I haven't put on any weight at all,' she said.

'Me neither,' said Leah. 'It's not very nice being told you have when you know you haven't, is it? This is my friend Shani. Shani, this is my gran.'

Shani stepped forward with a big smile and as she bent down, Ellen turned her head and raised her cheek for the kiss Shani placed on it. As Shani straightened up, she said, 'Hello Leah's gran,' but when she spoke, she was looking beyond Ellen, through the window into the kitchen where Ellen knew CJ and Clyde were, their laughter carrying through the window left ajar into the garden. She sighed deeply, looked at Shani directly and shook her head. She was seventy-one years old and had witnessed so many women in heat during that time it was just boring now; predictable and boring.

'That's not very nice, Granny,' Leah said.

'It's okay,' Shani said with a smile, but the truth was Ellen had spooked her. The old woman had looked at her like she'd read her mind and it embarrassed her to think that Leah's grandma had picked up on her attraction to CJ. 'It's really lovely to meet you, Mrs Fenton,' she said.

The back door opened and the adults inside came pouring out, led by CJ who announced, 'Everyone back onto the patio. The fireworks are starting.'

The folks on and around the patio space were suddenly as busy as guests at a wedding getting ready for the group photo, the children sieved to the front where they'd have the clearest view of the fireworks, as the adults moved towards the rear, and Ellen – on account of her age and the fact she was sitting on a chair – was jostled along with her seat from the back to the front of the patio alongside the grands and great-grands.

'I'm really sorry,' Leah said to Shani.

'You're crazy. This is amazing.'

'Growing up in care's made you over-sentimental about families,' Leah said.

'Do you know anyone less sentimental than me?'

'Fair point.'

Shani took a slow look around her. 'I can't stop staring. This is way better than every fantasy I had as a kid.'

'Bigger,' said Leah.

'Better,' Shani said.

CJ placed a firework into the holder he'd inserted in the ground near the back end of the lawn and shouted, 'Everybody ready?' Shani grinned at Leah then turned her head and shouted along with the children, 'Yes!'

'I asked, is everybody ready?' CJ said, cupping his hand to his ear. Like the audience at a pantomime, this time Leah, Shani and everyone else responded louder, 'Yes!'

'That's good,' said CJ. 'Because once we get going, there's no turning back.'

And though his eyes roved generally over the people now arranged on the patio in a neatly inclined mass, they intentionally paused when they got to Shani, who he thought was possibly the sexiest woman he'd ever seen.

Ellen had really enjoyed the fireworks. It was her favourite part of the November party they'd hosted every year for the last three decades, the fireworks. They were always good, because the adults each brought a firework along with them, and the initial ribbing over duff ones had evolved into a joking-not-joking-at-all competitiveness that ensured the standard remained consistently high. This year's fireworks had been spectacular, and now they were finished so was she. Claudette and Joycelyn weren't wrong; she had been up since the crack of dawn, waking at five thirty to get the soup on, hauling out her party pot for the occasion. She'd spent the entire morning peeling and slicing and chopping and stirring, wheedling and coaxing her legendary broth into a state of culinary perfection. She could see people grabbing cups of her soup from Claudette as she passed through the crowd carrying them on a tray, closely followed by Joycelyn who was carrying another tray of burgers, and Dumpling keeping up the rear with the condiments and serviettes. They stopped near the barbecue, at the group Leah was part of along with her no-good friend. The two young women had Iffy and Ibbs on a hip each and were in conversation with Linus, CJ, Franklin and Clyde. Ellen watched as Leah put Iffy down and set about sorting out a burger for her, then, as Dumpling laughed at something Franklin said, she heard her mother's voice inside her head say, *blood follow vein*. She looked around at all the people gathered in the garden, amongst them four children, ten grandchildren and the six – and counting – great-grandkids, and took a moment, as she did at every family event, to remember Clay, and all those loved ones up there resting with the ancestors – or, in the case of her mother, quickstepping like crapo on the hot coals spread over every inch of the terrible ground below; took a moment to experience gratitude, for all of this was her clan, the tribe she had raised with her bare hands, recognising that had she died when she was nineteen the majority of the people here would never have existed. Had she died at nineteen, Clyde would still have been running round the earth like some kind of crazed sex maniac, would still, no doubt, have had children with other women – *more* other women – but they would not have been these people here in the garden right now, the ones she was watching laugh, eat and make merry, the ones who, for her, had been the point of everything.

And suddenly, she was exhausted. The prep for this party had begun days ago, with a long stretch of non-stop organisation and proper hard grafting. Now the fireworks were over, it was time for the triple birthday celebrations for Claudette, Joycelyn and CJ to begin. The stereo volume had already been turned up. The hard drinking would start as soon as the easy food – the burgers and patties and soup – had been served, the signal for the commencement of proper food; the curry and rice, the saltfish and johnnycakes, the goat water and fried chicken and hard dough bread. She'd played her part. The girls could handle the rest of the evening without her. She decided she would have a cup of soup and a pattie, retire to her room to enjoy them in peace and leave them all to it.

'Here you go.' Ellen looked up at Leah who was holding a small tray with a side plate and a cup of soup beside it. On the plate was a pattie inside a serviette which was folded around it like a taco. 'Note I'm being nice to you even though you were very rude to my friend. Lucky for you, I'm not a grudge-holder.'

It was a struggle for Ellen to stop herself smiling. Her granddaughter had her faults, quite a number of them, but every so often her instincts were as spot on as any witch's. She took the tray Leah was holding out to her. '*Your* friend? I thought she was CJ's friend.'

The two women looked over at Shani as a loud burst of laughter came from the group she was standing with. As they laughed, both Shani and CJ were looking at each other.

'You know, you really didn't do a good job with Uncle CJ, a grown man his age chasing after anything in a skirt even when she's younger than half his kids.'

'Me?' Ellen asked, looking at Clyde who was standing beside CJ, the two of them rocking together as they laughed. Clyde's hand was on his son's forearm as he spoke to him. Perhaps sensing he was being watched, Clyde looked up and the smile on his lips swiftly evaporated as his eyes locked with hers. In response, she pushed up her mouth and savaged Clyde with a mercilessly slow cutting of her eyes. She handed the tray back to Leah and strained as she forced herself up and out of the chair she was sitting on. 'He's his father's son.'

'Where're you going?'

'Upstairs.'

'Okay,' Leah said, and fell in line behind her grandmother, following as she made her way slowly towards the back door. Just as Ellen reached for the handle, CJ materialised.

'Mum,' he said. Ellen looked at her son turned foot soldier. 'Dad wants to speak to you.'

'Not now,' Ellen said.

'I told him that already. Can he pass by tomorrow?'

Ellen nodded.

'What time?'

'Eleven.'

'Thanks,' Clyde said, from CJ's other side, smiling at Ellen, who turned her head away from him, opened the back door and stepped inside the house.

'It'd be great if my friend wasn't pregnant by the time I got back,' Leah said to her uncle and grandad as if she was joking, then entered the house also, pulling the back door closed behind her.

Clyde's face was too expressive. Ellen knew what expressive meant because once, after a woman who introduced herself as *Mrs* Etienne knocked her front door and told her Clyde had been having an affair with her, when Ellen confronted Clyde and asked him why he'd done it, he told Ellen she made him feel confused because she never seemed to be happy to see him or sad to see him go. He said her face wasn't expressive. She hadn't realised what the word meant then. She'd had to search Claudette and Joycelyn's room for the dictionary the school had given them and look the word up when she found it, which helped her understand that what Clyde meant was that her face didn't show her feelings. Ellen reached up and opened the cupboard the cups were kept in, astonished it had taken her till the ripe old age of seventy-one to finally recognise how overly expressive her husband's face was of every emotion he chose to convey.

It was something she associated most with babies and young children. Babies had very expressive faces. When they were happy and laughing, their expressions filled her with so much joy she couldn't stop grinning and laughing along with them. When they were upset, when their tiny mouths were downturned at the corners, their cheeks and forehead creased into folds of unhappiness, their eyes squeezed tight in an expression of wretchedness and misery, all she wanted to do was whatever would resolve the cause of their unhappiness: feeding, changing, burping, cuddling, jiggling them, kissing, cooing, entertaining them till they were better, their wretched expressions gone. It was strongest in babies that expressiveness, slowly reducing as they got older. Many adults grew out of it completely, but Clyde hadn't. His expressiveness was on par with that of Iffy, who was four, or Ibbs, who was two. When he looked sad, Ellen wanted to cheer him up. When he was happy, it was all she could do to keep her drawers up. There was no one who looked more honest when they were telling barefaced lies and she'd yet to see an adult look more remorseful than the soulless, heartless man her life had been bound to for the last fifty years. Clyde had an expressive face and today, now that she had worked out the source of his superpower, she was determined she wasn't going to be tricked by it.

Her resolution made, she prepared three cups for tea, but only poured the hot water into hers, leaving the other two on standby for the arrival of Clyde and CJ, his general. The two of them were cut from the same cloth and more inseparable than twins. Clyde had fortified his army long before Ellen had known she was in a war, and by the time she'd realised, it was already too late. CJ had said Clyde wanted to speak to her, but he would not come alone, of this she was certain; at eleven o'clock, her husband and son would arrive together.

She felt calm, but that meant nothing. How many times had she felt calm then let Clyde's expressive face talk her into doing precisely what he wanted? She had no idea the specific number of times that had happened, but she knew it had been every time. And it wasn't as if she'd headed into each of those conversations clueless. She'd always been able to read Clyde like a book, better than she could read the children she'd raised – for the most part – since they were babies. Like now, Ellen knew exactly what Clyde wanted to discuss with her. She was so confident of it that if she'd been a betting woman – which she absolutely was not, never had been and never would be – she would've been confident enough to bet her house. She knew what he was on his way to discuss and right now, her answer was no, but she still had to meet with him and look into that expressive face of his and stand her ground. She heard the unmistakeable sound of her mother's laughter. Instead of a joyful sound, it was cruel, not laughing with but at her, and Ellen felt even less sure of what her decision would be by the end of their meeting.

A few minutes past eleven, at the sound of CJ's key in the front door, she put the kettle on. When they entered the kitchen, CJ said, 'Hi Mum,' and Clyde said, 'Ellen,' with a nod and she responded by nod and asked, 'You want tea?' to which they both answered, 'Yes,' and sat at the kitchen table where she'd left a plate of biscuits in the centre to indicate that was where the meeting would be taking place, and not in the living room. The living room felt too much like a social visit, a room to get comfy in, relax. The kitchen table was for business, where serious discussions were held, important decisions reached, where thousands of games of dominoes had been played. As she put their cups in front of them and took her seat, Clyde sipped his and said, 'Mmm. Just the way I like it,' and Ellen looked at him, at his face, at the expression on it that assured her firstly that he'd missed her, and secondly that mistakes had been made and would be learned from; the lying dog.

'What was it you wanted to speak about?'

CJ got straight to the point. 'Dad wants to come back home.'

Ellen didn't take her eyes off Clyde. 'Oh?'

'He made a mistake. He's really sorry.'

Clyde was staring with fascination into his cup.

'You said it was time you had fun. You wanted somebody to make you laugh. Me never learn no new joke after you gone. You sure is back here you want to come?' Ellen asked.

'You the only woman me want. The only one ever understand me,' Clyde said.

'Took you a long time to figure that out,' Ellen said. 'Near 'nough two years.'

Clyde sniffed and looked up at her. His eyes were filled with tears, his mouth downturned like a crescent moon tipped onto its side. He began to search his jacket pockets for his handkerchief. As he sniffed again, CJ reached onto the worktop, lifted the kitchen roll on its holder down and placed it in the centre of the table. He tore off a sheet and handed it to his father. He said, 'Mum, Dad's said he's sorry. He knows he shouldn't've done it. He'll never do it again. Even if he wannid, he can't. Don't kick a man when he's down.'

Ellen recalled the gravediggers shovelling earth onto her mother's coffin. Then, like now, it surprised her that she didn't feel anything. Normally, she would have felt upset – yes – but also sorry for Clyde based on her belief in the truth of the expressions on his face. This time however, much as she rummaged around inside herself, she couldn't feel anything resembling an emotional response. Almost two years ago he'd moved out of the family home and in with Wilhelmina, Ellen's friend, Ellen's good good friend, her only real friend; moved out and in with the last friend Ellen had left. What Clyde had never understood was that the biggest part of what kept him and Ellen together was the shared life they had built up over the last fifty-two years, the children they had raised and the grandchildren and the great-grands. Ellen wanted all those generations to be able to come and visit and see and stay with them both in the same house. Back in the day, when Clyde first entered her and her world, she had considered her life an instant success and had always been content to have risen to greatness as a consequence of proximity. As the family had grown and the generations had increased, success – as she saw it – shifted, becoming increasingly evidenced by the fact they were still together, however hard the work had been to achieve that. She hadn't wanted to explain to Iffy and Ibbs that Nana and Pappy wanted to live in different houses now – *Does Pappy get his dinner at Uber Eats now, Nana?* She hadn't wanted to explain to her grandchildren that they had both decided it was better for them to live apart, or to listen to her children talking about Clyde as if he was a child instead of a hard-back grown man – *he needs to be free to find his way, Mummy* – or an insect – *the bee moves from flower to flower* – a saying she was positive Clyde had taught them. They'd shared their lives and created generations of family and that was what underpinned her desire to keep taking him back. But he'd been gone for almost two years this time and she'd been okay, better than okay, she'd been relaxed, free from the regular stress he was always putting her through. A year ago, she'd read in the newspaper that her grandchildren were the 'bounceback generation' that kept moving away from home, yet for financial reasons, kept returning. But what about the bounceback husbands who kept going off and coming back like raatid yoyos? What about them? In the past, this was the stuff Ellen would have been upset about, but today it seemed she genuinely didn't care any more. He'd done this too many times. She was no longer 'carrying feelings', as they would've said back home. In fact, sitting at that table, listening to Clyde's pathetic sniffing and watching the dabbing of the tissue along the bottom lids of his eyes, the only real feeling she could honestly say she felt was fatigue. She'd been there, done it, and had a shelf-load of T-shirts to prove it. Then she thought again about what CJ had said. She looked at her son.

'What do you mean?'

CJ asked, 'What?'

'You said even if he wanted to leave again, he can't. What did you mean?'

As if he'd been awaiting his cue, Clyde started blinking fast and his lips began to move soundlessly. Ellen was only just able to understand the words that suddenly burst from his mouth between a moist snort and the onset of some proper blubbing and bawling. 'It's cancer,' he said. 'Them can't do nothing.'

And with his own voice heavily choked with emotion, 'Dad's a dead man walking,' CJ said.

Later, after Clyde and CJ had left the house and she'd run herself a bath then got into it with a cup of hot chocolate to have a good cry, Ellen thought two things. The first was that Clyde had been wrong about her face not being expressive, and maybe that was because he'd never seen her crying in the bathtub or shower, because those were the only places she allowed herself to cry. She was positive it was because of her mother, who didn't believe in wasting good words when slaps were quicker, and after she'd slapped her daughter, if tears welled up in Ellen's eyes or – God forbid! – she did begin to cry, that was her mother's cue to give Ellen something to *really* cry about. So no, she didn't do public bouts of tears. Tears were saved for when she was in the bath or the shower for the simple reason that water got rid of the evidence. In the shower, she would cry as silently as she could while the water cascaded down her face and body, washing away the tears even before they'd left her eyes. In the bath, she filled the tub, got in, sat down, then wet a flannel, lay back and used the flannel to cover her face so that the wet flannel absorbed her tears while she got on with it. The only time she'd ever cried in front of Clyde was the day Clay died, and really, anyone could be excused for that. As she lay in the bath with the flannel over her face, she thought if Clyde could see her now, he would have to apologise for accusing her face of not being expressive.

The second thing she thought was that the anger imploding inside her chest was directed at the right person and, despite her tears, that struck her as interesting. That day when *Mrs* Etienne had knocked and told her about the affair Clyde had been having with her, Ellen had been livid, but not with Clyde: with the other woman. She could distinctly recall thinking the woman had knocked her door to try and break up her family. She had told *Mrs* Etienne to get her dirty lying mouth off her front doorstep. She'd said, in no uncertain terms, that only a truly wotless person could be turning up at someone else's home announcing who it was they'd been entertaining between their married legs. She'd told her she wasn't the first woman who'd thought she'd gone up in the world just because she'd moved to England and now owned the two pairs of drawers. She had asked *Mrs* Etienne whether she even knew how to spell the word *shame*? All those words spoken in anger towards the woman when she hadn't doubted for an instant that what she'd said was true. When Clyde returned home from work, Ellen hadn't even bothered to waste good breath asking him if it was true; she'd asked him instead why he'd done it. Even then she wasn't angry with him; she was genuinely confused. She'd never said no to Clyde in bed. Apart from the fear of pregnancy – she already had as many children as she'd wanted even before Clay was born – apart from the constant worry about falling pregnant and having yet more babies, she liked sleeping with him – very much. So, it was with hurt and genuine confusion she had waited for him to come in from work and asked him why he'd slept with *Mrs* Etienne. That was the day he'd extended her vocabulary by teaching her the word *expressive* and explaining to her that her face wasn't. Even after that discussion, instead of being angry with Clyde, she'd gone off to her bedroom to sit on the little stool in front of her dressing table and examine her face. With one single exception which she didn't really like to think about, that was how it had been for pretty much all of their marriage, her being angry with other women for coming on to her husband, her being angry with herself for her inability to keep his zipper up, her being angry with people who thought she was stupid for putting up with his behaviour or worse, pitied her. Only one time had she felt proper anger towards her handsome husband with his expressive face and it had been disastrous. Lying in the bath, however, thinking about what he'd put her through throughout their marriage, what – up to that very morning – he was still putting her through, the wotless shameless barefacedness of the man to leave the house he'd been living in with Wilhelmina for the last two years to ask to come back into the marital home so she could nurse him till his death, Ellen wanted to wring his bloody neck with her bare hands while releasing her rage in a billowing roar. This time the feelings felt right to her, like her emotions had been travelling on a bus on diversion throughout her entire adult life but the bus had suddenly reverted to the route it should have been on from the beginning, and she heard a gentle voice inside her head – she had no idea whose it was, but it was certainly not her mother's – as it whispered, *finally. About time.*

From the moment Leah opened her eyes, she knew she'd drunk way too much the night before and she immediately closed them again against the painful brightness of day and reached for the litre-sized bottle of water on the table bedside her bed, opened it by feel, chugged half of it, then set it back down. Lying on her back she took a moment to assess her body. Her head hurt, not just some parts of it, her whole head hurt, like her skull was a drum being beaten by a powerful musician. Even the channels of her ears and the cavities of her eyeballs pulsed, and her mouth and throat and the inside of her eyelids were as dry as if they'd been coated with volcanic ash. Despite the water she'd just drunk, her whole body felt dehydrated, but other than the impact of too much alcohol and terrible dehydration, she could feel no bruises or injuries. Moving on, she did what she always did when she awoke from a drinking blackout; she tried to piece together the previous night.

She could feel she was wearing loose pyjama bottoms and a T-shirt. That was good. That meant she'd managed to get herself upstairs to her room in the attic on her own steam and had sufficient wherewithal to get undressed and put her pyjamas on before getting into bed, as opposed to passing out. Fantastic! That was a great start. Then she remembered that Shani had been with her last night. Despite her senses telling her she was alone, she opened her eyes again and sat up. Shani wasn't in her bed or anywhere in the room. She picked up her mobile from the bedside table. There were two missed calls and one voicemail, all from her mum; no missed calls or messages from Shani. She lay back down and closed her eyes, trying to recall how the party had ended. Nothing. Shani leaving? Her mind was blank. She took a deep breath then began working through the evening chronologically.

They'd watched the fireworks in the garden. She'd left Shani downstairs when she came upstairs with Granny and saw her into her bedroom. Then she went out to the car and unloaded her stuff from uni, carrying it all upstairs to her room. When she went back downstairs, Shani and Uncle CJ were laughing and chatting together and she joined them for a bit but then wandered off because she was annoyed by it, not with Shani, but with her uncle, because she'd seen this kind of shit happen before, too many times; Uncle CJ's inability to rein himself in, and his monopolising of what was for him female fresh meat. She remembered leaving them to it but then, nothing. Then she recalled being at the drinks counter in the kitchen feeling tipsy and distinctly thinking she'd had enough and should stop drinking as she poured herself another drink anyway and knocked it back like it was an alcopop. She rolled over onto her other side. This was not good.

Her eyes were still closed, one of her hands on her head. Now she didn't want to remember last night at all, but it was already too late. Horrified, she had a flashback of screaming at Uncle CJ that he was the reason she didn't trust men – oh God! She turned over onto her other side hoping maybe that might be the end of it, but the clear memory of Shani touching her arm came to her, her friend telling her to calm down and that she, Shani, was an adult and could handle herself. Leah answered that it wasn't about her, it was about him, about men like him and she recalled that when she said it she was crying and people around her, including her mum and aunties, were trying to stop her, to pull her away, telling her she'd gone too far and she recalled herself telling them they were just as much to blame for him and for Grandad – shit! She'd even brought Grandad into it – that they were all part of the problem.

Her phone pinged. Leah opened her eyes and picked it up. A text message was on the front screen. From her mum again. It said *RING ME*. She put the phone back down and slowly sat up on the edge of the bed. Her feet moved around on autopilot, feeling for the slippers which were not there. She looked down. Couldn't see them, closed her eyes again, and held her head between her two hands, snapping them together to cover her face with her palms. She tried to remember Shani leaving but couldn't. Saying goodbye; nothing. Then she remembered Uncle CJ saying she had embarrassed herself and he was taking Shani home. Try as she might, she couldn't recall Linus and Iffy and Ibbs at all. She really hoped that meant they'd left by then and hadn't seen her shouting and crying and behaving like a crazy drunk.

'Oh God!' Leah stood up. She could see her slippers askew on the carpet beside the bedroom door and had an instant flashback to her hurling them last night as her mother and Auntie Joycelyn were leaving the room. The tune being beaten by the drummer in her head was reaching its crescendo. Her bladder was full. She needed the toilet then more water then some orange juice and a mug of black coffee with paracetamol, and she really *really* needed something to eat. It had been a terrible night.

She stood up, careful to make no sudden movements, opened the door and began her slow smooth descent down the stairs to the next landing. She was so absorbed in her own discomfort, it was only once she was right outside the bathroom door that she registered the sound which was clearly coming from inside that room and had been getting louder, and she found herself trying and failing to account for the sound, which sounded like crying, very distressed crying from a voice that was familiar and yet alien in relation to that sound. She tapped at the bathroom door, softly at first then much louder.

She said, 'Granny, is that you?' The crying stopped. There was a great splosh of water as if her grandmother had suddenly sat up in a full bath. 'Please say something, otherwise I'm coming in.'

'It's okay,' Ellen said. 'It's okay. I'm fine.'

'I can hear you're not,' Leah said. She reached for the door handle and grasped it, but before she could turn it, the sound began again and she realised her grandmother wasn't crying; she was laughing, hysterically. 'Granny, you sure you're okay?'

The laughter morphed into a fit of coughing before Ellen answered, 'I'm fine, girl. Go on about you business. I couldn't be better.'

The Big Dinner

February 2011

(Four years earlier)

Although the room in the attic was the largest bedroom in the house, Ellen had prepared the smaller of the three bedrooms on the first floor for Cassius and his wife. She hadn't put them in the attic because Cassius was seventy-four, and although his wife was almost a decade younger Ellen had worried that the stairs would be a problem if they needed to use the bathroom in the night, as the attic didn't have an ensuite, a decision she'd regretted since 1979, when they did the loft conversion for Claudette and Joycelyn to share after Dumpling arrived and they needed more space. They were fifteen and sixteen then, still young girls. Clay had just been buried and money was tight, and because she was still reeling from all those things that had happened in such a short space of time she really wasn't thinking straight, which is how the biggest bedroom in the house had ended up being the furthest away from the bathroom and toilet, and the least convenient for staying guests, especially if they were elderly.

She also hadn't put them in the medium-sized room on the middle floor because that had originally been CJ's childhood bedroom up until he began to have what Ellen referred to as his *woman-friends* stay over, when, to Clyde's amusement and Ellen's mortification, they discovered that the brick wall that divided their room from his, though strong enough to be one of the building's supporting walls, was useless at muffling sound, which meant they could hear the squeaking of the bed and the creaking of the floorboards beneath it in addition to the audible oral sounds of CJ and his woman-friends having sex in real time. In summary, Ellen hadn't put them in the attic on account of them being too old to go up and down the stairs in the night and she hadn't put them in the room next door to hers in case they were still young enough to be at the nookie. Instead, she was giving a final once over to the smallest bedroom, which she'd been preparing for days with clean sheets and towels and a thorough dusting, hoovering, polishing and airing.

It had been Dumpling's room before she swapped over with CJ when he became a man, and though not the biggest, it was still a decent sized double.

She'd had Linus carry the portable TV up from the kitchen and a battery-operated radio down from the attic, so that Cassius and Janet could comfortably pass time in the room if they wanted a bit of peace and quiet.

She'd also had Linus bring up the small round table that was normally by the front door, then bring down the two easy chairs so they could sit and have a drink or a cup of tea and read the newspapers or relax and WhatsApp their family in the States in comfort, and because it was March, yesterday she'd placed daffodils and water into the vase on the dresser so that in addition to brightening up the space, the yellow blooms had the opportunity to burst free from the shroud of their bud and begin teasing the air with their delicate talcum scent.

Though they'd spoken on the phone over the decades, Ellen had never met Janet in person, and as for Cassius, this would be his first visit to the UK since his last one in 1971 when Ellen had wanted to kill Clyde but couldn't because, to all intents and purposes, he was already dying. Ellen checked the watch on her wrist. CJ had picked Clyde up three hours ago and driven them both to Gatwick to collect Cassius and his wife and their baggage. They would be back in an hour or so. She stood outside the entrance to the room and took one last look about her before pulling the door closed. She hoped that they liked it enough to want to stay inside it as much as possible.

'Just gimme one good reason why I should go see him?' Leah asked, dropping her spoon into the mug she'd been stirring, her interest in the cup of hot chocolate she was making having evaporated.

'Because he's your dad,' said Claudette.

'Honour thy mother and thy father,' said Joycelyn.

'Auntie, stop it,' Leah said to Joycelyn, 'You don't even go church.'

'Why do you have to be so rude?' asked Claudette.

'Why do we have to do this on my birthday? Every. Single. Year.'

'Why can't you be like your brother?' asked Claudette, looking at Linus, who did go and see his father on his birthday each year and with whom every tiny thing did not always have to turn into a massive issue. Immediately, Linus picked up the final Digestive on his saucer, having already worked his way through the seven that had been on top of it, and with the focus of a surgeon in theatre mid-op, began dunking the edge of the biscuit into his tea. He loved his mum and he adored his sister. He hated these rows and couldn't bring himself to hurt either of them by supporting the other one. Leah often called him Switzerland, but at times like this it was not neutrality he was hoping for, it was invisibility. Even as he raised the biscuit and took a bite, he continued staring into his mug to avoid being dragged into the argument by accidentally catching someone's eye.

'What Linus does is his business. What I do is mine,' Leah said.

'It's one bloody day,' said Claudette, 'One bloody day!'

'Well, if it's no big deal, why doesn't he do it? Why doesn't he put himself out and come visit me one day a year?'

'It's a respect thing,' said Joycelyn.

'He's a sperm donor. I don't respect him.'

Claudette sucked air into her lungs sharply and

clutched at the area above her left breast where she could feel palpitations; actual palpitations. To hear the rude gal refer to Abraham – the man she had loved and shared her soul with – as *a sperm donor*. If he was a sperm donor, what did that make her? A receiver? The carrier? An oven? Not for the first time, she wondered whether Leah was actively trying to kill her. Arguing like the two of them were size. Like because she was eighteen now and an adult by law, she could do whatever she pleased and speak to her mother and her auntie anyhow she felt. 'Respect me and do what you're told!' said Claudette.

'I'm eighteen. You can't tell me what to do any more,' Leah said.

Claudette blamed England for filling kids' heads with rights, encouraging them to backchat adults, making them feel entitled to refuse to do what they were told. Kids back home just didn't behave like this. You think she could've been walking around Montserrat when she was a pickney telling old Mistress Fenton she didn't feel like fetching water? Or that she would go river to wash clothes when she was ready? Or that old Mistress Fenton couldn't tell her what to do? If she'd lost her mind somewhere and found herself standing in front of her grandmother chatting that rudeness to her face, she would've been roasted. Dead. She wouldn't have spoken to her like that then and she wouldn't – if the blessed woman was still alive – speak to her like that even now. Children were still children whether they grew bigger or not, and she would not allow anyone she'd been in labour with for almost two days to speak to her like that.

'As long as you're under this roof, you'll do what I say,' Claudette said.

'Then maybe I should go,' said Leah.

'Well, it's your choice,' said Claudette, feeling pressured to show no weakness in front of Joycelyn and hoping her strong words would force Leah to recognise what should be a natural hierarchy and just stop with all the facetyness.

Instead, Claudette's words landed on Leah like a slap. She knew her mother would never have said that to Linus. She had been relegated to her place as usual: lower and lesser. She'd always had to shout to be heard, fight to be seen, while all the men in her family had to do to qualify for unconditional respect was be born.

'Fine!' said Leah. She turned her back to the silenced room and slowly poured the lumpy hot chocolate mixture into the sink, blinking quickly while willing herself not to cry. Determined to show no weakness, she slowly tore a sheet off the kitchen roll and dried her hands before walking to the door and leaving the room.

There was silence for a moment then Joycelyn said, 'She ain't going nowhere. She's just giving it the biggun.'

Too quickly, Claudette nodded in response. Her throat felt physically blocked and she didn't trust herself to speak, but the truth was she'd never known Leah to change her mind once she'd made a decision, which meant the person who would need to do the compromising to sort this out was her. But she was the mother. It wasn't the natural order. And it would be embarrassing. She could feel Linus staring at her and she looked at her son, her sweet little man, so easy, so uncomplicated, wishing for the thousandth time that Leah had been born a boy as well.

'Well?' Linus said.

'She's out of order,' Claudette said.

Linus rose from his chair and took his cup to the sink. 'I'm gonna go speak to her. Everyone says things they don't mean when they're angry.'

Joycelyn took a sip of her tea, looked at her nephew and raised her eyebrows. 'Good luck with that.'

At the sound of the key in the front door lock, Dumpling was the first to stand, instinctively scooping her youngest, Fiona, from her lap to her hip as she did so. Frank Junior, who was seven, had been sitting on the sofa beside his grandma, but he was so impacted by his mother's excitement that he stood up too, impatient for the first glance of his great-uncle Cassius, his grandfather's brother, whose visit had been the subject of such intense talk for so many months that he had become a legend of a man in the head of the young boy. He'd heard how Uncle Cassius's son, Junior, had disappeared in Alabama when he was twelve and to this day had not been found – he'd had nightmares about it; lots of them. How Junior's mum, Auntie Shola, had died not even a year after when her heart cracked in two. He'd heard that Uncle Cassius got shot when he was put in the army and sent to Vietnam to fight in a war, and ever since then had three holes in him. Frank Junior had thought about those bullet holes a lot and in one of his dreams, saw his uncle standing in their living room in front of the window with the sunlight breaking around his silhouette like an eclipse, streaming three beams of light through the holes in his body, which bounced around the living room carpet, ceiling and walls like search lights. He'd heard and dreamt so much about his uncle he felt like he knew him, but other than seeing him a couple of times on his mum's laptop, he'd not yet met him in real life. Tingling with anticipation beside his mum and quite unable to stand still, Frank Junior began doing a crazy dance.

'Sounds like they're here,' Wilhelmina said, rising with her empty mug in her hand and reaching for the one on Ellen's lap also.

'Thank you,' Ellen said, smoothing the front of the frock she'd laboured over earlier, uncharacteristically undecided about what to wear. She was so glad Wilhelmina had come over to give her support, glad that in her sixty-seventh year – with a burial ground's worth of the bones of her former friendships trailing through her adult life behind her – she'd managed to preserve this one friendship for so long, with a good good friend who never got in the way and always did what needed to be done without first having to be asked. Ellen reached out her hand and squeezed Wilhelmina's wrist and her friend smiled down at her. Ellen smiled back. They could not have been closer if they'd been sisters.

Dumpling looked at Frank Junior dancing beside her and said, 'Stop it,' then opened the living room door and Cassius and his wife Janet and Clyde and CJ poured into the room with cases and bags and coats and hats and for the moment there was a blur of hugs, salutations and introductions and amidst the noise and chaos and raised voices, Ellen's eyes caught those of Cassius, identical to those of Clyde, and the dizziness that accompanied the disorientation she experienced, had she not already been seated, would have brought her to her knees.

'We been looking forward to this so long. How y'all doing?' Janet asked, materialising in front of Ellen as she stood, and embracing the sister-in-law she'd never met before in real life as tightly as if she were a lifebuoy.

'We're well,' Ellen replied. 'How was the journey?'

'Girl, it was long!'

Janet released Ellen's waist and, taking hold of her shoulders, she stepped back and examined her sister-in-law. Ellen examined Janet too; young-looking for sixty-five, neat and trim with a face made kind by laughter lines when she smiled and better looking than Ellen was, which was something Ellen was generally used to; she had many attributes, but good looks was not the one that first came to mind. Ellen considered herself a bit old in the tooth to be playing silly games with other women, so was surprised to feel the sting that accompanied her noticing how attractive Janet was. Sixty-five and young enough, Ellen suspected, to be at the nookie regularly. It had been the right decision not to put them into CJ's old room.

'You lookin' good, girl. Come here,' Janet said, then embraced her again.

'Thank you. And you,' Ellen said, trying to conceal her desire to wriggle away from the unaccustomed physical affection. 'Let me introduce you to my friend Wilhelmina, and Dumpling and the grandkids.'

As another round of introductions commenced, Ellen turned around away from the group and found herself face to face with Cassius and Clyde, both laughing in response to a joke she'd missed, each with an arm around the other that gave her an instant insight into what they might have been like as mischievous young boys.

'You could be twins,' she said, with a grin, but as Cassius grabbed and hugged her then released her, searching her eyes and not her form, she acknowledged that wasn't exactly true. Cassius was older and, unlike his charmed brother, life had tossed him masses of catastrophes to deal with. Though he was only five years older than Clyde, those catastrophes were etched into his face in the form of lines, wrinkles and saggy bags, and whereas Clyde's hair was greying around the edges and his sideburns in a way that made him look distinguished, Cassius's head of hair was a shock of silver so light it was virtually white. Their height and the shape of their bodies, heads, faces, features and skin colour were the same, but although he didn't hold and move himself like an old man, visually Cassius could still have been mistaken for Clyde's dad, and definitely looked too old to be wandering up and down stairs in the night-time to pee.

'I hope you taking me for the younger-looking twin,' said Cassius, without taking his eyes off hers, and for a moment Ellen wondered how different her life might have been with this brother, who was searching her face seeking clues as to how she was and whether she was happy and what was going on inside her, unlike the one whose only searching when it came to women was confined to the insides of their drawers. She didn't know what he saw in her eyes, but she believed he'd registered something of her unhappiness and for a moment she felt visible, façade-free, able to acknowledge and have acknowledged the pain she carried, the pain that was a fundamental part of the reconstruction she'd been undergoing for decades and which she'd come to hide as a matter of course. In that briefest connection, she recognised the tragedy of her life was matched by the tragedy of his and she experienced a moment of déjà vu during which she thought she might cry.

'You can be younger, I'll take better looking,' said Clyde, clapping Cassius on the back as he laughed hard. Ellen was thankful; it made Cassius look away from her and at his brother, allowing her to swiftly rub her index fingers under her eyes and sniff twice, instantly regaining her composure.

'Looks like we got double trouble,' Janet said, materialising beside her.

'Double trouble for true,' Ellen said. 'Come, make me show you you room, give you some time to relax yourself and settle in.'

'That'd be great,' Janet said. 'Feels like we been travelling for months.'

The two women picked up some of the smaller bags and packages and made their way into the hallway. Just as Ellen lifted her foot onto the first step, the doorbell rang. She smiled at Janet. 'Hol' on a minute,' she said, turning around and heading back towards the front door. She opened it to find Leah and Linus standing there, Linus carrying two suitcases and Leah holding a large crate of what looked like stationery, folders and text books, clearly having just stopped crying. Linus raised his eyebrows and gave his grandmother a look that said, *yes, this is a big issue.*

Clyde came out of the living room. 'I thought I heard the bell.' Then, spotting his grandkids, he said, 'Linus! Howdy. Come on in. Hey Leah. Say hello to your Aunt Janet. These are Claudette's kids.'

Leah and Linus entered the hallway, closing the front door behind them, both politely saying hello and giving hugs to their great-aunt.

'I was just taking Janet to their room.' Ellen handed the bags in her hand to Clyde. 'Take these up and show her where it is,' she said, then observed what was probably the biggest difference between the two brothers, as Clyde's gaze alighted briefly upon Janet's breasts before bouncing up to her face with a smile.

'Follow me,' he said.

Although Ellen didn't hear what Clyde said next, she guessed it must have been amusing because Janet burst out laughing halfway up the flight of stairs and said, 'You stop that.'

'Morning,' Wilhelmina said to Leah and Linus, then, looking down at their suitcases and paraphernalia, added, 'You better go on inside.'

As Leah and Linus pulled the two cases through to the kitchen, the sound of Janet laughing was heard again.

'We need to keep an eye on that one,' Wilhelmina whispered, with an upward glance toward the ceiling. Then, raising her voice to normal levels, said, 'I was gonna sort out some drinks, but looks like you need your space.' She walked back into the living room as Ellen began making her way to the kitchen.

Ellen had been born in Montserrat, during a time when people didn't speak to children about big people business. From her birth up until 1955, when her mother returned to the island to collect her from the next-door neighbour, Mrs Skerritt, she had no recollection of seeing or living with either of her parents. In fact, from the perspective of memory alone, it was as if she'd always lived with Mrs Skerritt. No one ever sat her down and explained that her mother and father were away on other islands trying to earn a living, or deemed it necessary to give her a date to look forward to on which they might possibly return. The day her mother showed up to collect her had been a perfectly normal day, without a single thing occurring or a single word said that might indicate something completely out of the ordinary was going to happen – and when it did Ellen had been astonished.

She'd been outside in the back yard handwashing laundry in the great metal tub. Mrs Skerritt had stepped out of the house and said 'Dry you hand. Somebody's here for you,' then proceeded to walk ahead of Ellen back into the front room where a woman was standing, very well dressed, very serious, a perfect stranger. Her first emotion had been fear, that unbeknownst to herself she'd done something wrong and was about to be in trouble. Only when Ellen looked from the hard-faced woman to Mrs Skerritt in confusion did she add, 'This is you mother.'

It seemed to Ellen that she should feel something other than what she felt when she looked back at the woman who was her mother, some tenderness or love maybe, even recognition, but the only thing she felt was curiosity. Her mother continued to stare at her a moment longer before looking away from Ellen, back to Mrs Skerritt then said, 'That's not what I was expecting.'

Such a big thing and yet she'd had no chance to prepare herself, like she'd had no advance opportunity to explore the fact her name wasn't actually *Ellen* till a few months later when her mother decided they were going to England and applied for their passport. Her mother had gone on her own into town to collect the passport, and when Ellen spotted the official-looking document on top of the chest of drawers in the bedroom she couldn't resist taking a sneaky peak. Inside, there was a photograph of her mother with an expression that captured her nature exactly, not just cold, but angry, as if she had physically felt the hard blow of the official stamp heavily embossed across her image. At the bottom of the page there was a section entitled 'Children *Enfants*' and the name Virgie Angela Silcott was handwritten under that section beside Ellen's date of birth.

'Mama,' she said, holding the passport out for her mother to see it, 'They put me name down wrong in the passport.'

Her mother didn't even pause in her stirring of the food in the doving pot on top of the wood oven in the outside kitchen. 'That's you name,' she said and Ellen felt her hair rise, the roots of the strands straightening till they were like spines of black sea urchins piercing her scalp. Her face blazed and the blood swirled beneath her skin like water in the rockpools at the top of the Great Alps.

'But me name is Ellen.' If her mother had been tuned in, properly listening, she would have heard the panic in Ellen's voice and maybe had some idea of the extent to which her daughter felt untethered, but at that time, unfortunately, the people around Ellen had no real sense of the fact children might have feelings.

'People *call* you Ellen,' her mother said. 'You *name* is Virgie.'

'So why people . . .' Ellen stopped mid-sentence as her mother gave her the look that clearly asked, *you gonna keep pushing till I box you down?*

No one explained to her that when babies became ill it was because they'd been given the wrong name and the jumbies were unhappy about it. Changing the name didn't just pacify them; it also made it difficult for Death to find the child. She would learn about this as an adult, because no one, not even her mother, deemed it necessary to explain something so bewildering to a child, although it was such a significant issue, leaving Ellen so confident the name in the passport wasn't hers she could hardly sleep or concentrate in the run-up to leaving the island. She was convinced that on the day they were supposed to begin their journey to England, someone would check her mother's passport, realise a mistake had been made and stop Ellen from boarding the boat, that she would become an observer to her mother's departure, left behind without a parent again. When that didn't happen she was convinced the mistake would be discovered when they arrived in England, and when that didn't happen that she would be found out when she started school. In the four years she attended school in England, she felt like an imposter every time her official name was called out.

The time Ellen had spent living with Mrs Skerritt was time spent pulling her weight. She cleaned the house and swept the yard and carried clothes to river to wash. She gathered eggs and shelled gungo peas and pounded cassava for bread and she did what she was told because that was what children did and she didn't ask questions because it was not expected. To this day she had no idea why her mother and Black Joe were no longer together or where he'd been throughout the entirety of her childhood. No one had taken her and sat her on their lap and explained it was impossible for the majority of the island to find work in Montserrat sufficient to live off, that they'd been forced away from the island through poverty, her father included.

As a consequence, Ellen had spent long periods piecing together fragments of information about Black Joe from things she'd overheard in conversations amongst the people around her. He was as dark as she was. He'd been a motherless botherless boy, raised by one of his aunts. He was friendly and good with his hands, good with making and fixing things, always ready to help out older people and mothers with a little groundwork: hoeing, tilling, planting. She'd had to form an image of him from virtually nothing, scraps, and the image she had fashioned was of a kind and helpful man. Did she think he could have done more to see and spend time with her? Yes. Did she think he could've sent her gifts, maybe useful things like shoes or clothes? Of course. But did she love him despite his failings? Yes, she did. If she opened the front door and he was standing there, would she shut the door in his face? No, she would not, because whatever happened, come what may, Black Joe was still her father. Without him, she would never have existed.

Ellen watched Leah sobbing and wiping her eyes as she explained what had happened that morning, as if what had happened – that is, being told to go visit your father once in a blue moon – was one of the most terrible things in the world that could befall a person, as if she, at the age of eighteen – only just! – had been promoted to judge and jury over the relationships of the big people around her. Of all her grandchildren, this one tried her patience hardest. Growing up her whole life with not just her mother, but an entire family. All those aunts and uncles and grandparents spoiling the girl from birth non-stop. She'd never had to make a choice between her family going without or going someplace else to make money. Her life had never been interrupted. She'd never had to sort through her children like laundry, trying to work out which ones to take with her, which ones to leave behind. She'd never had to put up with the caca Ellen's generation had put up with after they arrived in England, never had to look at all those nasty signs and prejudiced people, then swallow and smile and still talk politely to them because you needed what they had. She had no idea of the experiences that stripped a person's dignity, no idea that where there was no respect out of doors it was even more incumbent on those inside to give every man his little measure of respect; every single one. Because of her irritation, Ellen's voice was hard when she interrupted Leah.

'You are me granddaughter. Right or wrong, me nah go put you out in the street.'

'Thank you, Granny,' Leah said, sniffing, smiling and wiping her eyes.

Ellen nodded at Linus. 'Take you sister's cases up to the attic.'

Linus stood. 'Yes, Granny.' He picked up the suitcases and began lugging them in the direction of the door. Leah also stood.

'Not you,' Ellen said.

Leah sat back down.

'I'm not gonna take you side over you mother. She ask you to go see you father; you need to go see you father ...'

'But ...'

'Don't but me!'

Leah paused, fired up again at being backed into a corner over the same issue and ready to meet the fight, but floundering because she was no longer just dealing with her mum; she was dealing with her grandmother. It was one thing standing up to and raising her voice to her mum and an entirely different matter raising her voice to Granny. Also, she couldn't ignore the possibility she could be made homeless twice on her eighteenth birthday. 'Okay,' she said.

'Today,' Ellen said.

'All right.'

'I'm gonna need you to pick up some shopping for me later.'

'Sure.'

'And to give me a hand with the dinner on Saturday.'

'Okay.'

'And you need to sort things out with you mum.'

'Oh my God! Anything else?'

'Don't make me catch any man-friend in this house.' Ellen raised a finger, halting Leah's response. 'And I'll have none of that lip.'

Leah glared at her grandmother as she stood. 'Thanks for letting me stay, Granny. Really appreciate it. I'll just go clap the ball and chain round my ankles myself.'

Cassius and Janet had arrived on the Monday and from the Monday to the Friday, with the rhythm of a man in fulltime employment, Clyde had taken Cassius out from morning till night, with no regard for the fact Cassius had visited England with his wife; taking him to the Antigua Association for dominoes and lunch, or to his favourite bookies, where he introduced Cassius to a number of friends in similar circumstances – retired from work and keen to get out of the house and from under their wives' watchful eye. Late afternoon they'd return home for dinner, before Clyde and usually CJ took Cassius out to their local pub, to meet up and have a laugh with Franklin, James, Backfoot and the remainder of Clyde's social circle. Oblivious to the fact Cassius had been pretty much teetotal for the last four decades, and as a consequence had accumulated little tolerance to alcohol, they pressured him to join them in necking the liquor, only to bring him home properly wasted after both Ellen and Janet had gone to bed, laughing their heads off about his inability to hold his drink, before helping Janet to get her husband out of his clothes and into his pyjamas and bed.

For her part, Ellen hung out with Janet, and often Wilhelmina, the women visiting the markets and malls and family houses: lunch at Claudette's, dinner at Joycelyn's, an evening at Dumpling's. She even – for the first time since 1972, when Ellen went to the pictures with Clyde to see *The Harder They Come* – went to see a film on the Friday evening; Leah took the three older women to a special screening of *Waiting to Exhale*, which they all enjoyed immensely, before returning home and having a couple of late tipples before night's end. Which was why, on the Saturday morning, after Ellen had got up, brushed her teeth and taken her bath, had finished creaming and dressing herself and was sitting at the dressing table fixing her hair, she was surprised to hear a quiet tapping on her bedroom door and even more surprised after she said, 'Enter,' to see Janet come in, her eyes red and swollen, crying too much to be able to speak coherently. She knew Clyde and Cassius were already up and out and that Leah was with Claudette and Joycelyn downstairs in the kitchen getting the day's big dinner on the way. The only thing she could imagine was that Janet and Cassius had had some kind of argument, a bad one from the looks of it, maybe about him spending so much time with Clyde and so little with her. She'd seemed okay with it all, seemed happy and jolly enough when she'd been with Ellen, but you never could tell with women. Some of them would be smiling in your face while the hands you couldn't see were pressing hard on the knife in your back.

Ellen went downstairs, made them both a cup of tea and brought them back upstairs with a couple of biscuits on a tray. She did her best to calm down her sister-in-law, then asked her to start at the beginning. Before Janet began to speak, she glanced at Ellen as if ashamed and instinctively Ellen felt a sickness and anticipation in her stomach that was familiar. As Janet spoke, she didn't interrupt, just sipped on the tea in her cup and listened.

For the life of him, Clyde had no idea how Ellen knew he had slept with Janet, but there was no doubt she knew, and also, that she knew he knew she knew. It was the steadiness in her gaze when she looked at him, a detachment which remained even after he'd tried bussing a little joke with her, and it was a bad end to what had started out as such a lucky morning. He'd decided to take Cassius out and leave the women in peace to get on with preparing the big dinner without the two of them underfoot. He'd gone with Cassius and CJ to the bookies and then on to their local pub for some celebratory tipples after both Clyde and Cassius had backed a 30–1 outsider who had galloped home to come in first place. They'd been in great cheer when they arrived back at the house, in good time to catch a little fresh before dinner, which is precisely what Clyde had done, before entering the kitchen humming and rubbing the last of the Astral Cream into his hands. Then Ellen speared him with that look.

Unusually, he felt bad, in part because Ellen knew about it, yes, but also because there were a number of reasons Janet should have been off bounds and the whole messy business should never have happened.

Number one: Janet and Cassius were guests in their home and Ellen had gone to a lot of trouble to welcome them and make them feel comfortable during their stay. It was unfair to her for all her efforts to be cancelled out by his inconsiderate actions.

Number two: although it was impossible to stop himself sleeping with other women, since 1971 he'd drawn a line at sleeping with them in his marital home following an unfortunate incident when Ellen caught him in bed with Irene, one of his colleagues from work – well, colleague and good good friend, up until then – and to his shock, had chucked ice-cold water over her and, because he was on his back beneath her, had inadvertently chucked cold water over him also, before proceeding to throw Irene's clothes out the bedroom window like a complete madwoman. It had been left to him to recover them, running down the stairs and out onto the street like a madman himself, wet and barefoot, wearing nothing but a hand towel clutched tightly about his waist to cover his deflated dignity. Irene's pantyhose had been snagged mid-air on the aerial of a passing Ford Granada and were gone for good. The rest of her clothing he'd had to snatch with the one free hand available to him before rushing back into the house to physically prevent Ellen pushing his good good friend out the front door in her birthday suit. Since then, not sleeping with his lovers in his marital home had become a personal rule he'd observed diligently, though it was a personal rule Ellen had openly scoffed at when he'd slipped up once and accidentally referred to it as one of his positive traits.

And then, finally, number three, and probably most important of all: Janet was Cassius's wife and, as Cassius was his brother, even Clyde recognised she should've been a no-go zone.

Clyde found himself listening intently to the sounds inside the house, all normal multigenerational family noises; in fact he could hear Cassius' voice, loud and laughing, and he knew that there were only three people in the house who knew what had happened: Ellen, Janet and himself. Then, recalling again what had happened to poor Irene, he wondered where Janet was.

'She's inside. At the table,' said Ellen as she turned away and Clyde made his way slowly to the dining room, as perturbed as ever by her ability to read his mind.

*

As he entered the dining room, he raised his hand at Cassius, who was sitting at the head of the table in the seat he himself ordinarily sat in but that he had vacated and bequeathed to Cassius for the duration of his stay.

'Come, take you seat, man,' Cassius said with a smile, indicating the seat to his left, on the other side of the table, forcing Clyde to sit directly opposite Janet, who gave Clyde a polite nod by way of a hello, then busied herself looking down the table as if deeply interested in the other conversations being had there.

Dumpling and the family members closest to them began laughing at a joke someone had made, and though Clyde was so deep in troubled thought he'd missed the punchline, their laughter brought him back to himself and the role he was supposed to be performing as host of this meal, so he picked up his drink, said cheers and clinked his glass against his brother's and somehow, without looking at her, clinked glasses with Janet, then swigged a large mouthful of his whiskey over ice.

On account of her status as an honorary family member, Wilhelmina had been invited, and along with Linus and the rest of the women had pulled out the extensions on the formal dining table, and brought the regular kitchen table they usually ate at into the dining room and extended that as well. They had draped it all in matching tablecloths so it looked like one long banquet table, then prettily dressed it with the good crockery, cutlery and glasses and two centrepieces of candles and fresh flowers that reminded Clyde of the church altars of his childhood. And sin. The women had finished putting out the salads and coleslaws and potato salads and were bringing out the hot dishes, filling the middle of the table with steaming bowls and platters of the feast they'd been cooking up since morning.

On the other side of the table, Wilhelmina materialised between Cassius and Janet with a large dish, still hot from the oven, filled with macaroni cheese, and Clyde could not fail to notice that though she had smiled at them, when she looked at him her face was vex, proper vex, and under any other circumstances, the way she cut her eye after him would have been his signal to get cracking, out and away, were he not sitting at the table awaiting the commencement of the dinner in honour of the brother he'd not seen for over forty years. In fact, putting the dish down, she almost placed it on top of the back of his hand, which was palm down on the tablecloth and would probably have sizzled like a piece of jerked pork had his reflexes been a fraction slower, and that was how he knew there were not three but four people in the house who knew about what had transpired between himself and Janet. As he regularly did whenever he felt his tribulations rising, Clyde looked down the dining table to CJ, who had Jayden on his lap and was speaking to his nephew, Linus, who was opposite him beside Violet, the eight-month-pregnant push-up-face girlfriend. Clyde waited patiently till CJ looked up at him, then raised his glass in his son's direction.

Clocking the look and realising something was up, CJ raised his own glass in response without pause in his conversation. Jayden was standing on his dad's lap, fifteen months old, vigorously bending his knees so he was bobbing up and down as if jumping, though his feet didn't leave CJ's lap at all. CJ laughed at Jayden's antics while trying, without success, to catch Violet's eye. For some reason CJ had never been able to understand, he was obsessed with women who didn't respond to his charisma, especially when he'd targeted them and purposely turned it on. He'd turned it on with Violet for the two years Linus had been going out with her, yet for some inexplicable reason she hated him. CJ continued explaining to Linus that he didn't need to worry about the baby during the first year when the baby was being breastfed – he couldn't resist a quick glance at Violet's breasts but was confident neither of them had noticed.

'Everyone's got their special role,' CJ said, 'Yours is to feed the family and make sure the bills get paid.'

'I'm on maternity leave from work,' Violet said, without cracking the scarcest hint of a friendly expression. 'I ain't exactly destitute.'

Linus felt the rising tension and in a desperate attempt to diffuse it, laughed aloud though no joke had been made, then put his arm around Violet and hugged her closer to him despite her initial resistance. He leaned his head against hers. 'Richer or poorer,' he said. 'Thick or thin.'

'You planning to breastfeed too?' asked CJ, then laughed heartily at his own joke. Linus laughed as though this too was funny, though he really didn't think it was funny at all and he was wishing Uncle CJ hadn't come and sat down this end of the table, which he'd chosen very specifically because he'd seen Uncle Cassius up the other end and assumed that Grandad would be sitting with his brother and as a consequence Uncle CJ would be sitting up that end too, as Uncle CJ and Grandad were always together and his intention had been to sit as far away from them both as possible, because underlying all the laughs and jokes and backslaps they considered him nothing more than a Joey. Linus would do anything for the women he loved; for his mum, for Leah and now for Violet, pregnant with their baby, his first love and the only woman he'd ever slept with. In the eyes of his uncle and grandad, he was quite some distance away from being a real man.

Jayden stopped jigging and stood still on CJ's lap with an expression of intense concentration on his face. A moment later, CJ's face creased up in disgust, surreptitiously sniffing his son's nappy area before sharply leaning back away from it. 'Shit!' he said. 'This is really bad timing, Jay.' He looked firstly at Violet then Linus, giving each of them the charming helpless look he'd inherited from his father, which usually resulted in a laugh and an offer of help from whoever he aimed it at. 'He needs changing,' CJ said, as Violet's expression hardened further. Resigned to his fate, CJ stood up and didn't bother saying anything more as he walked away.

Claudette was carving the lamb, Joycelyn was decanting the roast potatoes into four bowls and Ellen was ladling her legendary lamb gravy into gravy boats when Wilhelmina returned to the kitchen. As soon as Ellen saw

Wilhelmina's face, she wished she hadn't told her about Clyde and Janet, because she always took it hard, Clyde's infidelities, was always furious about him cheating on her. The truth was it made Ellen feel good, like there was someone who recognised she deserved much better than a man whose only skill with pants was the speed he could get them off, yet a man who for the most part she couldn't blame, because the one fact life had taught her was that the women were just as bad as the men, often much, much worse, so in the spirit of fairness, she never held Clyde solely responsible. Wilhelmina's rage always made Ellen feel seen, but today she could do without everyone else seeing, because all she wanted to do was get the big dinner safely out of the way without mishap.

'The macaroni cheese needs a spoon,' Wilhelmina said.

'Don't worry youself,' Ellen said, 'Leah's sorting the spoons.'

'So what should I do?'

'Put your feet up. Relax youself.'

'Go on inside, Mrs W,' said Claudette.

'We've got this,' Joycelyn added.

'Go,' Ellen repeated and quietly breathed a sigh of relief as Wilhelmina turned and went back out the door. Nothing spoiled food faster than grudge-holders in the kitchen.

As Ellen began wiping the splashes off the gravy boats, she wondered whether Cassius had told Clyde what Janet had confided in her, that although there was plenty of love and affection between the couple, there was no sexual intimacy, hadn't been for the majority of their marriage, which meant Ellen's diplomatic concerns around which bedroom to put them in were all for nothing. She really needn't have worried on that score at all. She suspected Clyde had known and that it had excited him, the idea of delivering a little famine relief, though he was hardly to blame if his brother wasn't giving his wife the good good loving, and Janet herself had said she held herself as much to blame for what happened. The thing that most troubled Ellen was that she had no idea how Cassius would take it if he found out.

She'd gone with Clyde and CJ to see him in the States back in 1970, when his wife Shola had newly passed, less than a year after his son went missing. He felt guilty for everything then, for being away in the army fighting wars that had nothing to do with him personally while his wife had been left back in the States where a real war against coloured people was being waged, raising their son on her own. Ellen had observed him closely back then and though he'd been in the army for years, she could see no aggression in him, nothing hard, nothing to suggest he was capable of killing people when ordered who had done him no harm. Back then he had been soft and kind and sad. The other time she'd seen him was that time Clyde was in hospital and they'd all thought he was dying. He'd flown out straight away to support them and only returned to the States when it was evident Clyde was recovering. He had married Janet a few years after that in a private ceremony and had been intending ever since to bring her to England so they could all meet in person. It was obvious he was stronger now, happier, but nothing of what she knew about him helped her make an informed guess as to how he might react if he found out what had transpired between his brother and his wife. Janet had wanted to tell Cassius, *need to* were the actual words she'd used, and the two women had discussed it for a long time before deciding it was probably best not to tell Cassius till after the big dinner. That was the agreement. Ellen had referenced the planning and prep and hard work that had gone into this meal, said she would be rewarded for her efforts only when she looked down the table and saw everyone enjoying the food, but the truth was she preferred, if at all possible, to contain all confessions to a time when the house was not filled with every single person in the country they were related to. She really hoped Janet would keep her mouth shut about it forever, but failing that, she hoped Janet's conscience would allow her to keep it shut at least till everyone had finished eating and gone home, and when she said after *everyone* had gone home, she meant Janet and Cassius especially. As far as Ellen was concerned, the best place for Janet to deliver that confession to her husband was back home in the States after their return from an otherwise successful family reunion.

When Wilhelmina entered the dining room, marched straight towards Janet and sat down beside her, Clyde experienced a wave of stress so intense, his instinct was to cry for help.

'You lookin' tired today, Miss Janet. You never sleep good last night?' Wilhelmina asked.

'Well ... it's ... ahm ...' began Janet.

Cassius laughed and put his hand onto Janet's shoulder, massaging it affectionately. He indicated Clyde with a nod of his head, 'That man's a bad influence. Got me up and down all day and half the night, waking my po' wife in the early hours when he finally get me home. No wonder she can't get no sleep.'

To Clyde's enormous relief, the chair beside him was pulled out and CJ sat in it. 'I've come to join the grown-ups,' he said.

'W'appen to Jayden?' asked Clyde, ecstatic to have something else to talk about.

'Candice is changing him,' CJ said, ecstatic to have bumped into his niece with such perfect timing.

As Ellen put the last of the gravy boats down on the table and sat down beside Wilhelmina, Clyde stared at the gravy boat in front of him. Anything rather than look at the brother he had wronged, or Janet, Wilhelmina, and now Ellen sitting in a row opposite him.

'My, my, my,' said Cassius, looking at the abundance of dishes running the length of the table, then at Ellen, 'This's a mighty feast you cooked up. Feels like Juneteenth.'

'I had some help,' Ellen said, then glanced down the table, checking whether Claudette, Joycelyn and Leah were also seated. Seeing they were, she picked up the crystal tumbler in front of her and rapped her knife against it, and a Mexican wave of shhes rippled down from the top of the table to the bottom. Then Ellen glanced at Clyde, gave him a nod and he stood.

'I ain't a great one for words,' he said.

'Unless you're making an excuse,' said CJ, to laughter.

'Or persuading someone who ain't even drink to *just have one*,' said Cassius.

'Or if he's had a puff,' said Leah from the far end of the table, triggering a collection of responses which were an almost equal combination of laughter and expressions of horror.

'But you all know how happy I've been to see me one brother after so much time . . .'

'And Janet,' said Wilhelmina, 'Don't forget how happy you been to see her.'

For Clyde, it was a moment of terrible panic. First of all he laughed, then immediately reined it in because he could hear how excessive and phony it sounded. Then, his mind simply went blank. He knew he was supposed to say something about Janet, but there was nothing in his head. 'Yes,' he said, 'Janet, me sister-in-law, thank you. Thank you very very much, very . . .'

'Much?' said Wilhelmina.

CJ stood up. 'I've got this, Dad.' And Clyde collapsed into his seat with relief. 'I know what Dad wannid to say. Thanks Uncle Cassius for travelling cross half the world to be here and spend time with us. It's been too long . . .'

'That it has,' said Cassius.

'Next time will be our turn. We'll come and see you guys soon . . .'

'Y'all family. Come anytime you ready,' Cassius said.

'And thank you Aunt Janet, for coming, yes, but also for taking care of Uncle for us all these years when we were too far away to do it ourselves. I'm naturally gonna say you're a lucky woman to be with Uncle Cassius, well, cos he's my uncle . . .'

Above the laughs from the table, Cassius said, 'And cos man like me's in short supply.'

'But what my dad would also've said is that Uncle's very lucky to have you . . .'

To everyone's astonishment, Janet pushed herself away from the table with a howl and dashed towards the dining room door. In the silence, everyone listened to the sound of her feet running quickly up the stairs and across the landing, followed by the slam of her bedroom door.

Then, Cassius stood up. 'Excuse me,' he said and left the room and the sound of him pounding up the stairs could be heard.

'What's going on?' asked CJ. 'Was it something I said?' He looked at Ellen. 'Should someone go up there?'

'It's man and wife. Leave them to it,' said Wilhelmina.

'We should probably eat,' Ellen said, then when no one responded, she added a little more forcefully, 'I said *eat*,' and the stilted sounds of forced jovial chatter began to combine with the noises of people beginning to dish up.

'Dad?' CJ looked down in bafflement at his father, who had raised his hands to the sides of his head covering his ears and was staring down at the plate in front of him. In Clyde's mind this was a very bad development, and the number of people in the house who knew what had hitherto taken place was likely in the process of increasing from four to five.

'Okay,' said CJ, 'I think I'm gonna go up anyway.'

As CJ moved his chair back from the table and began

to turn around, he halted at the sound of the bedroom door slamming and a cacophony of stamping feet and raised voices crossing the landing then coming down the stairs. Cassius burst into the room, with Janet close behind him. Cassius surged forwards, almost falling, and Janet was forced to relinquish her grip on the back of his jacket. On the other side of the table, Clyde jumped up and began to run along the backs of the chairs of the family seated on that side, changing direction like a football player with a ball, and Cassius began running along the backs of the chairs of the family seated on his side like a player on the opposing team marking him. After a few moments of this Cassius ran out of patience, suddenly jumping up onto and over the table, breaking plates and glasses and raising screams from the family members sitting closest by. The screams galvanised CJ, his sisters and Linus into action, and as they began to run towards the pair, Cassius grabbed his brother from behind, twisted his arm up behind his back and used his other forearm to press against the back of Clyde's neck, forcing him face-first up against the wall, bashing his nose against it.

'Traitor!' he shouted. 'You goddamn traitor!'

CJ began to struggle with Cassius, trying to pull his forearm back and off his father's neck to release Clyde, who looked as though he was genuinely choking. The blood streamed from his nose onto his clothes. The older grandchildren were herding the littlest ones and the great-grandchildren seated closest to the action, guiding them around the table to the other side and safety. Clyde collapsed to his knees as CJ managed to break his uncle's hold, then wrapped and locked his arms around his uncle's body from behind, firmly restraining him till he finally stopped resisting. By then, Cassius was openly crying and repeating to Clyde, 'You're supposed to be my brother, man, my brother.'

Ellen looked over at Janet, who was still standing just inside the door bawling her eyes out. She looked at Wilhelmina, whose face was alight with glee, and for the first time in all the years they'd known each other, Ellen felt so angry with her she could have merrily strung her up.

'This is ridiculousness,' Ellen said, for the umpteenth time, with no expectation it would make the slightest bit of difference.

CJ was carrying their cases and Cassius and Janet were holding the remainder of the other bits and bobs swiftly packed, some of it clearly just grabbed and shoved into carrier bags.

'Come and stay at mine,' Claudette said, standing in the kitchen doorway. 'It's no bother.'

'Wasting your money on hotels. You don't need to do that,' Joycelyn said, from beside her sister.

'I'm sorry, but we do,' said Cassius.

'Everybody makes mistakes,' Ellen said, staring at her brother-in-law, who had not looked at or spoken to her since the incident.

CJ, reading the room and seeing no possibility of compromise at this point, opened the front door. 'I'm gonna put the cases in the car,' he said.

Cassius followed him out. Janet stopped at the front door and looked at Ellen. 'I'm so, so sorry,' she said, then paused because she was a hugger and ordinarily she would have enveloped Ellen in a great hug, but the rules had shifted now, possibly to Do Not Touch. Finally, she turned around and went through the front door as well, closing the door and pulling the drawbridge up behind her.

'Clear as day that one was a homewrecker,' said Wilhelmina.

'Gotta be her fault,' said Leah. 'S'not like Granny's got a homewrecker living here.'

And before Ellen could come up with a reply to Wilhelmina, who she considered responsible for this mess, or the facety granddaughter always talking like she and everyone around her were size, they'd both walked back into the dining room where the clean-up was still underway.

Ellen went into the kitchen where what had been salvaged of the food was being dished up onto paper plates and being eaten on laps and in the hands of people sitting and standing around the kitchen, living room and garden. The voices around her in the kitchen and the ones that could be heard about the house were subdued and oddly respectful, quieter even than if everyone had been gathered for a family funeral. Two plates had been dished up and set aside under cover for her and Clyde on a large tray. She took two glasses from the cupboard, filled both with ice and poured Hennessey into one and Baileys into the other, shaking a little off the top of each bottle first for the jumbies, though it felt like a waste of time pacifying them at this point when it looked to her like they had already unleashed their mischief for the day; like putting fence round the kitchen garden after the donkey already nyam off the vegetables and mash up the place. Then she put the glasses alongside the plates of food and as she began lifting the tray, Leah materialised beside her and took it from her hands.

'I'll help with that,' she said.

Ellen followed her granddaughter out into the hallway. She knew Clyde would be upstairs in their room and that he would be devastated.

'You okay?' Leah asked.

'Of course I'm okay,' said Ellen, her tone intentionally brusque to bring the uninvited conversation to a close. 'I can manage from here,' she said to Leah as they reached the landing at the top of the flight of stairs.

'You want me to get the door?'

'I said I can manage,' Ellen said.

Ellen took the tray and looked at her granddaughter pointedly till she turned around and went back down the stairs. She walked to her bedroom door and stood outside it, rolling her eyes, entirely unsurprised to hear a variety of gasping, inhaling and sniffing sounds coming from inside the room. Her husband, the great man, lady killer, love king, bawling like girl pickney, not because of the terrible fight with Cassius, or the broken tables or plates or glasses or ruined dinner, or the fact he'd betrayed her again. His tears were for himself, because everyone had seen and now everyone knew what he'd done. He was crying because there was no spin or joke or explanation he could levy to absolve himself. Now he was waiting for her to bring his food and his drink and some kindness and understanding that he might pull himself back together, and she knew she was not being forced and that no one expected her to do it and that her doing it was a matter of personal choice and she expected no sympathy from anyone for her ridiculous position around Clyde's shenanigans, in which she'd long recognised she'd been mostly complicit. She lifted one of her feet and firmly kicked the base of the bedroom door as her hands were too full to get the handle.

'Clyde? It's me. Come open up the door.'

Golden Child

2000

(Eleven years earlier)

Dumpling had never had a birthday that hadn't made her feel wretched, but her twenty-first was by far the worst she'd experienced. She'd hardly slept the night before, tossing and turning from the early hours till six-thirty before finally accepting night-time was over. Then, though it was February and dark as night outside, she'd lain in bed for over an hour without turning the lights on, for fear someone would notice them and realise she was awake. Instead she had pulled the covers over her head and used her torch to illuminate the photograph she couldn't stop looking at, the one she kept in her bedside drawer and got out whenever she felt sad, and on all her birthdays. If the woman in the photo looked like anyone, it was Eartha Kitt. The image was a black and white one and in it, the woman's face was fair and framed by meticulous voluminous curls, the same jet black as her eyebrows, lashes and pupils. She was young, eighteen, but in her eyes there was the suggestion she knew more of life than she should have had to, combined with a steady determination. Only after the battery in her torch died did she get up, go into the bathroom, lock the door then stand in the shower, crying her heart out. Half an hour later she was back in her bedroom, creamed and dressed, trying to pull her hair into a ponytail in front of the dressing table mirror while also trying to pull herself together. She needed to get her game face on so that when she went downstairs she'd be able to respond with a smile to all the birthday wishes, laugh along with all the good-natured birthday jokes and not present a depressed and despairing front to the people around her who loved her and wanted this birthday to be special. But the fact was she could not have what she wished for most, which was for the woman in the photograph to be present on her birthday, and she had never been able to have her with her on her birthday because she'd died twenty-one years ago while giving birth to Dumpling.

Dumpling knew the reason this year had been the hardest was because her mother, Francesca, had been only twenty when she'd died and it felt somehow as though death had frozen her in time at that age forever, which meant that this birthday she was older than her mother had ever been, which was so wild it was impossible to get her head around. She was also acutely aware that even though Francesca had not lived to see her twenty-first, during the time she *had* lived, she'd lived considerably more than Dumpling. She'd left her home in Dominica and travelled on her own across the world to a country where she had no family. She'd found a home and a job to sustain herself and a man she was so in love with she became pregnant with his child. Had she not died, she would have been a mother by the time she was twenty-one. Dumpling's guilt was overwhelming. Mother killer. Both the cause of one death and replacement for another on the same day. Her obligation to make good on her mother's sacrifice, be worth it, was such a heavy weight it overwhelmed and paralysed her, and instead she squandered the life she did have and added that to the growing pile of everything else she felt guilty about.

Despite now being legally old enough to do pretty much anything she wished, Dumpling had done nothing. Four years on, she was still working as a store assistant at Woolworths, still living at home, the family baby and Daddy's little girl, still wondering where the great love of her life was and waiting for her destiny to begin. She tried not to think about how disappointed her mother would have been to see what her daughter had made of the gift her death had given her.

Hair finished, Dumpling stood up. Carefully, she dabbed the bottom lid of her eyes and slapped her cheeks to get the blood flowing, then she sniffed and blew her nose into the handkerchief she always kept tucked into her bra. She looked at her reflection and suddenly grinned, then immediately stopped because she looked macabre. She tried again, a gentler smile this time, that stretched her mouth less wide. The result was better, more natural. Determinedly, she held that smile in place as she turned and walked out of the room.

'She's coming! She's coming!' Leah squealed with excitement. She raced back into the kitchen with her cousin Candice grinning and running behind her and both girls crashed into their Uncle CJ, who was leaning against the breakfast counter chatting on his phone and holding a mug of tea.

'Oi!' he said, holding the dripping mug away from his clothes and looking for something to wipe the spills off his shoes.

'You two, slow down,' said Claudette, glancing at the clock on the wall impatiently, because Dumpling must surely have known they were all waiting downstairs for her. She'd heard her go into the shower over an hour ago. It was just bad manners to keep everyone waiting this long. She looked at her mum who was uncharacteristically chipper, her arm draped around Linus's shoulders, whatever she was saying making him laugh; at her dad who was halfway through the buttered slice of hard dough bread in his hand and was doing a skank to the ska being quietly broadcast from the radio. Had it been her or Joycelyn who'd done this, Claudette was confident no one would be standing around the kitchen acting like waiting was fun. But then if it was her or Joycelyn's birthday, would the whole family have come round first thing in the morning when they knew full well they'd be seeing them later anyway at their birthday party? If it was her or Joycelyn's birthday, would either of them even have had a birthday celebration all of their own that they weren't obliged to share with one or more of their siblings? No, they would not. But there was no point saying anything. This was how it had always been. There were two camps amongst the siblings: those who had been blessed with birthday parties for them alone and those who never had anything – including a bed – that they did not share. There were those who were called out for every tiny thing they did wrong and those who could do no wrong. She and Joycelyn had always been in the cursed group and CJ, Dumpling, and for a time, Clay, were in the other.

'Did you hear?' Joycelyn said to Leah and Candice, who hadn't stopped running, had merely slowed down a bit. They slowed further to a rapid walk.

Joycelyn was irritable and impatient because she knew Claudette was irritable and impatient. It was almost nine and they were due at the hairdressers with Dumpling at ten. They needed to get Dumpling out of the house and keep her out of the house for the whole day so Dad and CJ could shift the living room furniture around to create a dancefloor in the centre and get cracking picking up the shopping, drinks, cake and decorations in good time. Then they'd still need to get to the barbers for a shape up and be back in time to get washed, dressed and ready for the surprise party at seven, but the Golden Child was taking bloody ages to show up.

Joycelyn loved the term *Golden Child*, the secret name she and Claudette used between themselves for their younger sister, because she'd come up with it herself and it was one of the few original thoughts she'd had that was worthy of longevity. The name suited Dumpling down to the ground for a number of reasons. Number one: she was the only one of the sisters born in England, which meant she had never had to be separated from her family for years on end before being sent for to join parents she'd been apart from for so long they no longer felt like an actual mother and father any more, but more like a new pair of strangers she had to get to know and adapt to. Or, before she could even properly get to know them, have her mum give birth to a new baby brother, relegating her straight to the back of the queue she was entitled to be at the front of. Number two: as a child, CJ was disciplined by his father, which meant he wasn't disciplined at all. Joycelyn and Claudette had been disciplined by their mother, which meant they got lots of beatings. However, even though Dumpling was not Mummy's *real* daughter, so if anything she should have been in line for more beatings than Mummy's actual blood kin, Dumpling had for some reason been exempted from beatings and punishments of every kind. In short, she'd been completely spoilt. The two older sisters had deemed this yet more unfairness heaped on top of being left behind in Montserrat for nearly five years, then being brought over to do cooking and housework and still being expected to continue in that role while Dumpling played around with her dollies and CJ played around with his woman-friends. Then number three: Dumpling truly was golden. Her hair was less kinky and longer than theirs. She had a figure that was better than either of theirs had ever been, and whereas Joycelyn and Claudette were dark skinned, their complexions only marginally lighter than their mother's, Dumpling's complexion was the same as both Daddy and CJ's: the colour of gold. These accumulated injustices had left the two older sisters carrying feelings which were rarely raised with their parents because they had been brought up to honour their mother and father that their days might be long and to know their place. They were, however, discussed between them both when they were alone, often after they'd had a couple of drinks and some new offence had reopened their collection of unhealed wounds. Overall they were unified in their agreement that it was their mother who was and had always been in charge, the decision-maker and disherouter of discipline, whereas their dad was genuinely loving, kind to everyone – including them – so although it was the two parents who had left them behind in Montserrat and who spoilt Dumpling more than the daughters who hadn't been Brought In From Outdoors, they held only one parent responsible, and that was Ellen.

The first thing Joycelyn noticed when Dumpling walked into the kitchen was the huge smile plastered over her face, which she knew would've pissed Claudette off even more, particularly as it wasn't accompanied by an apology for unnecessarily keeping everyone waiting, but that didn't surprise Joycelyn at all. Some people only thought about themselves. That was Dumpling to a T.

'About time,' said Claudette as everyone said variations of 'happy birthday' at the same time.

'Late as usual,' Joycelyn said, then hugged and kissed

her youngest sister like everyone else, because unlike Dumpling she *did* think about other people and it would not be good form to show bad face and ruin the special day which the whole family had been planning for months as if it was a family wedding taking place instead of them all celebrating a birthday.

Ellen lit the candles with the matches she'd been holding for the last half hour then watched as Linus carefully carried the cake to the table. People said when it came to the children and grandchildren you weren't supposed to have favourites, but the fact was people were human and humans had preferences and she preferred Linus over all the other grandchildren. Linus was her favourite and despite what everyone thought, it wasn't just because he was a boy. Everyone in the family assumed she preferred the boys over the girls and she had to admit that her spirit did take more to the boys, but that wasn't the only reason. It was also because he was the family member who most reminded her of Clay. Linus was so easy to be around, happy to help with whatever he was asked to do, and he did things his uncle and his grandfather would never dream of, like helping her to make Dumpling's birthday cake yesterday, whisking the butter and the sugar by hand – which, even though she owned a Magimix, was Ellen's preferred method; old-skool stylee – without complaint till it was creamed to her satisfaction.

Yes, Claudette or Joycelyn would have done it had she asked them, but they were females; Ellen expected their help in the kitchen, whereas Linus was a young man. When he helped in the kitchen, he did it from the goodness of his heart, from kindness. That was the quality in him that reminded her so much of Clay; he'd been such a kind boy. So different to Clyde and CJ. In fact, after he was born it felt as though she and Clyde each had a son; CJ was his and Clay was hers. She'd never felt like that with any of the other kids. CJ had always been his father's son, and she hadn't carried then given birth to Dumpling, and that was aside from the fact that Dumpling had always been Clyde's because Dumpling *was* Clyde's. And there was a hole the size of five years in her relationship with Claudette and Joycelyn which she was not convinced time would ever sufficiently patch up.

When they'd sent for the girls in 1972, they'd asked an old neighbour of Ellen's, Schoolteacher Liz, who they'd heard was coming to England, to chaperone the girls on the journey. Ellen had been excited for weeks before their arrival. Up until then they'd been renting out two of the three bedrooms in the dilapidated house they'd bought three years earlier, and they'd been using the money they'd received in rent to make the property properly airtight and habitable. One of the bedrooms had been occupied by the Griffiths family, the husband, wife and daughter, who had given them notice they'd managed to find themselves a flat – small but just about affordable – and would be moving out. The other one had been occupied by Wilhelmina Brown, who Clyde said had been recommended to him by someone at work, and who had become a good good friend of Ellen's before moving out and into a council flat of her own around the corner from them. It was Wilhelmina who had helped her, over four months, to sort out the newly empty room; repainting, recarpeting, assembling two new single beds, one for the girls to top and tail, and one for CJ who would be sharing the bedroom with them and who she would be very glad to get out of the middle of her marital bed. She had bought bedding and put up new curtains and fashioned a wooden cupboard in one of the alcoves which she'd shelved then painted herself by hand. She had shopped for all the things they would need, clothes, especially warm ones; socks and hats and scarves and shoes and coats, items she had been intending to buy a couple of sizes too big so they would get maximum wear out of them as they grew. But when she was in the shops, it seemed that English clothes for girls came up in sizes that were very large indeed, and because she didn't want them to look ridiculously swamped in oversized clothes at school, she'd ended up buying their clothing in the exact size for their ages, which looked as though they would still have quite a lot of room to grow into. So much thought and work and conscious effort and attention to detail had gone into Ellen's preparations for her girls.

In contrast, Clyde had done no preparation at all. The only thing he did was on the morning they'd set out from home to begin the drive to Tilbury to collect the girls, when he pulled up outside the newsagents, popped inside with CJ, and came out with the most ridiculously full carrier bag of sweets Ellen had ever witnessed, the price of which he refused to share, no doubt because he knew that had he done so she would have blown an English gasket.

On arriving at their destination, they parked up and walked along the dockside to where the ship was already anchored and waited for the girls to disembark. For Ellen, it would become a matter of astonishment every single time she recalled that on that day it was Schoolteacher Liz she had recognised first, not the children her body had given birth to, who were little more than babies when she'd left them and had grown into big children she knew nothing about; not a thing about their tastes or personalities, whether they were funny or cheeky or shy. They'd become fully formed without her, emerging from the gangway between the ship and the docks as if they were twin new-borns who should have weighed seven and eight pounds but surprised her by arriving aged seven and eight years; perfect strangers she needed to get to know again from scratch. Looking at them, she realised there was every chance all the clothing she'd chosen so carefully would only just about fit, that she'd completely underestimated how much they'd grown since she'd last seen them.

Before their arrival, when she had thought about the moment of their reunion, she had imagined it quite differently to how it had turned out, and it wasn't till later that she realised she hadn't accounted for the change in them at all, nor herself. Claudette and Joycelyn had been two and three years old when she'd left Montserrat, and CJ hadn't yet learned to walk. Her relationship with them all back then had been a physical one. There was always one of them on her lap or on her hip or back, always one of them wanting a kiss or cuddle or to be heist up. The four of them would sleep at night together in one bed, a tangle of arms and legs and bodies intertwined like mangrove roots. On the day the girls arrived, when Ellen looked at them, she realised that way of being with them had long crept past on tiptoe, that she would need to find a new and different way.

Clyde, on the other hand, had no trouble whatsoever. He screamed when he saw the girls, grabbed each of them in turn and hugged and kissed them and threw them up in the air, making them squeal and laugh breathlessly, making CJ laugh too, while she stood watching her crazy husband, more childish than the children themselves, wondering if he was going to kill them by accident and at one particularly reckless point, whether he was going to spin around with his daughters till they all ended up falling over the edge of the dockside into the Thames. Because of this, the first words the girls heard from her lips were ones telling Clyde off and asking him to put the girls down and leave them down and pointing out that they were young ladies now, and after he had done that and nudged them in her direction and her daughters took reluctant steps forwards then gave her a hug, she felt awkwardness in the stiffness of their bodies which had forgotten how to effortlessly interfuse with hers, had fallen out of practice. Suddenly, with a feeling akin to grief, Ellen found blessed distraction in CJ distributing so many sweets to his sisters that they could barely carry them all without regularly dropping some, then somehow having to pick the dropped sweets up with full hands, and despite the fact the girls would only say thank you once and very formally when they entered the bedroom it had taken Ellen months of thought and time and money to arrange to perfection, the girls laughed and said thank you over and over again to Clyde almost every step of the journey to the car and virtually every mile they travelled on the drive back home for the sweets he'd bought and given them. Her daughters had walked back into her life and instantly become daddy's girls. All the kids had been Clyde's kids till Clay. Ellen had worried and carried him to term and for the entirety of the six short years he'd lived, he'd been hers and hers alone.

The family gathered around the table stopped singing 'Happy Birthday' as Candice, in a moment of overexcitement, blew out the candles on the cake. Then Ellen moved closer to the table, relit the candles and joined in as everyone began singing 'Happy Birthday' again to Dumpling, who, Claudette noted, cried actual tears of joy, which Claudette thought was just a bit extra, a little bit attention-seeking on a day she was already guaranteed everyone's attention anyway, so there was really no need to overdo it.

'Happy birthday baby,' Clyde said and kissed his daughter on the top of her head. Ellen went back to the counter to pour the boiled kettle into the cup already prepped for Dumpling with the teabag, milk and two sugars, only to discover Wilhelmina had beaten her to it, had already poured the hot water from the kettle. She handed the cup to Ellen without a word, just a smile, reminding her again of how much she valued the dear friend who never got in the way and always did what needed to be done without first having to be asked. Joycelyn cut the first slice of cake and handed it to Dumpling, then began cutting slices for everyone else.

'I hope your wishes come true auntie,' Leah said and was swallowed up by her aunt in a great hug. Auntie Dumpling was hands down her favourite aunt, though she'd had to learn the hard way that it wasn't a polite thing to say openly. She genuinely hoped Auntie Dumpling's wishes really did come true as her own wishes at Christmas had not come true at all. In fact, quite the opposite. After what Leah and Linus had considered a year containing a few hiccups but otherwise near-exemplary behaviour from them both, they had written letters to Father Christmas asking for bikes for Christmas, and on Christmas morning after they woke up early and snuck downstairs into the living room as quietly as they could, Leah could not contain her shriek of joy as she spotted the sparkling new frame of a black Mongoose Villain with golden Christmas bows stuck to the handlebar, till Linus sat on it and Leah realised there was only one bike in the room. Finally, she spotted her gift, a wrapped box beneath the tree that could not possibly contain a bike. When she opened it, she discovered a pink Barbie Typewriter, which she'd still not touched two months later. It had been a devastating trauma on what should have been one of her two happiest days of the year – her birthday being the other one – a trauma that resurfaced every time she saw Linus's bike leaned up at home or him riding it, and her heart was filled with genuine hope that nothing that terrible would befall Auntie Dumpling on her special day.

'Thank you,' Dumpling said to her niece, kissing her again and smiling while wiping away tears. 'Me too,' she added, knowing full well it was impossible for her recurrent birthday wish to come true, that it had been impossible from the start.

Ellen moved back from the group gathered around the table to stand beside Wilhelmina, feeling a familiar sadness at Clay's absence combined with a profound sense of achievement on account of all the generations before her. The last of the children was now a fully-fledged adult. She'd done it, despite all the difficulties, despite having to do much of it alone while Clyde was busy elsewhere, they'd made it, she and Clyde, which meant everyone else had made it too. She watched as Dumpling popped a bit of cake first into Leah's mouth and then into Candice's, who was standing beside her, head raised with mouth opened wide as a hungry baby bird, as Clyde snatched the phone from CJ and began speaking into it, as CJ wrestled with him to get it back.

'Boys will be boys,' Wilhelmina said, with a laugh.

Clyde had been in a playful mood for weeks, with everyone, including Ellen. They'd made love early that morning, trying to hold down their laughter for fear of waking Dumpling in the bedroom next door to theirs. She loved him most when he was like this, when he wasn't ducking and diving, telling her silly lies and being caught out in those lies so easily it exhausted her. Did that mean he wasn't seeing anyone else? She had no idea. Too many times throughout their marriage she'd thought he was being faithful, only to discover he was not. Now she tried to just not think about it because thinking about it made her feel as though there was an unresolved issue she needed to make a decision about. But for better or worse she'd made her decision, decades ago, back in Montserrat in 1963 when she'd allowed the most beautiful man she'd ever seen, whose name she didn't know, to lead her back into her home and onto her bed then demonstrate how glorious he could make her feel; her, Black Ellen, whose mother had lived with so much physical pain because of the sickle cell disease, and who had relieved and distracted herself – maybe even entertained herself – by transferring that pain to her daughter via words Ellen could not forget, whether she forgave her mother or not.

Like when she'd just got her first full-time job at a puzzle factory near her home, counting the puzzle pieces inside each box before it left the building, easily the world's most boring job, but it was her first *proper* job and Ellen had been excited about it. She'd used some of the money she'd saved from her paper round to buy herself some smart new work clothes and knowing what her mother was like, she'd purchased everything with her in mind, opting for looser frumpier options than she might otherwise have selected had she merely been pleasing herself. It had been a weekday and a workday for her mother and because she hadn't expected her home for another couple of hours, Ellen had been trying out her new clothing, in front of the only full-length mirror in the house, which was in her mother's room. She was examining her slightly more sophisticated look when, unexpectedly, her mother walked in. Ellen's smile vanished and she stopped posturing and posing immediately, knowing that for reasons she'd thought about many times without progressing any further in her understanding, every display of joy in Ellen enraged her mother, as though she considered happiness itself sinful, despite not being a churchgoer or practising Christian. As a consequence, she was not surprised at the anger she could feel emanating from her mother as she stood still just inside the bedroom door, with an expression on her face that wasn't shock at finding Ellen in her room without her permission, but one that suggested she'd always expected to catch Ellen in there doing things behind her back, that she'd always known her daughter was hiding a shady world that she revelled in whenever she was alone. She looked Ellen up and down, her rage increasing as she took in every detail of her new attire, and when she spoke, her words were a sharp hard expulsion.

She said, 'Plenty man might sex you, but none a'them will marry you.'

Ellen had been only fifteen then, fifteen and wondering where her place in the world was, trying to work out what direction she needed to head in to be sure she found it. After delivering those devastating words, her mother had simply left the room, but her words didn't follow. Instead, they stayed behind and embedded themselves in Ellen's head her whole lifetime, and sometimes when she'd been doing something completely unrelated, innocent even, like washing the dishes or painting her nails, or combing the hair of one of the elderly residents at the Heights, she would hear those words in her mother's voice inside her head from nowhere, and every time they hurt then made her examine them again, what they meant, the precise meaning, questioning again not the fact that her mother had thought those words, but that she'd spoken them. Some of the explanations she came up with took her to very dark places. The most charitable conclusion she'd entertained was that the bloody witch never wanted to imagine – never mind see – her own child experience a better life than the one she had lived herself and every so often, when the girls dug up yet another ancient resentment relating to their being *abandoned* – the actual word they'd used – it was on the tip of her tongue to tell them that for some people, being left behind was the happiest part of their childhood, happier than the life they were subjected to after being sent for or collected; that they had no idea whatsoever how lucky they were.

In the midst of Clyde and CJ's tussling, Clyde stopped resisting, allowing CJ to reclaim the phone, then looked at Ellen and began to dance-walk over to her, in time with the music's beat but moving as if he was an elderly arthritic man. As Ellen rolled her eyes, Wilhelmina laughed out loud then took Ellen's hand and started dancing with her, mimicking Clyde's movements, forcing Ellen to join her till Clyde reached them, at which point Wilhelmina stepped back so Ellen and Clyde were facing each other. The track on the radio ended. Arema's

'In Love' began to play, and Ellen and Clyde paused then started to dance again, this time without eye contact, each staring over the other's shoulder, their bodies almost but not quite touching, their arms straight down at their sides, dancing like the other's mirror image, in perfect rhythm apart, as synchronised as if the two of them had been dancing together a lifetime, which of course, they had. Then CJ pulled Dumpling up to dance, then everyone else joined in, some imitating the same dance, others whooping and cheering Ellen and Clyde on, everyone laughing to be partying in the kitchen on a Saturday morning at nine a.m., and as CJ turned the volume on the radio up, Ellen hoped with all her heart that the old bitch could see her right now, could see her handsome husband, her handsome son and grandson, the life she'd made for herself and her family, hoped her mother had the ability to reach into her soul and witness the expanse of the joy inside her, so infinite that even the pain of remembering Clay could not dispel it.

The party broke up when the track on the radio finished and CJ turned the radio back down to regular listening levels.

'Shame we're not gonna be here tonight,' Ellen said to Dumpling. 'Woulda been nice to have a little get together, everybody celebrating you special day.'

'We can celebrate next year,' Clyde said.

'Honestly, it's fine,' said Dumpling, relieved her sisters were taking her out for dinner later with just a couple of friends, which would be massively less stressful to navigate than the entire family and a full-on party, a possibility she had been dreading for months. It was wonderful to be freed from the oppressive shadow of that worry, to be able to relax, not to have to go to the extreme effort of geeing herself up to an Academy Award-winning performance of a regular person celebrating their birthday and having the time of their life.

'Really is a shame we didn't think about it before,' said CJ.

'Honestly, don't worry about it,' said Dumpling and she wondered if she would ever be able to tell her family how she honestly felt on her birthday. She tried to remember how the subject of her mother had become taboo, trying to recall the specific moment she had realised this, and as usual drew a blank. No one had ever said she couldn't talk about her mother, but at the same time no one in the family ever spoke to her about her mother either. Sometimes she thought she would be driven crazy by the silences and no-go zones and the invisible distances it felt like she alone was always trying to close.

In her twenty-one years, she'd only once asked her dad about her mum, even though the wondering had become near obsessive. At that time, the only thing Dumpling knew about her for sure was that her mum and dad had fallen in love, and after she died it was too painful for him to even think about. That was why he never mentioned or discussed it. Also she knew she had been created in love because she had been born on the day of the year most significant to love: Valentine's Day. Beyond that she basically knew nothing about her mum apart from her name, Francesca, and there were thousands of questions she wanted answers to. Like, what kind of person had she been? Had she been kind? Gentle? Happy? Patient? Did she laugh a lot? What was her favourite food? Her favourite drink? Was she excited to be having a baby? Once she'd made up her mind to ask her dad, it felt as though she'd then had to wait for years for the perfect opportunity to present itself, a moment when they were alone in the house so no one could interrupt or derail their conversation once it started. She didn't know why it was so important that no one else was there or even around to overhear. Whenever she thought about discussing it in front of the family, she remembered the moment she'd found out, which had happened when she was five or maybe six. She'd been arguing with her sisters. She couldn't recall why. She'd been a kid so maybe she'd gone into her sisters' room and touched their stuff or not wanted to share her sweets or was just generally being obnoxious. Anyway, whatever it was, in her memory, she told her sisters she was going to tell her mum.

'She's not your mum,' Claudette said.

'*Your* mum's dead,' said Joycelyn.

A decade later she was still trying to find the vocabulary to describe the extent to which those words had impacted her, like a hard physical blow winding her, but also the way the severity of her response had come from a place that knew something had always been afoot, that there was a reason why her sisters were off with her. They never physically hurt her and they weren't off all the time; sometimes they were really kind and thoughtful, playing with her, plaiting her hair over and over as if she was a little dolly, into hundreds of beautiful styles, bringing her home sweets and treats and small gifts, but that day her sisters' words broke her because she had never felt like she properly fit in.

She remembered crying as she ran to Ellen and told her what had been said. What she had wanted was to be told that her sisters were lying, but instead Ellen called her sisters downstairs, slapped them both and asked if anyone had given them message to carry, which was absolute confirmation for Dumpling that what they'd said was true. Ellen really wasn't her mum, which meant her sisters were only her half-sisters and CJ was only her half-brother and Ellen wasn't related to her at all. The only person in the family with whom her relationship was as she had been raised to believe was Clyde.

Years passed with no additional information whatsoever, then one day she was fifteen and the moment finally arrived. After months of practising the most gentle way to approach the question so her father's feelings weren't hurt, after making them both a cup of tea and taking a seat with him in the kitchen, her mouth fell open and the words tumbled out and onto the table between them before she'd even had a chance to take a sip.

'What was she like?'

Clyde looked confused.

'My mum.'

'You mean when she was young?'

'My real mum,' Dumpling said and felt herself blush when she heard the word *real* which she had consciously intended to avoid because it sounded so ungrateful, so dismissive of everything Ellen had done, when she had in fact voluntarily stepped into Francesca's empty shoes and raised Dumpling better than she had raised her own daughters, so much so that Claudette and Joycelyn despised Dumpling for it, even though she'd never asked to be put on a pedestal or for any special treatment.

'I meant my birth mum,' she said, then watched a series of uncomfortable expressions cross her dad's face as he contemplated the question.

For a moment he examined Dumpling's face. 'She was a nice girl. Pretty. Like you,' he said.

His words brushed over the surface of her unanswered questions without impacting it in the slightest, then dissipated into the air. Had her mother been clever? Funny? Serious? Girly? Emotional? Had she liked walks or music or chocolate or flowers?

'Did she see me? Before she died. Did she get to hold me?'

'I wasn't there. They rang me at work to come to the hospital and get you.' Then, seeing something of the disappointment on her face, Clyde said, 'I don't know what to say. I was married, you know? We never lived like man and wife or nothing.'

That moment had been devastating for Dumpling. She'd been psyching herself up to it her whole life, this asking, to get answers, only to discover there was nothing, absolutely nothing more than her mother's name that she would ever know. Years of thwarted wishes and imagination bubbled up and overflowed from inside her and she cried like a hurt child, loud, raw and uninhibited, able to see with her own eyes how distressed she was making her father feel but unable to stop. Clyde stood and went out of the kitchen. He returned with some toilet paper in one hand and a passport in the other. He handed both to her. Dumpling blew her nose then opened the passport to her mother's photo. She straightened an index finger and gently touched her mother's face. Francesca Isadora Dupres.

'That's all they gave me,' Clyde said.

Something like hope died inside Dumpling that day. In the years she'd been plucking up the courage and waiting for the perfect time, she'd imagined a rippling effect of actions in her mind that answers to some of her questions would have initiated. For example, if her dad had given her details of one of her mother's friends or someone who knew her well, she could have tried to find and speak to that person, which came along with the tantalising possibility that she might somehow be able to find her way to her mother's family, because she must have had some, back in Dominica, parents, maybe siblings. It wasn't impossible, the idea that Francesca might have had another baby before she'd had Dumpling and had done what Clyde and Ellen had done and left the baby with someone back home, freeing herself to be able to come to England and work and earn money and have a go at a real chance to support herself and her child. Dumpling's ripples had led her to explore the possibility that she had another entirely formed family out there in the world somewhere, people who had known her mum and could maybe talk about her or show Dumpling photos, maybe take her to the house her mother had been born in and grew up in, or to the part of Dominica that had the view she'd loved most, a family who could bridge the chasm between how she felt about her mother and what she knew. There were so many possibilities she had expected to evolve from her discussion with her father, like rivers from streams. Instead, every hope she'd ever had on that front had come to an end as effectively as if a tombstone had been dropped on them.

After she'd been given her mother's passport, she'd looked carefully at Dominica in the geography textbooks and atlases at school. It was one of the largest islands in the Caribbean. Although English was its official language, the majority of the island spoke French patois, which she didn't speak. They had reduced in frequency but Dumpling still had nightmares about arriving in Dominica alone and trying to find Francesca's family, her family, with her only language, English, while increasingly impatient people around her responded in patois till she awoke in a state of panic. She'd had to accept that apart from her looks she was nothing like her mum, and didn't have half the courage her mum must have possessed when she'd travelled more than 4000 miles from Dominica to England on her own in search of opportunities, and because Dumpling lacked that courage, half her ancestry was dead to her. She tried not to think about it, but when she did she was positive that the lethargy she had felt since, the tearfulness and lack of joy, was a form of depression, and that she would never be able to shake it off.

'Earth to Dumpling. Come in, Dumpling,' said Claudette.

Dumpling looked up at her.

'She's asking if you're ready to go,' said Joycelyn. 'Our appointment's at ten. The hairdresser's not gonna hang 'round waiting the whole day.'

'Sorry. Yes, I am.' Dumpling stood up from the table. 'Thanks for coming over this morning and making my day so special,' she said to everyone in the kitchen, relieved that the most social part of the day was now behind her. She did a circle of hugs and kisses as Claudette and Joycelyn waited for her with their coats and shoes on, holding their bags by the kitchen door. Then she turned to leave, blowing kisses into the barrage of goodbyes.

Dominoes

1981

(Nineteen years earlier)

The crack of the domino combined with the loud smack of palm on wood as Backfoot delivered his double-five tile onto the kitchen table with an overarm swing.

'Lord have mercy,' Franklin said, 'is cricket you ah play?' His expression was serious. Clyde and James laughed aloud.

'Leave the man,' said Clyde, slapping his domino down. 'You no see him ah bowl?' James and Franklin laughed.

'You face favour bowl,' Backfoot said as Franklin clapped a domino down.

Wilhelmina, who was standing beside Ellen as she stirred the goat water in the doving pot on the stove, laughed aloud. 'But what is this? Game or war?'

Backfoot nodded his head towards the assortment of coins which had been tossed into the centre of the table. 'You know how much money these mandem already fleece me for?'

'Ah no fleece we fleece you. Is game we ah play.' James picked up a domino from the undealt dominoes face down on the table then slapped it onto the table with a flourish.

'But how dis man always have the double six?' Clyde asked.

'Ah cheat him ah cheat, man,' said Franklin.

'True you no know some people just born with plenty plenty luck,' said James.

'Only man with no skill need luck,' said Franklin.

Backfoot looked at Wilhelmina as he delivered another overarm swing and his domino crashed onto the table. 'This is war,' he said.

Wilhelmina raised a brow. 'Unu should be making love, not war.'

Backfoot winked at her. 'First things first,' he said. 'Let me win back me money.'

At the sound of the front doorbell Wilhelmina straightened up from her relaxed lean against the countertop to go and answer it. Ellen put a hand out, halting her. 'Don't bother youself. I think I heard the girls coming down the stairs.'

'You sure you hear them?' Wilhelmina asked, as a roar went up from the men sitting at the table followed by loud laughter.

'I'm sure.'

As Gloria stepped into the kitchen, followed by Claudette and then Joycelyn with Dumpling on her hip, the crisp cold breeze that entered the hallway when the front door had been opened rushed ahead of them into the kitchen like a hurricane wind, scattering the stagnant clouds of cigarette smoke that were layered in the air above the kitchen table.

'Evening all,' said Gloria, pausing at the table and resting her hand on Franklin's shoulder.

He glanced up at her briefly. 'You a'right?' Gloria nodded and responded to the men at the table who looked up and said variations of hello then immediately looked back down as Backfoot delivered another domino onto the kitchen table with an overarm swing.

'But who call this man Backfoot? Should'a call him Front Arm,' said Clyde and as the room laughed, Gloria walked towards Ellen and Wilhelmina.

'Evening Gloria,' said Wilhelmina. 'Is only now you coming from work?'

The question was delivered in a perfectly ordinary tone, so much so that outside of Wilhelmina and probably Gloria, Ellen was the only other person in the kitchen who picked up on the subtext and only then because she was already aware of how high up in her stomach Wilhelmina kept Gloria. The words were aimed at putting Gloria and what she was wearing down. It was also low, because Gloria was a good-looking woman, her body fit as any young girl's, with good taste and the ready cash to indulge those tastes. She was bejewelled about the wrists, neck and fingers as usual and wearing super-high wedges with a leather skirt and silk blouse, fur coat draped over her shoulders beneath immaculate freshly hot-combed hair; in summary, looking nothing like a person who had just finished work then made their way straight over to a friend's house.

'I was off this afternoon. Doctor's appointment,' said Gloria, her tone neutral as she handed Ellen a bottle slickly wrapped in an off-licence sheet, which Ellen was confident would be Gloria's favourite tipple: gin.

'Thanks,' Ellen said, as she took the bottle, unwrapped it, twisted open the cap and shook a little of the gin off the top of the bottle for the jumbies. She respected Gloria's brave front. Not for the first time she wondered if that was what kept her feeling sympathetic to Gloria, the fact she'd had to learn to navigate strange waters as a woman, had learned through trial and tribulation how to fix her face to hide her feelings, how to deliver her words evenly with an absence of the passion churning up inside her. Ellen knew precisely how hard-earned that skill was, the turmoil and upset that were par for the course. But Gloria's lack of emotion wasn't enough to appease Wilhelmina.

'You pregnant?' Wilhelmina asked and Ellen felt she had gone too far, because everyone knew Gloria and Franklin had been married for must be five years now and, so far, there had been no babies; and everyone also knew there was nothing that would make Gloria and Franklin happier than to have some babies underfoot. Anyone with a bit of compassion in their soul would know the subject was a sore one for them both, yes, but for Gloria in particular, as Franklin already had two children living back home in Montserrat with their mother, clearly inferring that all his equipment was in perfect working order and so any problem bringing more Frank Juniors into the world was down to Gloria.

'Claudette, hang Gloria's coat outside,' Ellen said, 'and come wash the rice when you finish.'

Without looking at her mother or replying, Claudette began walking towards Gloria.

'No,' Gloria replied to Wilhelmina, with the tired smile of someone responding to a painful question from a well-intentioned person. She shook herself free of her coat which Claudette, standing behind her, walked away with. 'Not yet.'

'Hand me a glass,' Ellen said to Gloria. 'Let me get you a drink.'

Gloria turned around and opened the cupboard on the wall behind her. It was a Friday and pretty much every Friday friends gathered at Ellen and Clyde's because they had the space for it; to have some food, a little drink and a laugh. Some came for the dominoes, or to drop off their Pardner money, for the music that was so familiar to them all and sometimes the dancing that listening to the music organically evolved into. There were regulars and people they only saw every now and then, friends who popped in, passed through, stopped by just for the company, to be with other people who looked like them, for the release that came with that, the relief, the ease. As exiled countryfolk, the opportunity to just be themselves was something greatly relished and, like Gloria, the Friday crowd eventually grew to find and know their way around Ellen's kitchen, and certainly the cupboards that housed the essentials, the glasses and the teacups, as well as if they lived there. Ellen took the glass Gloria handed her.

There were times when Ellen just did not understand Wilhelmina. She knew women did this, acted up around men, joked and shamed and put each other down while vying for the spotlight, the men's attention, but in Ellen's experience it was usually women who were either interested in those men or insecure about their relationship with their own men and saw other women as a threat to that. Ellen looked across to the table, at the men gathered there, wondering which of the men's attention Wilhelmina was trying to divert away from Gloria and onto herself. Though Wilhelmina enjoyed the odd flirtatious joke with Backfoot, there was no chance of a relationship between him and her friend because Backfoot was a hard man, a hard drinker, hard smoker and hard gambler and Wilhelmina had turned down too many men with far fewer failings to end up falling into a relationship with someone on a full-speed trajectory toward their own self-destruction. She also wasn't interested in James who was a nice enough man but dull, particularly around women. That left only Franklin and Clyde. Ellen studied Franklin anew. He was a big man, taller than Clyde and wider in a way that made him look powerful. She looked at Clyde. It wasn't so obvious at that moment because he was sitting down and the tabletop completely hid his stomach, but over the last year or two he'd begun to develop a paunch around his middle, one Ellen equated with a five-month pregnancy. Franklin in comparison looked fit. Side-on to Ellen's view, his stomach appeared flat and watching him, she had to admit he was easy on the eye. Perhaps sensing he was being observed, he looked up at Ellen, caught her eye, nodded and she nodded back then quickly looked away. He was not as attractive as Clyde – very few men were – but he was still handsome in his own right. Maybe there was an attraction there she'd failed to notice. Perhaps Wilhelmina really did have a thing for Franklin?

As much as Franklin was a decent-looking man and good company, he was married to Gloria – though no one knew better than Ellen how difficult it could be to get your man to keep the zip of his pants up even when you were married to them and giving them regular nookie and doing everything you could to meet their every need; cleaning their clothes and cooking their favourite foods just the way they liked it. Even when all of that was being done it still didn't guarantee they would be faithful, and that was after you factored in having four kids with them. Without the kids – yes it was wrong and tough to swallow – but without the kids no one expected fidelity from such a man. If such a man played around with other women, none of their manfriends would bat an eyelid. Even worse, if the man played around with another woman and she was to become pregnant, well, for Gloria, that could be game over.

Ellen handed Gloria her drink, gin and tonic with plenty of ice. Gloria raised her glass to Ellen and

Wilhelmina, who raised her glass then chugged down the contents. Ellen picked her own glass up, said cheers, then took a mouthful. She watched as Gloria took a sip and had to acknowledge that as sound as the logic of her thoughts was, Gloria had one thing Ellen did not: good looks. Male or female, you could not look at Gloria and fail to notice that not only was she a very attractive woman but she was also impeccably turned out. That didn't guarantee that Franklin wouldn't play away from home, but it did skew the possibilities of Franklin leaving Gloria, because she was a catch. Other men noticed her, did a double take, checked her ring finger out. It also meant it was conceivable that Gloria herself might decide to act if his behaviour became outrageous and, who knew, she could even end up with someone better than Franklin, a scenario Ellen did not apply to herself as just being married to Clyde had exceeded every expectation she had ever had on the relationship front, and just as she had never anticipated she would end up married to a man so attractive that, even from the very beginning, the moment they'd met, he'd exceeded her wildest dreams, she was under no illusion: she knew that the possibility of her becoming the wife of another man of equal beauty was nil. As her mother had so helpfully pointed out: sex, yes, but marriage? No. It was a sequence of thought that she tried not to have too frequently, because it usually ended in her wondering if that was part of the reason Clyde slept with other women, whether he'd had the same thoughts about their relationship and arrived at the same conclusion.

She took a large mouthful of her drink and deliberately parked her thinking process, glancing around for something else to focus on.

'Let me have a little hold,' Gloria said to Joycelyn, holding her hands out to Dumpling, who, though technically no longer a baby, was never more content than when she was being passed around from one person's hip to the next, who was so overindulged that at one point Ellen had had to insist she not be picked up at specific times of the day in order to ensure she spent enough time on the floor that she would be able to learn to walk confidently, and had then had to enforce the ban during a long period of Dumpling sitting on a single spot having a meltdown. Dumpling smiled and stretched her arms out towards Gloria.

'Hello beautiful,' Gloria said, as she took her and smoothly shifted her over onto her hip, then opened her handbag, took out a lollipop and held it up. 'What's this?' she asked Dumpling, who looked from the lollipop to Ellen with intense longing till Ellen rolled her eyes and said, 'All right.'

Dumpling grinned and said, 'Thank you, Auntie Gloria,' and as Gloria put her down on the ground, turned her full attention onto watching the lollipop being unwrapped.

Claudette returned to the kitchen and Gloria moved out of her way so she could get to the pots in the base cupboard behind her.

'The hard dough bread needs cutting,' Ellen said to Joycelyn. Although Joycelyn didn't answer her mother, she immediately began to move towards the drawer the knives were kept in.

Ellen heard the sound of the front door slamming closed and knew CJ had arrived home, which was confirmed a moment later when he entered the kitchen with a young woman. The two of them immediately became the focal point of the room. The young woman was fit and what was proving to be CJ's type – very curvaceous with big bum and breasts – and her assets were being flaunted in a skin-tight red dress. The men at the table greeted CJ jovially whilst eyeing up the young woman. After the greetings and handshakes between the men, Clyde said, 'You not gonna introduce you friend?'

'Sorry,' CJ said. 'This is Roxanne.'

Roxanne smiled at each of the men around the table as they introduced themselves to her, and for the first time since Claudette and Joycelyn had entered the kitchen with Gloria the sisters exchanged eye contact with each other, equally mortified now the woman who had looked a bit familiar had been named. Roxanne was two years older than CJ and had been in Claudette's year at school. The last time Claudette had seen her, Roxanne had been shrouded in an oversized school blazer that had been purchased so large initially she never fully grew into it before leaving school, accompanied by the knee-length, pleated-all-round uniform skirt, and her hair, like Claudette's own, had been plaited as per a mother's strict directive into a school-appropriate style. Neither of the sisters missed the fact that her face was made up, the entire range of make-up having been applied: foundation, blusher, eyeliner and shadow, mascara, the full works, even though she and Claudette were the same age.

'What a pretty girl,' Ellen said, as CJ brought Roxanne over to introduce her now to the women.

'Nice to meet you,' Roxanne said quietly, as if overcome by shyness, though Ellen could see nothing shy about the way the tricky girl was dressed, with her titties and batty out of doors. Nonetheless she liked CJ's taste, liked that his type appeared to be not just coloured women but coloured women with dark skin. It felt like a compliment to Ellen each time she met his womanfriends and he'd gone dark, especially when her son was such a lady-killer he could pretty much have anyone.

'Very pretty,' Gloria said.

'Thank you,' Roxanne said.

'Nice, CJ,' said Wilhelmina, looking at Roxanne and then at CJ as if his new girlfriend was an accomplishment to be proud of, and one that reflected positively on him.

'You want a drink?' Ellen asked Roxanne.

'Can I have a brandy and Babycham, please?' Roxanne asked, which was how every woman in the room knew the girl didn't have any broughtupsy, because anyone with even a little home training would've known not to ask for brandy *and* Babycham the first time they were introduced to their boyfriend's parents. Out of politeness, she should've asked for a glass of sarsaparilla or a bottle of Cherry B or just the Babycham on its own, even if moving forward no one ever again saw her sober.

Before Ellen could open her mouth, Joycelyn turned

around and went to the cupboard to get a glass for their visitor.

'I didn't know you knew my younger brother,' Claudette said to Roxanne, who looked at her properly for the first time, shrieked 'Claudette!' then embraced her, which Claudette considered quite the overreaction considering they were never really close at school and barely spoke. She was surprised Roxanne even knew her name.

'Oh my God! I never knew he was your brother.'

'Well, we never used to hang out with the people in his year being that they were a lot younger,' Claudette said, making the point that Roxanne at seventeen was going out with a fifteen-year-old boy, a very handsome boy, smartly dressed and with the confidence of someone much older than himself, but a boy two years younger than herself nonetheless. In her view, it was embarrassing. Girls their age seeking romance looked to proper men and older boys, lowering their bar gradually to a reluctant acceptance of boys their own age, but two years younger? Definitely not.

'Oh my days,' said CJ. 'You two know each other?'

'You better mind youself,' said Backfoot.

'You in trouble now,' Clyde said.

'Stop it,' said Gloria, laughing. 'Let them be.'

Joycelyn stepped forward and handed Roxanne a glass. 'He's my younger brother too.'

'Thanks,' Roxanne said as she took the drink. 'We never met, did we?'

'Joycelyn was in the year below. She's in the fifth year now, the year above CJ,' Claudette said.

'Nice to make your acquaintance,' said Joycelyn, giving Roxanne a hard-faced stare.

'But CJ, you a badman, already a deal with older woman,' said Backfoot.

'Chip off the old block,' said Wilhelmina.

'The apple never fall far from the tree,' said Franklin.

Ellen didn't join in the laughter, as she was two years younger than Clyde and it felt to her like the joke was related to his seeing and sleeping with other women who were older than himself which, as funny topics went, wasn't the most amusing punchline she'd ever heard.

'You know what,' CJ said, 'We're going upstairs for a little bit of peace.' He looked at Roxanne and flicked his head as if to indicate *come on*.

'Enjoy you *piece*,' Frank said, and the men laughed as CJ and Roxanne exited.

The entire incident had left Claudette seething with rage. She looked at Joycelyn and saw her feelings reflected in her younger sister's face. Then each of them turned around and carried on with the tasks they had been getting on with when CJ and Roxanne had made their entrance.

Neither Claudette nor Joycelyn was engaging in small talk or chit chat with their mother. Their day had started with such happiness and optimism, which they'd fully expected to culminate in a wonderful evening that would forever define the exact moment they went from being girls to women. The whole thing had begun the week before when their dad had received his Pardner Hand and, being his typically kind and generous self, had given them both a crisp ten-pound note which they'd spent down the market on an outfit each and a communal stock of makeup, including lipstick, mascara and blusher, all of which had been safely put aside specifically to be worn that very Friday. Claudette had initiated it. She was seventeen, had left school and was at college studying childcare. Although two of the tutors were male, all the students were female and, despite having been there only two months, in terms of life experience, it was very apparent to her that she was lacking in advancement of every kind on the growing-up front. She was one of only a handful out of twenty-four girls who had never had a boyfriend and three of that small handful were forbidden to have one by their religion. Whereas Claudette – though her mum and dad had sent them to Sunday school when they were little – couldn't really describe herself as religious. But it wasn't exactly that which had started her thinking about the world and her place in it, nor was it the fact that some of the girls on her course not only had boyfriends but had also had sex. It was the fact that she hadn't ever felt as if she was on a road and heading in a direction in which anything like that could become a possibility. Claudette had had men eye her up, naturally, when she was out, on the street, on the bus or train or in shops, but none of that had led to her being chatted up. Despite no longer being an actual schoolgirl, she hadn't taken even the first step towards finding and being in a relationship. Only once had she ever received flowers on Valentine's day, and she'd been ecstatic for days till Joycelyn fessed up she was the person who'd sent them.

She was convinced something had messed up time and their actual ages in their mother's head and that it was to do with those years they'd been left behind back home like shoes that rubbed your corn, while CJ was taken with their parents despite him being the baby and the one who needed the most looking after, even though they were older and would be off their parents' hands far quicker in terms of going to school and childcare no longer being an issue. She was convinced that in order not to feel guilty about it, their mother's mind had simply erased those years and subtracted them from their actual ages, because that was how she treated them, like they were girls of twelve and thirteen instead of sixteen- and seventeen-year-old young women. They were still not allowed to go to friends' houses without permission or to hang out with other young people on the street, to eat other people's food or borrow anything from anyone. They weren't allowed to say *yes* if offered a biscuit without their mother giving them an imperceptible nod first. They were not allowed out late or to chat to boys or go to raves or clubs, just stuck in time, unable to draw breath if their mother said *no*. In short, while their dad was *illegally* teaching CJ to drive and sharing his weed and cigarettes with him and he seemed to have the same freedom to come and go as their dad did, Claudette and, as a consequence, Joycelyn, felt like they were suffocating. Once and for all, that needed to change.

Earlier in the afternoon when they'd arrived back home, Claudette from college and Joycelyn from school, Ellen was waiting for them both, to wash and season the meat, grate the carrots, cabbage and onions for the coleslaw, run to the shops for milk, mayonnaise and soda pop, then give the kitchen and toilet a quick once over, topping up the toilet paper and putting out a clean towel and a fresh bar of Imperial Leather on the side of the toilet sink. Afterwards, the two young women had retired to their room to begin the exciting process of getting ready, in the knowledge they were going to look amazing and – in an effort to creep out from under Ellen's skirts – like stylish young women, instead of as continuations of the girls they felt their mother had always kept them as and would be happy to continue keeping them as till they died from old age, still spinsters.

They'd donned the slim-fitting pencil skirts that smoothly sheathed their forms and the perfectly coordinated tank tops they'd bought in different colours to emphasise their individuality – Claudette's in brown and Joycelyn's in beige. The V-neck tank tops fit snugly, and once they were dressed in their splendid new finery they marvelled at the instant transformation not just from girls to women, but from girls to hot women; sexy young women looking good. Then the sisters had hot-combed and styled each other's hair before finally sitting down to complete their process of transition through the careful application of the new makeup.

On their own, neither would ever have been fearless enough to make an appearance in this new and transformed state, but what courage they lacked as individuals they found in their combined reserves, because there were two of them, because they were sisters and so close in age, because CJ, who was younger than them both, was already being initiated into the adult world of men and bringing his woman-friends home, and because Claudette and Joycelyn were united in their agreement that their time to take their place in the adult world had arrived some time ago and been completely ignored by the family. When they'd finished, aware the doorbell had rung a number of times and people had already started to arrive, the two girls made their careful way down the stairs in the tottery winkle-pickers that set their new look off to perfection.

They paused for a moment outside the kitchen door, hearing the ordinary entertaining noises of clinking glasses and the pot lid being replaced, the oven door opening then closing, listening to the sultry vocals of Shirley Brown and the chatter and laughter of the men on the other side, their voices raised in order to be heard. The sound of the tipping of the dominoes onto the table from its bag seemed to suggest the right moment to enter, the casting off of childhood and the start of their new life as young women coinciding with the beginning of the game. However, when the two young women opened the kitchen door and passed through it, their entry also coincided with the final track on the tape cassette coming to an end and the perfect silence of everyone inside the kitchen as they paused what they were doing and stared at them. It was such a floodtide of silence that it stopped their forward momentum and the two girls stood still just inside the kitchen door, somehow looking around without catching anyone's eye, smiling the smile of young girls unused to being the centre of attention and slightly awkward to find themselves in that position even though they had initiated it, both engaged in their own battle under the intense scrutiny not to give in to the instinct to squirm.

The men were sitting at the table smoking and drinking in advance of the start of the dominoes game, Backfoot among them and the first to recover. 'But look p'on these two beauty queens,' he said.

Next Clyde spoke, as if he'd genuinely been trying to recall if he'd forgotten something, some special event which required the complete transformation of his daddy's girls into hardback women, complete with breasts adoor. 'Is where you both going?'

Then Wilhelmina laughed and said, as if she was speaking to Ellen but loud and directly to the room, 'But Ellen, me never realise is three big woman ah live here.'

During the uncomfortable laughter that followed, the girls looked at Ellen, whose face was a picture of fury. She was giving them *the look*, and in this instance it meant *You better get your asses upstairs and take off those skirts tight round you batty, and the low-cut tops with half you titties hanging out and wipe the paint off you faces and fix the hair on both those heads back into a style that I think is appropriate, and what's more, you better do it right now!* The look continued in its message by adding *Doing all of that does not mean this matter has come to a close, because believe me, this is not finished with. You can be guaranteed the three of us will be revisiting this issue tomorrow.* Having received that entire message, articulately conveyed by their mother through eye contact alone, Claudette and Joycelyn bowed their heads, turned around and walked back out the room.

Of course, the absolute worst part of the saga was that after they'd travelled back upstairs, taken off their shoes and clothes and makeup and brushed and clipped their hair back up into ponytails, had a cry and quiet rage against the unfairness of everything in their world, which seemed related to the fact they were girls and nothing further, and stoked the resentment they had always felt towards their mother, who in their view had been singularly responsible for everything in their lives that was bleak and old-fashioned and stacked so heavily against them, after all that, they'd had to come back down again looking like schoolgirls; and that return to girlhood, back to their place, was singularly the most embarrassing experience of their lives. They'd been brought up to respect adults and elders, to listen when they were spoken to, to do what they were told when they were told to do it, and on top of that, to honour their mother and their father, which meant they had been effectively silenced and had all agency taken away, to such an extent that when they returned back downstairs, not only did they not protest or demonstrate any unhappiness about what had happened to them, but they were careful not to meet their mother's eye, worried some residual resentment might be accidentally conveyed, which they knew their mother would have no qualms about addressing on the spot in front of everyone.

Joycelyn washed her hands at the sink and left the

tap on and Claudette moved alongside her, with the big rice pot in her arms, one-third filled with rice, which she placed under the running water and began to rinse. Though they were side by side, they didn't look at each other or even risk exchanging a glance of solidarity, knowing how eagle-eyed Ellen would be. They'd had the audacity not just to challenge her authority but to do so in public.

A roar went up from the table and as three of the men groaned, James grinned and laughed and gathered up the money in the centre.

'This can't be right!' Backfoot said.

'The man ah use obeah,' Clyde said.

'Is skill me ah use. Skill and plenty plenty luck,' James said.

Franklin slapped the rest of the bones in his hands down on the table in a gesture of defeat.

'Me nah play no more. Only had me pay in me pocket one night and this man a'ready looking to clean me out,' said Franklin as he stood.

'Let me put on a tune,' Wilhelmina said, making her way over to the stereo on the side and looking though the cassette tapes. She ejected the one inside the machine and put in another. After a brief interlude of white noise, Al Green began to play. Wilhelmina started dancing. Then Gloria began to dance, slowly incorporating into her dance the move from where she had been standing to where Dumpling stood sucking her lollipop. She picked Dumpling up and continued dancing with her. Franklin stood up at the table and danced his way over to them. Immediately Dumpling stretched her arms out towards him. Gloria resisted handing her over, turning so Dumpling was out of arm's reach.

'It's me who buy you the lollipop,' she said.

Dumpling began to make sounds of resistance and stretched her hands out more desperately towards Franklin.

'You can't bribe her with no lollipop. Gimmee me girlfriend,' Franklin said.

Gloria kissed Dumpling on the cheek as she handed her to Franklin who put his hands around Dumpling's waist and raised her into the air as the small girl shrieked and laughed.

'She's such a little flirt,' said Wilhelmina.

'Takes after the father,' said Ellen, rolling her eyes.

Gloria took hold of one of Claudette's hands and one of Joycelyn's. 'Come on,' she said, 'You can finish you chores after.'

The two girls began to dance with her, then Claudette put down a piece of fancy footwork and Gloria and her sister laughed and cheered her on. James came forward and took Joycelyn's hand and began to dance with her as Wilhelmina turned the music up and everyone else in the room bobbed in their seats or got up and joined in.

Dumpling's Arrival

1979

(Two years earlier)

'You sure you don't want me to walk with you?' Wilhelmina said, when they reached the bottom of the road.

'I'm sure,' Ellen said. She needed to be alone.

'As God is my witness, I could wring his blasted neck!' Wilhelmina said as the two women embraced. Then they parted ways; Wilhelmina headed off to the left, to walk the fifteen minutes to her house, and Ellen headed off to the right, in the direction of the high street.

It wasn't especially late, but it was already dark. Ellen had decided to head towards the high street because she'd told Clyde and the kids she was going out to pick up some shopping and there were a number of shops on the high street that would be open for another hour or two, which would give her ample time to have a wander and a think. Though she appreciated Wilhelmina's support, she was so sensitive to the hurt Ellen experienced, such a good good friend, that she frequently took Clyde's bad behaviour even worse than Ellen did. Her performance and cussing clouded Ellen's thought process and made it difficult for her to think straight. And boy did she need her head clear to think, because what had happened over the past couple of hours was not a new version of the same old problem, it was a completely different problem that came with lifetime consequences, and it had arrived straight on the back of the other terrible lifetime consequences that she was still struggling to come to terms with.

The evening was cold and, though it wasn't raining, the air was damp. She did up the top button on her coat, pulled her scarf down a little lower on her forehead and upturned her collar before briskly walking on and attempting to begin the process of making sense of what had happened.

The day could not have started more normally. She had known it was a Wednesday, but she hadn't recalled it was also Valentine's Day, as whilst Clyde had been very quick to embrace the pub culture since their relocation to England, he had been considerably slower embracing British romantic traditions. Ordinarily the kids would have been in school except it was also half term, which meant they were off. Ellen had been on the early shift at the Heights that week so had got up at five as Clyde was leaving for the sorting office. Now she was wondering whether Clyde really had gone to work at all. This was the problem with being married to what Wilhelmina called *a habitual liar*, that she often found herself having to go over the fine detail again and again with the advantage of hindsight, trying to see whether everything had been as innocuous as it appeared when it had happened in real time, trying to spot any meaningful holes.

Ellen thought back further, to Clyde's behaviour the previous evening. He'd been out drinking at the Prince with his friends till late. He arrived back home just before ten, which was a little early for him, so she had only just finished painting the nails on her left hand but hadn't yet started her right, and she would have described his condition as drunk but not paralytic. She heard him come in and then heard him go outside into the back garden where she knew he was having a puff, and so she took her time painting the nails on her right hand and had completed the job by the time he came upstairs bringing an aromatic cloud of minty-spliff cologne into their bedroom with him. He'd been merry, very merry, merrier than he'd been at any point over the previous four months, much more his old self, had bounced back to being able to compartmentalise his sadness, which had pleased her no end, because nothing was more wretched than Clyde's face when he felt sad. It was impossible not to want to assist him back to happiness with every remedy she had at her disposal, and that feeling was even stronger when she felt responsible for his sadness, which she did, regarding Clay.

Then he got in her way till she gave up trying to finish putting her rollers into her hair and indulged instead in eating the prawns he fed her, which he'd bought from the cockles and whelks man outside the pub. He was happy and funny and kind to her, and though she was sad because of Clay, she really couldn't say that was the reason Clyde was being kind to her, because he generally was a very nice man. He had his faults for sure. It was true she couldn't really trust a single word that came out of his mouth and yes, he took off faster than Speedy Gonzales after anything in heat, and he wasn't good with money or even particularly grown up when it came to being a husband and father, but on the positive side he was really handsome, very sexy, good company, and he made her laugh. He'd joked around and fed her prawns, then they'd had one last drink for the road before heading to bed where they'd indulged in the good good loving before falling asleep. In the morning getting ready, he'd been in great cheer, humming out of tune as he bathed and brushed his teeth and got dressed. Everything added up. Nothing was out of place or suggested in retrospect he was heading off to join another woman first thing in the morning to hold her hand as she delivered his child. She had no reason to disbelieve he'd gone to work that morning. Nothing pointed in any other direction. All things considered, that part of the information he'd given her was probably true.

However, he'd also told her that he'd had no idea Francesca was having his baby. Though she had no evidence to contradict this, with everything Clyde said she was forced to take into account the fact he was a habitual liar. If even Clyde himself had not known Francesca was having his baby then died in childbirth, how would anyone else have known Clyde existed and that he was the father? And how would that person have known Clyde worked at the sorting office, or the actual times he worked, or even which sorting office he worked at or where it was, never mind have all the knowledge necessary to run down there to bring Clyde word his child had been born and the mother was dead? If Clyde himself did not know he had impregnated that woman, how would anyone else have known or traced the baby girl back to him? And that's not to mention of course that if he had no idea the woman was carrying his baby or that it was due and as he had said, someone had shown up at his workplace out of the blue and told him the person who had just had his child was dead, would he have shot off immediately to the hospital? Or might he have stated the blinding obvious, namely that they had the wrong man? As far as Ellen was concerned, it made more sense to her that he had known full well Francesca was pregnant; he just hadn't expected that when she was giving birth she would die.

'Evening Mrs Fenton,' said a woman walking towards her with her shopping bags.

Ellen nodded her head. 'Mrs Roy. Family all right?'

'Yes, praise Jesus. And you? Everybody managing okay?'

For a moment, Ellen felt like she was in tailspin, in a panic as to how Mrs Roy could have found out about the baby girl already when Clyde had only just brought her home and as far as Ellen was aware, none of the family had spoken to anyone else about her. Then she realised she had completely misinterpreted Mrs Roy's words. She hadn't been asking about this newest situation, she was talking about the other recent past one. Now she could see concern on Mrs Roy's face at her delay and difficulty answering such a straightforward question. Because of her delay she now felt obligated to give an explanation. 'Everybody's well. I'm just tired, y'know? The kids and work and everything when me head still fog-up.'

'The Lord never give us more than we can bear,' Mrs Roy said.

Ellen nodded despite her scepticism, now just wanting to get away. 'Amen. Say howdy to Mr Roy.'

'Will do,' said Mrs Roy and Ellen smiled and began to walk on, relieved to be out of the conversation and wondering what on earth she was going to tell people like Mrs Roy – who would know without a shred of doubt she had not been expecting – where the baby girl had come from. And the thought devastated her, because the mere fact she was considering how she would explain to everyone where the baby girl had come from meant that she had already made the decision to keep her, and as crazy as it would sound if she tried to explain it to anyone, Ellen felt as though she had betrayed her own self, as if she had just accidentally found out about a decision she'd made behind her own back.

She looked over the road to the Prince, on the corner of the block opposite. If it were any other evening she would have been tempted to go over there, to go in and have a double – maybe even triple – gin and tonic. Today however she knew there would be people there whom she and Clyde knew and she really had no idea what she wanted to say to anyone who knew her and Clyde yet, especially as the news would have spread like wildfire amongst Clyde's friends and acquaintances. She didn't want to make an even greater fool of herself going into the pub and not mentioning the great bomb that had dropped on her home while speaking to people who were probably already gossiping about the husband she'd been married to for eleven years, who was – theoretically – sleeping in her bed every night but had still brought his outdoors baby indoors. No. She wasn't yet ready to have that conversation with anyone. Not till she had regained her composure and worked out what she was going to say. She continued walking till the Prince was out of view and behind her. Ahead she saw Mr Brewer, the husband of her next-door neighbour, walking in her direction on the same side of the street she was on. Instinctively she turned towards the road and, finding it blessedly clear, crossed quickly, thereby avoiding having to speak to him, for now anyway. He'd no doubt be hearing the baby girl cry later on that night when the street was quiet and the cries of babies sounded loudest, would hear it through the supporting wall that divided their homes, and Ellen knew with certainty that Mrs Brewer would be over in the morning, her face lit with curiosity, her hands clutching an empty sugar bowl.

Her change of course landed her on the pavement outside Sid the grocer's where Sid himself was leaned up against the doorjamb. He smiled at her as she approached.

'Evening, Cherry Blossom,' he said, 'Nippy night, innit?'

'Yes, it is,' Ellen answered returning the smile. He always seemed such a pleasant man, Sid, so friendly. He regularly stood in the shop doorway when there were no customers inside and said hello to everyone who passed by, and he seemed to have no awareness that calling coloured women 'Cherry Blossom' was rude. It was a feature of some English people she'd got used to, a way of being that was as much a part of who they were as the seed was a part of the ginnip; it wasn't impossible to separate the two, and when you managed to do so successfully the results were great, but it could also be quite hard work for very little return. It was a feature that made people who otherwise seemed genuinely nice deeply offensive by accident. However, she did know Cherry Blossom was the brand name for the nation's number one shoe polish, and she also knew it was not acceptable for anyone to call her that, so unless it was some kind of emergency or she had no other practical choice, she never spent her money in his shop.

'Have a good evening,' she said and as she passed, he tipped his cap. It felt like a reprieve to have had a little think about something normal in the midst of the crazy situation she found herself in, lovely for her mind to be distracted momentarily by a bit of regular everyday prejudice, and she felt sad the conversation had ended so quickly.

That morning, Ellen had got up and bathed and dressed and poked her head around Claudette and Joycelyn's door and woken them up because she needed to remind them to pick up the oxtail for dinner and to ask the butcher to chop it into medium-sized pieces and she needed to emphasise one last time they were not to take their eyes off him while he was chopping because more than once he had weighed her meat for her and afterwards, somehow in the chopping, pieces of the meat he'd charged her for had ended up on the floor instead of in the bag. Ellen knew a number of other women who'd had the same experience, so particularly because the girls were young – which meant he'd think them naive and be emboldened – they needed to keep their eyes on him the whole time. She would be the first to grudgingly admit he was a talented butcher and he managed to chop meat up with plenty skill and the minimum splintering of bone, but he was also a crook. Then, reminder successfully delivered, she'd tiptoed past CJ's room, because she knew he'd still be sleeping, and departed for work as normal.

Ellen sighed deeply when she thought about her job. She'd been working at the Heights for more than ten years. She'd started out as a care assistant, doing the back-breaking work of taking care of the residents, all of whom were white, while the majority of the care assistants, all the cleaners and the cook were coloured and mainly from the Caribbean, though there were a couple of Nigerian women, one Ghanaian and two Indian women working there as well. It was the lifting that made the work so hard and there was so much of it to be done: lifting residents on and off the toilet and in and out of beds and chairs and baths, for meals, TV and bed changes. Some of the residents required a number of bedding changes each day, and more than a handful of those changes were deliberately engineered by some of the openly prejudiced residents, who purposely soiled themselves out of resentment, and to make the jobs of the staff they despised as difficult as possible. Yes, all in all, it had been very hard work.

Yet it would be a lie to say she hadn't enjoyed it. It didn't offer anything like Clyde's job at the sorting office – fixed shifts and decent pay both for overtime and for working unsociable hours – nor did it come with a fantastic pension scheme, but she had enjoyed the company of women like herself, exiles from their homelands struggling to work and raise families in the absence of grandparents and the familial support they'd left behind in the migration to Great Britain. It wasn't as good a job as Clyde's but she'd been promoted to supervisor two years ago, the first coloured supervisor the home had ever had and second in charge only to the care home manager, Mrs Mannering, who Ellen got along with well. Ellen enjoyed her position as a supervisor and she was very good at it. Funny that amongst all the things Clyde had said when he brought the new baby girl home out of the blue to live with them for the rest of everyone's lives, he hadn't mentioned giving up his job to look after her, and of course he wouldn't be the one giving up his job because although her job was more senior to his and came with more responsibility, his brought in more money.

Ellen turned into the VG Shop she shopped at regularly and walked straight to the baby section near the back, which wasn't large by any means, but did stock infant formula. All her kids, including Clay, had gone from breastmilk to goat or cows' milk, so although she knew of formula, she'd never used it. She turned around the tin in her hands and read the instructions on the back to see whether it was suitable for newborns. If you could use the word *lucky* in this context, they'd been lucky that Francesca had bought some baby things, which Clyde had collected from her place, a room in a shared house. She had already been behind with her rent and the landlady had refused to let Clyde into the room unless he brought the rent up to date. Not wanting to be that person, yet unable to unsee the holes in his story, Ellen had asked Clyde how he knew where Francesca lived. He said he'd only ever been there one time, that it had been late at night and he'd had a lot to drink and although he could remember roughly where it was, he couldn't remember the name of the street or the house, but the hospital had given him the address. She'd asked him if he was saying he'd only ever seen Francesca that one time, and with his characteristic ability to anticipate the corner her line of questioning might back him into, he'd paused for a moment then said he'd seen her twice; the night he'd met her and one time after, when she called on him at work and told him she was pregnant.

'I thought you didn't know she was pregnant,' Ellen had said.

Clyde responded quickly that although she'd told him she was pregnant, he couldn't believe it, after all he'd only slept with her the once and he didn't even really know her. In his view, the baby could've been anyone's. Ellen had not asked what had changed his mind, because the answer was blatant; the baby girl was a cute little dolly, her skin colour the exact same as Clyde's and the top strip of her ears the same colour as the rest of her face which meant she'd stay that shade. Besides, her features were a carbon copy of her dad's. There could be no doubt in the mind of anyone who'd seen her that she was Clyde's child.

Ellen thought this part of Clyde's story was probably true. For obvious reasons she had no doubt he was capable of sleeping with a woman he'd just met without knowing anything about her, though she had no idea why he would be under the impression having sex with someone the one time couldn't lead to that woman becoming pregnant with his child, because that was exactly how Claudette had been conceived. From personal experience he should surely know that one time was often all it took. Though she had managed to resist the urge to tell him so, she hadn't been able to stop her mind running on Francesca, the wretched girl, hardly much older than her own daughters, living alone in a different country, unable to say no to one of the world's most charming men, only to find herself pregnant and him married, then having no one to rely on or help her in this freezing cold country, away from her family, giving birth alone while knowing she was facing complete destitution. Even had she not died, it would have been difficult – probably impossible – for her to manage. Then, unusually for her, as she hadn't been to church since 1962, when she'd attended her mother's funeral service, she suddenly found herself wondering whether the moment of the conception of this baby had been God's will. Whether it had also been his will for the baby to be raised by her, in order to balance the books, an opportunity for penance and a chance to put things right? If she had been religious, she would've answered yes, that was exactly what had happened. Instead, she berated herself for thinking foolishness at her age. It was more likely to be the result of good mischief of the jumbies, in lieu of the bad mischief, the terrible mischief levied upon her for a silly mistake.

There'd been no formula in Francesca's room, only clothes and nappies. Presumably she'd been expecting to breastfeed. The formula in Ellen's hands was suitable for newborns. She put a couple of tins in her basket with a pack of sterilising tablets, some bottles and a brush to clean them. She would not be able to bring herself to send a newborn baby to a childminder and even if she could find one at such short notice, a complete stranger who could take the baby in, she didn't want to. She'd done it, reluctantly, with CJ when he was three, and most importantly, when he could talk, and even then she had stressed over what was happening to him when he was away from her and what kind of care he was receiving behind her back. But a newborn? She'd never done it before and couldn't do it now. She would treat that motherless child the same way she would treat a baby she had given birth to herself. Something had given her another chance; God, karma, fate? Mischief of the jumbies, the good kind this time? This was a chance to move beyond her grief, and the possibility both broke her heart and re-joined the fragmented pieces into something that might alleviate the guilt she felt.

And so it was settled. She would not return to work. She would phone in tomorrow morning and hand her notice in with immediate effect. It would cause problems for a few days, but in the long term Mrs Mannering would simply replace her. It would also mean she didn't have to explain Clyde's greatest betrayal to date – or the consequences that were costing Ellen the life she had formerly crafted – to all her colleagues, who were under the impression she had her head screwed on.

Had she known today that she would never be returning, she would have said goodbye to the residents properly. It was impossible to work in a residential home for ten years without getting attached to some of them, even some of the facety ones, not the ones who were proper prejudiced, but the ones with a little character, who made the workday interesting. Like Mr Arbuthnot who was always telling the care workers he was going to marry one of them as soon as he got out of that place and his lucky wife would be able to retire and focus on some *real* wifely duties. Yes, he was a dirty old man, but he was a charming dirty old man who made her laugh. She would have said goodbye to him and to some of the others and definitely to her colleagues, some of whom had been there since even before she started working and had become like family, not family family, but work family, people you spent time with and got to know. Instead, she'd just shouted a general 'see you tomorrow' to anyone and everyone as she tugged her coat on and took her bag out of her locker, walked to the entrance and paused at the top of the steps to get her umbrella out, putting it up and over herself before setting off into the pouring rain.

The journey home from work had been a wet and miserable one, stopping off at the top of the market where there was a Jamaican fellow with a stall selling hard food, picking up some green bananas, sweet potato and dasheen for her and Clyde to eat with the oxtail they'd be having for dinner, and some potatoes for the kids, all of whom could not have had a more English palate had they been born to and grown up with Mr Arbuthnot. She'd been splashed by the filthy rainwater raised by a passing car as she stood waiting at the bus stop, the water dripping down her coat and tights till it filled her shoes, which she'd had to take off one by one and empty, then continue to stand in, her toes freezing, till the bus arrived, packed. She had stood in the centre aisle all the way home, the rasping chesty coughs of other passengers all around her, the insides of the windows steamed up and the air inside the bus both cold and damp. By the time she arrived home, all she wanted was a quick wash to clean the Heights off her, then a change into something warm and dry and a cup of something hot before getting on with the dinner.

She remembered how surprised she'd been to see CJ. Not that it was surprising to see him at home, but because during school holidays he was preoccupied from morning till night with his friends, and would ordinarily be playing out with them somewhere, in the park or over the estate or, on days rainy as that day had been, together in his bedroom. Instead, CJ was on his own, not on his own in his bedroom, but on his own in the living room. That was unusual and though she hadn't given it much thought at the time, she had clocked it. Also, when she'd woken the girls up in the morning, as well as asking them to buy the oxtail, she'd asked them to clean and season it, so it would be ready for her to begin cooking when she got in. However, when she arrived back home, they were both in the kitchen, and they'd not only cleaned and seasoned the oxtail, but Claudette was browning the meat in the frying pan and Joycelyn was cutting up the onions, garlic and sweet peppers to be fried in the same pan after her sister had finished, which would be the beginnings of the flavoursome stock. Her first thought was that they'd done something wrong and were sweetening her up in advance of her discovering what it was. It wasn't that the girls didn't help her in the kitchen – that was a matter in which they had no choice – but normally they were like budding lawyers, doing only the exact thing they'd been asked to do, nothing more, and at each stage Ellen would have to ask them to do the next thing. So their willingness was another unusual thing she'd noticed but at the time it had only occupied a brief moment of thought before her mind had moved on to something else. She had left the shopping on the side in the kitchen and headed up the stairs toward her bedroom.

The girls' bedroom was the first room she encountered at the top of the stairs, the door a few steps straight across the landing, and because it was open, Ellen could see the vase on the bedside table next to the girls' double bed. Normally it was in the front room filled with an assortment of plastic flowers, but today it had six real red roses inside it. In Ellen's opinion, the vase was too big to display only six stems, but Claudette had been too excited to hear what Ellen was saying the day before, which is how Ellen knew she'd lied when she said she had bought the flowers for herself with her pay from the little Saturday job she'd been doing at Woolworths for the last year. She had never known anyone to be so excited about receiving flowers they had sent themself. She knew they had been given to Claudette by a boy – maybe even a man! – as a Valentine's gift, though they had arrived the day before Valentine's Day. Despite Claudette's denial, she had reminded her daughter that she better not be in any nastiness with anyone, boy, man or beast, because if she was and Ellen found out about it, she would ship her back to Montserrat to live out the rest of her years. Nothing she said though had quashed Claudette's pleasure in the flowers and as Ellen arrived at the top of the stairs, she could see that the tight heads had relaxed themselves and started opening, occupying their space in the vase better than they had the day before and beginning to look quite beautiful.

*

Ellen was suddenly aware of an Indian woman tidying up the shelves beside her in a way that registered as slightly awkward. She knew the woman was the wife of the shop owner and when she looked up into the curved mirror above the shelves in front of her, the shop owner himself was staring at her but quickly looked away. She felt the rising annoyance she always felt at being watched and followed in shops, a factor she could never entirely adapt to but which had become a normal part of her everyday shopping experience in England, and ordinarily she would have considered putting down her basket with the products still inside it and walking out. However, she realised she'd been absentmindedly walking around the VG Store examining products she wasn't particularly interested in buying because she wasn't yet ready to begin the journey back home, and once she had paid for her purchases, it would have been ridiculous to get any further away from home while she was carrying heavy bags of shopping. She acknowledged that on this occasion her behaviour would have made her look suspicious. Also, she really did need the infant formula, so couldn't abandon it and storm out of the shop in a huff. Instead, she made her way to the till and paid for her goods, bagged them up, then exited the shop and began walking back towards home, her thoughts returning to the sequence of the day.

Once she'd washed and changed her clothes, warm and dry after her great wet escapade, Ellen had sat at the table in the kitchen drinking her tea, relaxing in the knowledge that once she'd finished drinking it, the browned oxtail was already on the stove cooking down and all she'd need to do was peel the potatoes and hard food, make some dumplings and put them on to boil. Then the doorbell rang. She hadn't considered it could have been Clyde because he had a key, which she could only recall him having forgotten maybe two or three times in all the years they'd been together, and he always used his key when he arrived home. Had he had his key, she would have known it was him, because she could tell which member of the family had arrived home from the way they let themselves in the front door.

Only Claudette opened and closed the door in what Ellen thought was a normal way; you heard the key enter the lock and the front door open, followed by the normal sound of it being closed. Joycelyn somehow always managed to get her key into the lock without making a sound, and the only thing that alerted you to the fact the door had been opened was the draft that entered the house and the noise of the street outside before she silently closed it. CJ opened the front door as if he was being chased by the police. She could be so specific about his style because once he actually had opened the door after running away from the police and on that occasion, he rammed his key into the lock, turned it and at the same time applied the force of his shoulder against the door so it sprung open noisily and was then loudly slammed shut. He'd told her that he'd just turned onto their road and was walking home when a Black Maria had pulled up alongside him and two policemen had jumped out and told him to effing stop. He said he'd decided to run instead because a friend of his had been stopped when he was returning home from a football match and, because he hadn't run, he'd been taken into the back of the vehicle and had been given such a beating that his Arsenal scarf was red from end to end, on account of his blood covering all the white parts. Anyway, Ellen had gone to the front door and given the police a piece of her mind and they had retreated and left CJ alone. When he had entered, she hadn't been aware there was an emergency of any kind because how he opened the door when the police were chasing him was how he'd always opened the door before that day and he still opened the door that way to this day. Clyde had a number of keys on his keyring, so his opening of the front door was distinctive as a consequence of the jingle-jangling noises which sometimes went on for some time when he had a few drinks inside him, and meant most of the time he couldn't sneak into the house without everyone knowing who it was even if he'd wanted to.

Ellen heard CJ open the front door and she had been puzzled, cocking her head and listening hard for a clue as to who was at the door. But hearing no voice and also hearing the front door close, and not having heard the jangling of Clyde's keys, she had assumed it must have been Wilhelmina who regularly stopped by on her way home from work. She had been looking up, expecting her friend to walk in, when Clyde entered.

When she thought about it now, she realised it was no coincidence CJ had opened the front door and let his father in, and it must have been why her son had been in the front room on his own to begin with; he'd been waiting for his dad to return home with the new baby so he could let them both in. Then she realised the new baby was why Claudette and Joycelyn had been sweetening her up by getting on with cooking the dinner without her having to ask them first, and for a moment after she'd had that revelation she stopped walking because the feelings that accompanied that realisation momentarily overwhelmed her.

It was not the first time her children had taken their father's side, but it was the first time to her knowledge they had joined forces with him and worked as one behind her back and against her. She could see no other way to interpret what had happened. There'd been times in the past when she knew the kids had not been entirely truthful with her, but it had always been around far smaller issues. Even if she tried, it would have been impossible for Ellen to count the number of times CJ had lied to her about where he had been and what he'd been doing, the number of times he told her he'd been late from school because he had been in the library doing homework with his friends. Had she been a betting woman – which she was not, never had been, never would be – she would have been prepared to bet her house on the fact he'd never voluntarily stepped inside the school library in the three years he'd been at that secondary school. Then there'd been silly lies when she'd given him a time to get home and he had come back hours later; how the bus had broken down, how someone had been hurt and he'd had to wait with them for the ambulance, how he'd got lost and just couldn't find his way back. And not to forget the lie he'd given her a number of times now about how his watch had stopped so he hadn't realised the time. She wasn't even going to start on the number of times she'd smelt cigarettes on the boy and, on at least two occasions she was absolutely certain of, weed. Both the cigarettes and weed she'd spoken to Clyde about, pointing out that CJ was still only thirteen, and he'd laughed so heartily she suspected Clyde was proud of the boy. Because of that, Ellen had stopped even treating the matter as an issue; after all, the girls were her domain and Clyde was supposed to be shaping and guiding their son. For all she knew, it was probably Clyde who was giving CJ the cigarettes and the weed; she wouldn't put it past him. She'd also stopped making an issue of the fact CJ had starting bringing what she called 'woman-friends' to the house *to do revision* and taking them into his room and closing the door.

Then of course there were the silly collective lies over the years that she'd seen through though left unchallenged. Like she had always known that Clyde frequently took the kids to Kentucky Fried Chicken, even though she had banned them from eating the unwashed unseasoned undercooked nastiness. In that case, it wasn't lies that effort and imagination had been put into, like the ones CJ told; instead they were blatant lies the children told after Clyde had brought them back home and none of them wanted any dinner or – unlike every other day when they were full-scale attempting to eat the family out of house and home – they only wanted a tiny portion because they were just not that hungry. She knew full well Clyde had told them not to tell her they'd had Kentucky, but she hadn't considered those lies to be lies on Clyde's side against her. They were lies the kids had told for their own benefit, so that their dad would continue buying them the fried chicken they loved.

What had happened here was different. They weren't covering their own arses or protecting their treats or privileges. This time, they'd all taken their father's side. Against her. For that he must have told them in advance, before she came home from work, already told them he'd had relations with another woman and for them to have colluded as they clearly had, presumably none of them had been horrified – as Wilhelmina had been – that their father had been sleeping around and cheating on their mother. None of them. At that moment, when she'd been sitting on a chair at the table in the kitchen looking up at the doorway wondering who had just come through the front door, she'd been the only person in the house who didn't know the answer.

Clyde had entered the kitchen carrying something the size and shape of a wrapped bunch of flowers in his folded arms and an expression on his face that was a cross between a smile and a grimace. It was an expression he used on her the same way the girls used the cooking of the oxtail or tidying up more than she'd asked them to: a brazen attempt to sweeten her up in advance of her discovering whatever they were hoping to conceal or not get into as much trouble for. It was an expression he used on Ellen regularly, but on this occasion she had been wrong-footed and for that, she blamed Claudette's roses upstairs. She thought he'd bought her a Valentine's bouquet, despite the fact he'd never done it before, ever, and that the smile was his discomfort, not at playing the romantic – after all no one was more skilled at chatting women up than Clyde, no one was capable of encouraging the average decent woman to drop her drawers faster – but because he was normally most romantic when he had some kind of confession to make to her.

Ellen was working through what had happened with the finest of retrospective toothcombs, but at the time it had all happened much too quickly for any real-time analysis. The girls were cooking down the oxtail. She was drinking tea at the kitchen table. The doorbell rang. CJ was in the front room and so he answered it. She was wondering who it was when Clyde stepped into the kitchen carrying something which he held out to her, and she smiled at him as he unfolded his arms and handed her what she thought was a bouquet, and she looked down into her own arms to discover a baby, a tiny sweet baby, clearly just born, and Ellen was so astonished she was speechless, just looked back up at Clyde who was still wearing that expression of discomfort.

He said, 'The mum dead.'

'Poor baby,' said Claudette.

'What a cutie pie,' said Joycelyn.

'Her cheeks,' said Claudette, 'Just like little dumplings.'

Ellen had looked back down at the little baby in her arms and knew it was her husband's child. Clyde's daughter looked like CJ as a newborn, like Clay. The baby girl slowly opened her eyes and as they met Ellen's, in that roving newborn baby way, Ellen felt a cramping sensation in her womb, stronger than the cramps she regularly felt a few days before her period started, more like the painful contractions she had experienced while breastfeeding after giving birth, and the grief that was still ballooned inside her, that she had not yet finished putting to bed, built up to a roar that sent her blood racing, her pressure soaring, that sent a rolling wave of goosebumps over her skin. She experienced such a dizzying surrealness she wondered if she was going pass out.

'She belong with her family,' Clyde said.

'We're her family,' said CJ.

As Ellen turned into the top of her road, she thought about Claudette saying *her* when Clyde hadn't told them the baby was a girl; *her* cheeks, she had said, and she wondered when Clyde had told the children and what he had said to them? He would have known she was going to finish work at two, that the earliest she'd be home was three. Maybe he'd phoned the house and explained everything to CJ and CJ had explained everything to the girls, that another woman had died having their father's baby, or maybe Clyde had come home with the baby before she got home for a live rehearsal, everyone going over their parts till they could deliver them after their mother returned. Maybe Claudette had practised saying *those cheeks* in rehearsal but slipped up during the live performance. Maybe Clyde had explained to them that they were all the baby's family, all related by blood, that she was *his* daughter and *their* sister and they all needed to help him, to take his side, leaving their mother, the only family member without a blood tie, outnumbered and unsupported. He wouldn't have been able to go outside and sit in the car till he saw her arrive because the car was still impounded by the police, but it was very possible he'd gone to the Prince and CJ had rung him at the pub when Ellen was upstairs in the bathtub washing the Heights off her skin.

As Ellen continued walking, she felt the most alone she could ever recall feeling in her lifetime. To be perfectly honest, the fact of Clyde bringing another child into the world was not a surprise to her. It was something her mind ran on frequently. How could it not, when the technology had yet to be invented that could prevent the zip of her husband's trousers coming down? Of course it was something her mind had run on, many times, something she had even thought he was going to say to her on a number of occasions when he'd had that expression on his face that was half smile and half grimace and told her he had something to tell her. Other women might laugh at her behind her back or worse, feel sorry for her, but Ellen had always known who she was married to, the kind of man Clyde was. And CJ was already his general, had been for some time now. She'd allowed Clyde to raise their boy and he had raised him in his own image; CJ and his father shared the same mind. That he would take his father's side against her was something she would have expected. Under the circumstances, how could he not?

But when it came to Claudette and Joycelyn, she

felt she had been properly betrayed. They were not their father's; they were hers. It wasn't their father who had sent barrels of food and clothes and all manner of household items for them when they'd been left back in Montserrat – towels and sheets and tablecloths, cutlery and crockery – or who'd explained to them what the blood between their legs was, or who'd bought them pads and bras or taught them how to wash out the crutch of their drawers over the sink each morning. It wasn't their father who'd taught them how to cook or properly clean or sew. They should've been her team by birthright; it was their place, where they belonged. She heard the sound of her mother laughing, not with her but at her, without kindness, without humour, and the feeling inside her was intense and too recently experienced for her not to recognise it as grief. She felt it rise and swell within her and she wondered whether there would ever come a day when, apart from Wilhelmina, she would ever be able to trust any other woman in the world.

She opened the garden gate and walked the path to her front door. She put her shopping bags down onto the doormat and felt around inside her handbag for her keys. The lights were on in the front room and hallway, and from inside the house she heard the unmistakable sound of the baby girl bawling. She'd been severely punished for the horrible mistakes she'd made in the past, but this tiny girl was a clean slate. She would treat this baby better than she had treated any of her own and this one child that had not come from her womb would love her better than her own blood kin. She felt another contraction in her womb, not as sharp or painful as the first, but she was still able to identify it as the physical reaction of a mother's body to her newborn child. Her hand closed around her keys and she pulled them out of her bag, put them into the lock and turned them.

Clay

October 1978

(Four months earlier)

Ellen had just begun painting the thumb nail on her right hand when Clay entered the front room making vrooming noises and running his favourite Matchbox car up and down the length of his arm. It was a metallic green superfast Porsche turbo that CJ had given him on his sixth birthday, and Clay was so attached, he even slept with it. Her work at the Heights meant she took good care of her hands and part of that was ensuring she kept her nails clipped as low as possible, not just for neatness – though she did think her short nails looked very neat and tidy – but because that way they were easiest to keep clean in a job that necessitated her washing her hands sometimes upwards of twenty times a shift. She'd only been a couple of weeks into the job when she realised that the work would finish her hands off for good if she didn't take care of them, so she started carrying cream around with her and applying it every time she washed her hands. Then once a week, she gave her rough hands a treatment which began with removing the last lot of nail paint, trimming and filing the nails down, then washing and drying her hands and slathering them in cream before giving them a luxurious massage. Finally, she would paint her nails, and normally she would do it in her bedroom or the kitchen and never under any circumstances in the front room where she was now. But on this occasion she'd broken the house rules she had herself set because the painting of her nails was one of her rare indulgences, and another of her rare indulgences was the thick white shagpile carpet that had been recently laid in the hall, the stairs and on the front room floor, and sitting in her front room which had been carpeted so gloriously whilst treating herself to one of her favourite indulgences was irresistible, despite the fact she knew she would have blown her top and gone straight back to her roots with the cussing had she happened across Claudette and Joycelyn in the front room doing the exact same thing. Sitting on the sofa doing her nails, bottles of varnish and methylated spirits and a bag of cotton wool on top of the towel draped over her lap – just in case! – with her bare feet out of her slippers, toes scrunched into the sweet dense pile, was as thrilling for her as she imagined it might be in heaven itself.

After the upbringing she'd had, it greatly amused Ellen that she could imagine nail varnish in heaven at all, and amused her further still that nail varnish occupied a position of such high esteem for her, virtual reverence, when she didn't really think of herself as much of a girlie girl. She hardly wore makeup as such. It was another in the long list of things her mother hadn't approved of. In fact her mother had considered make-up frivolous and was enraged by the women who did wear it, in a way Ellen had never properly understood. As a consequence, she never dared experiment with make-up as a teenager, even during those years when it was the most popular pastime of virtually all the young girls around her at school, disregarding the possibility throughout all of the years she lived with her mother. Only at the age of nineteen, after her mother had died, did she give it a go, and her first attempts were clumsy and unsuccessful, so much so that not only did she think make-up didn't suit her, she thought it made her look like a clown. It was years before she tried it again and only then because Wilhelmina persuaded her by offering to apply it and refusing to accept no for an answer, and when Ellen saw the result she'd been forced to grudgingly admit she liked the overall effect. She still didn't wear much make-up, just a touch of lipstick when she was working, a little more if it was a special occasion, her definition of which was an occasion so special it involved her visiting the hairdresser to have her hair done. But she fell in love with nail varnish the first time she tried it.

'Can I do it?' Clay asked, and when Ellen looked up at him, he contorted his face into an expression of longing and added, 'Pleeeaase.'

Instead of laughing, she slowly shook her head and

because she hadn't said 'no', Clay knew that meant 'yes'. He slipped the Porsche into the pocket of his shorts, knelt down at her feet on the white shagpile carpeted floor, took the bottle and brush from her hands and carried on painting her nails.

Ellen marvelled at his concentration, the slow precision of his strokes, and her heart was full of both tenderness and worry as she watched her boy. Claudette and Joycelyn were out down the market doing the regular Saturday morning shopping and wouldn't be back for another hour or so, and Clyde was at football practice with CJ. Had any of them been at home when Clay asked if he could paint her nails, she would have said no. In the girls' case, one of the reasons was because instead of them being grateful for everything she'd done for them, the sacrifices she'd made, and the things she'd had to do to ensure they could be with her and would not go without, the girls – she was sure – were actively watching and tallying up a list of grudges against her, and although they loved Clay – it was impossible to not love Clay – they'd made it clear that in their minds she treated him differently to how she'd treated them, which was hardly surprising considering they'd spent the bulk of their childhood back home without her. In Ellen's mind, that was like comparing coconut water with sand, and on its own wasn't sufficient reason for her to say no; but when she had so vocally, on so many occasions, outlined all that was forbidden in the living room, and expressly included any painting of nails by anyone anywhere near the carpet as one of those forbidden activities, for the girls to witness Clay putting nail paint on her fingers in that space, would, she was confident, have blown their minds.

For completely different reasons, she would also have said no had Clyde been at home because Clyde didn't like Clay involved in what he called woman-business, didn't have a framework for understanding why his son would want to be. He understood men like himself very well, the ones who laughed loud and entertained the crowd, who were opinionated, played dominoes, who gambled, drank and womanised, men like the ones CJ was on a trajectory to become. CJ was his father's son, made in his image, in looks, actions and mindset. Though Clay looked more like Clyde than CJ, in fact looked more like Clyde than even Clyde did – of which she was mightily glad – in personality he was nothing like Clyde, nothing at all. If anything, he was the complete opposite. She knew it and she knew Clyde felt it.

The result was an ongoing hearty effort on Clyde's part to encourage Clay to toughen up, to take part in more masculine pursuits, combined with an unspecified disappointment when he saw Clay initiating or involved in woman-business. For the most part, till recently, it had been okay because Clay had been too young to notice or understand, but now he was six, he'd begun to register Clyde's disappointment and though he still didn't quite understand it yet, he was trying to. Ellen had been dreading the day he worked it out and what that would mean for her sensitive boy, whose main ambition in life seemed to be pleasing everyone. So far, she had resisted making efforts to try to change Clay's nature. She had especially resisted any attempt to try to change it so it was more like Clyde's, but it felt like the clouds of a battle were slowly forming, gathering closer the older her son got. Each time she thought about it, it worried her, so she did what she had become so skilled at during her marriage, and decided to just not think about it. She'd already put to bed bigger worries around Clay. She would do the same with this one, when the time was right.

'Oh no!' Clay said. He put the brush back into the bottle and pulled a bit of cotton wool off the roll. He opened the methylated spirits, put the piece of cotton wool on the open mouth of the bottle and tipped it, then began to clear the varnish from the finger he'd just painted, which had spilled over the edge of the nail onto the surrounding skin, and he did it as gently as if he were cleaning a wound. Throughout the entirety of Ellen's life, no one had ever spoiled her like this, and she loved it. She relaxed her thoughts and her shoulders and felt the tension drain from her body as she gave herself permission to simply enjoy the experience.

CJ had no interest in doing anything like this, nor did his father. It wasn't a matter of Clyde being horrible to her, because he wasn't, but he pleased himself in everything. He'd never hit her, very rarely even shouted, but only because it pleased him not to be that kind of man. He wanted to be loved by all, needed to be thought of as decent, generous and good and that was what motivated him, not a desire to be the kind of husband he thought Ellen would like him to be. His primary instinct was to please himself, and getting involved in woman-business simply didn't please him.

Ellen couldn't comment on whether the girls had been interested in nail polish when they were Clay's age as she'd not seen either of them during the years they were six, but she could say they'd been interested in nail polish from when they arrived in England. They did their own and each other's hands, and if Ellen was present in the place they were doing it they would do hers too, but they didn't seek her out, they didn't search the house to find her so they could pass time doing something nice for her. Only Clay did that.

Clay finished repainting the nail, cleanly this time. He sat back, shifting the weight from his shagpile-cushioned knees till his bottom was resting on his heels, then he raised his eyes to hers, proud of himself and his accomplishments, looked up at her with his father's face, lit by kindness, and waited. Ellen straightened her arm and carefully examined the tips of her spread fingers, rotating her hand at the wrist as diffused daylight bounced off the glossy surfaces.

'Not bad,' she said, and Clay's pleasure was evident in his grin. He knew this to be great praise from the woman whose guidance most often took the form of pointing out what had been done wrong rather than right. He was so easy, so easy to make happy, so happy making others happy, and his joy was contagious. Ellen smiled back.

Clyde stood at the side of the pitch with the other parents. The match was in the last fifteen minutes of the second half. His hands were jammed into the pockets of his coat, because although they were still a couple of months away from proper winter, the fog hadn't yet lifted entirely and the air itself was freezing cold. He was grateful that the rain which had been falling for most of the week had stopped, but it had left the ground so soft that most of the boys on the pitch were covered in mud from head to boot. He saw CJ looking at him and he raised his hands and gave him two thumbs up on autopilot, though he wasn't sure what for as he'd been so preoccupied with his current problem that he hadn't been able to properly concentrate on the match. In fact it had been days since he'd been able to concentrate on anything other than his problem, not that any of that time spent thinking about it had yielded any solutions or been useful in any way, as his problem showed no sign of disappearing despite him racking his brain non-stop about how to make that happen.

Worry was a very unusual state for Clyde, as throughout his life there hadn't been much for him to be concerned about. From time to time of course there'd been things his mind ran on, like the time he had appendicitis and thought he was going to die and was convinced God had meted out a deserved yet terrible punishment on him for having had sex with two women – three if you counted his wife – in his marital bed during one week, and he'd sworn to God that if he survived he would be faithful to Ellen and Ellen alone for the rest of his days – though he considered that promise invalid once he'd survived the surgery and the anaesthetic had worn off and the doctors explained that what he'd been suffering from was an acute medical condition and nothing to do with the wrath of God at all. With the exception of a few extreme occurrences like that one, intense worry was quite an unusual state for him and, in his opinion, one that did not suit him at all.

What did suit him was being able to come and go without concern, being able to do what he felt like with little real consequence, and that was what his life had been like up until Monday morning when his governor at work had collected him from the sorting floor and walked back with him to his office, explaining there was a young woman named Francesca waiting in there who was insisting on speaking to him and refusing to leave till that happened. On the journey to the governor's office, he'd been racking his brains because he couldn't actually recall anyone named Francesca, although that wasn't much of a surprise because he was such a lover of women, so many of them over so much time and not just – as some people believed – in the physical sense. There were friends of Clyde's who imagined he slept with an assortment of different women every day, who didn't understand that what he enjoyed most was the thrill he received from women's attraction to him. This meant that although he had in all honesty slept with many women, the number of women he'd flirted with, chatted up and been chatted up by was infinite, and the majority of them – without some kind of prompt – were very difficult to recall. Of course, there were exceptions, highly memorable women like Cisely, who he'd tried to break up with because he'd felt – quite rightly as it turned out – that there was something a bit unbalanced in her. She'd begged him to let her love him one last time and he'd reluctantly agreed then allowed her to tie him to the bed first, whereupon she refused to untie him for three days.

After he'd finally managed to convince her to let him go and made his miserable way home, he'd then had to present himself at the local police station where Ellen had reported him missing, not because he hadn't come home for seventy-two hours, but because during that time none of his friends had seen him. He'd been tempted to tell the police the truth, but then he thought about what he would have said if another man reported such a story to him. Then he thought about what his friends would have said if he'd reported the same story to them. Then he wondered what the local and national newspapers would have to say if Cisely was charged and taken to court and the two of them had to give evidence as to what had gone down; and it was clear to him he would be a laughing stock up and down the land, except in his own home where he suspected there would be little laughing done. In the end, because he had to say something to avoid being charged with wasting police time, he'd lied and said he'd had a blackout from what the police recorded as Excessive Consumption of Alcohol, though he'd known and spent a lot of his adult life with some very hard drinkers and despite his strongest efforts to recall even one who had blacked out for three whole days, he simply couldn't. Had his governor told him Cisely was in the office waiting to speak with him, he would have had no difficulty recalling her whatsoever. But Francesca?

As he walked back to his governor's office his poor brain was working harder than a team of regional letter sorters trying to recall the woman who went by that name, which sounded vaguely familiar, but not familiar enough for him to be able to put a face to it.

As the crowd about him began to cheer, Clyde joined in loudly to disguise the fact he'd been paying hardly any attention to what was going on in the match, and he felt a horrible guilt when he realised some of the players were running up to, hugging and jumping onto CJ, whose team had widened their lead by one more goal to lead by 2–0 with only ten minutes to go, and that his son had scored what would doubtless be the winning goal less than thirty feet away from his face, but he'd been so preoccupied with his tribulations, he'd missed it. He overcompensated by yelling his head off and letting rip his loud and practised whistle, generating so much noise that when CJ eventually managed to drag himself out from under the scrum, he immediately raised both arms in the air and grinned at his dad. As the ref blew his whistle and the game continued, Clyde's thoughts immediately returned to Francesca and the fact she was having his child.

When he'd entered the office and saw her, he knew she was someone he'd met, but he couldn't recall any of the detail beyond that, just that she looked familiar. As soon as the governor left the office, Francesca had come straight out with it and told him she was having his baby and it had shocked him so much that he'd said two things which even he had to admit were below the belt. The first thing he'd said was that he couldn't remember her at all. She'd begun to cry straight away and that was the cue that transported his memory back to being in her bed in the early hours of some morning several months ago. He'd awoken in a strange dark room needing to pee but had no idea where the toilet was. When he checked his watch and realised it was after two in the morning, he decided to get dressed and go home and stop off to pee somewhere along the journey. He was doing his best to get dressed quietly when she woke up and asked what he was doing. He'd told her he needed to get home, that his wife would be vex he'd been out so late.

She'd replied, 'Your *wife*?'

And then she'd begun to cry, the same crying she was putting down in his governor's office, lacking in any dignity or control. She cried like a child, hurt and uninhibited, loud and howling. She'd called him a liar and said he'd used her. He said he'd told her he was married but the truth was, he wasn't sure he'd said those actual words, because he couldn't even remember chatting her up, though he vaguely recalled walking with her to the house he was now inside and nearly jumping out of his skin when a car beeped at him while they were crossing the street. However, he was confident he would not have lied and said that he wasn't married. Drunk or not, that he knew, so she must have just assumed he wasn't, which meant the misunderstanding wasn't really his fault. She was still crying when he left her place and by then, he'd already moved on in his mind, thinking about how late it was and trying to get home as quickly as possible while praying Ellen was – and remained – fast asleep.

If she was awake, he knew she wouldn't say anything because she never did, verbally. Hers was a language of facial expressions and gestures: a deadpan stare with both brows raised, shrugging his hand off her shoulder, a single eyebrow cocked in response to his explanations, the pursed lips and slow cutting of eyes in response to his apologies, loudly kissing her teeth during his declarations it would never happen again. His mind had moved on to these more pressing concerns, those things that made him feel uncomfortable and would require him to make good for as long as it took to get Ellen back to being herself again so he could stop feeling bad. In short, he'd left Francesca crying at her home months back and, up until he made her cry for the second time in his governor's office, he'd wiped the experience clean from his mind.

Once she'd started bawling loud enough for the entire sorting office to hear, Clyde had grabbed and cuddled her, acknowledging that it was coming back to him and yes, of course he knew her. Then he'd had to comfort her till she calmed right down for fear the governor would return to find out what the hell was going on in there. It was after she finally stopped the noise that he'd said the second thing, which was equally shameful. He admitted he could now remember her, but asked if she was sure the baby was his. In retrospect he could see it hadn't been a nice thing to ask, though she hadn't started crying again when he said it. Instead, she'd pulled away from him and grabbed the lapels of his work jacket then, realising she lacked the necessary strength to successfully shake him, had released his clothing, screamed *cochon!* and slapped his face.

In complete desperation, he'd told her he was a married man and there was nothing he could do for her. That was when she pulled out the knife and for a moment Clyde thought he'd had it, then she began to force the knife into his hand, and he realised the weapon hadn't been brought along to kill *him*. She told him he might as well kill her and the baby there and then because it would be quicker and less painful than allowing their deaths to drag out. Francesca had pulled her blouse up, exposing her belly so that he could plainly see that what should've been a flat stomach on a small-framed woman of her size was now softly rounded. She told him she would lose her job and she wouldn't be able to pay her rent. Then she said there was probably no need for her to worry about rent anyway, as once the landlady found out she'd be out on the streets. She'd asked him what she was supposed to do, and for the first time since entering the office, Clyde answered with absolute honesty when he said he did not know. She'd given him a piece of paper with her address on it and told him he needed to come and see her at the weekend, otherwise she would kill herself and both she and the baby would haunt his backside for the rest of eternity. She swore it on her baby's life. Clyde had been raised on an indulgent diet of stories about ghosts and hauntings, about jumbies, duppies and Jack Lantern, about revelations, death and madness, and although he didn't generally consider himself to be a superstitious man, the threat terrified the living daylights out of him. Which meant he had to do something, whatever that something was, and he needed to do it fast as he was already on day one of the weekend.

He was quiet on the way back home and for most of the journey. CJ talked non-stop about his moves, his strategies, his glory, till finally, close to home, Clyde was pulled out of his reverie by silence and the dawning awareness that CJ had asked him something.

'Beg you pardon?' Clyde asked.

'Whassup?'

'Nothing.'

'Don't tell me that. Is mum divorcing you?'

Clyde laughed aloud. 'But what kinda question you asking me?' When it occurred to him that divorce wasn't as ridiculous a possibility as he would've liked it to be, he stopped laughing, shook his head and added, 'Not yet.'

'Then what?' CJ asked.

Clyde loved this boy and he did not doubt CJ loved him equally in return. He knew CJ had his back, that he could count on his loyalty, that he would never tell anyone in the world what had been said between them, but this confession was on a deeper level and would require him to ask his son not to say a word to a very specific person: his mother. Clyde was aware that he himself had lied to Ellen so many times during their lives together it would be impossible to tally them up, but in his mind those lies had been necessary to protect Ellen from hurt.

Asking CJ not to say anything to Ellen was not for Ellen's protection; it would be to cover his own arse and he felt terrible about it. The trouble was, though he felt terrible, the idea of unburdening himself had become very enticing and resisting enticement had never been Clyde's forte. The conundrum solved itself, however, when he had the very practical idea of allowing CJ to make the decision for himself.

'It's something I can't tell you mum and it would be wrong for me to ask you to lie to her.'

'I won't lie. I just won't say anything,' CJ said.

There were very few things in Clyde's life that had genuinely made him cry, though he had become adept at bringing himself to tears in discussion with Ellen, usually about his transgressions and accompanied by what he hoped sounded like heartfelt apologies. On this occasion however, his eyes unexpectedly filled with tears, blurring his vision, forcing him to swerve without indicating as he pulled the Cortina over to the kerbside, and the driver behind him demonstrated his disapproval with both his horn and a few choice swear words as he drove past them. As neither were wearing seatbelts, Clyde leaned over the handbrake and gearstick unimpeded and crushed his son to his chest. Finally, he wiped his eyes, turned the ignition off and began to speak to his blessed boy, conscious only of his relief at finally being able to discuss his issue with another living person.

When Ellen heard the front door open then slam closed, she knew it was CJ who had entered and therefore Clyde would be with him and she wondered why they were back from football so early, as they usually stopped for lunch at Kentucky or Wimpy and normally didn't get home for a couple of hours after football practice ended, and she was about to tell Clay who was resting on his knees still holding the bottle of nail paint to put it away when CJ paused in the doorway of the front room with his father behind him, and everything went out of Ellen's mind as she realised CJ was standing on her beautiful new white shagpile, covered in mud.

'Lord Jesus Christ!' she cried out. 'But look at this!'

The contents of Clyde's bowels instantly became liquid, and he wondered how Ellen had found out about Francesca and how Francesca had found out where he lived and whether she had shown Ellen her suggestively rounded stomach when she had visited his home and the full weight of his bad luck bore down on him; that all this had happened just as CJ had helped him to come up with a plan to sort everything out. 'It wasn't my fault,' he said.

'Of course it's your fault,' Ellen responded without lowering her voice. 'You should'a stop at the front door and make him take off them boots.'

Clyde recognised his mistake and had he not been so stressed out for almost a week anticipating the collapse of his life, he might have felt relief that Ellen was talking about mud on the new carpet and not about another woman carrying his child. Instead, the additional and unnecessary fright he'd experienced on top of everything else he was going through made his blood boil.

'Me no know why you buy the blasted stupidness in the first place,' he shouted.

Still holding the bottle of nail varnish in his hand, Clay stood up so he was standing beside Ellen and took a step closer to her because he'd never seen his father this angry before. Clyde clocked his movement.

'Bwoi, get upstairs and find somet'ing sensible to do wid youself,' he said.

Clay didn't move. Gently, Ellen put her hand on his back and nudged him forward. When he looked up at her, he had tears in his eyes. 'Go on up,' she said. Clay started walking towards the door, past his brother. In the silence, Ellen could hear his little feet pounding the stairs as he burst into a run.

'Four kids but you wanna put down white carpet,' Clyde said.

Watching him, Ellen found herself experiencing something very unusual: unaccustomed shock at her husband's behaviour. She'd been with him for fifteen years now and for many of those years had been of the opinion there was little her husband could do that could surprise her because she knew him and his ways so expertly, had come to know his ways from even before she'd been together with him as a couple. After the day he'd stopped outside the boundary of her property back home and taken her inside and they'd done what they'd done, she hadn't seen him for almost a year. Montserrat was a small Caribbean island, thirty-nine square miles, small enough for people from the larger islands to joke that big news there didn't have to travel far, and it was true that it was a very difficult place to keep people out of your business. By the time Claudette was born, there were few people who did not know Ellen had delivered Clyde's child, or that there was another woman on the island who had also recently delivered another child of Clyde's, a baby boy named Carlton. Some of the older women and some of the younger women – who Ellen thought were probably jealous that Clyde had slept with her instead of them – pushed up their faces whenever they saw her, looking down their noses at her big stomach and then her baby as if they were so much better, not because they'd been pious enough to avoid fornication outside of wedlock themselves, but because they hadn't been stupid enough to get pregnant so everyone knew about it. But the honest truth was that Ellen wasn't ashamed about what she'd done at all. When she realised she'd missed her period she'd been ecstatic. She was proud that someone as attractive as Clyde could see enough in her to be attracted to it, to her, and she was quite content to find herself pregnant with his child, had been quite content at the idea of raising his child on her own, because her expectations had already been exceeded, she who had been raised to believe no one would love her, who had hoped but never dared to dream, till she lowered a coconut pod from her lips and found herself blinded by Clyde's image.

In the weeks after, Ellen had heard he'd left the island, that he was off working in Suriname or Aruba or possibly Curaçao. She'd never been some silly girl with a head full of foolishness who'd walked blindly into her relationship with Clyde. She'd known exactly what she was getting into from the start. She didn't see him again till Claudette was almost three months and when he returned and she fell pregnant again, she knew exactly what she was doing. Same thing a year later when he returned and she fell pregnant again. Had that been the entirety of the basis of the relationship between them for the rest of her life, she would have been content to remain in Montserrat to bring them up on her own. She would have been satisfied. She had no expectations of marrying and she had no ambition to return to England, where her mother had taken her and she'd experienced the most miserable years of her life. But Clyde changed everything. When he began pressing her for more and more details about living and working in England, when he realised she had enough money put aside to get them both there, when he decided to head to the Motherland to make his fortune and he asked her to marry him and go with him, by then, she knew him and she knew exactly what she was signing up for when she said those yeses, and she said those yeses despite the fact she had vowed never to return to England where her mother had been buried and would be able to find her. Marriage to Clyde was beyond the greatest thing she'd ever imagined; she couldn't say no. She married him knowing exactly who he was, and just as she resisted changing Clay's nature, she'd never had any desire to change Clyde's, to clip his wings or neuter him. She loved him as he was and it was a matter of pride to her that while other women fancied the pants off him, it was *her* he'd chosen to marry, *her* home, *her* bed he returned to and slept in at night. She'd thought there was little her husband could do to surprise her, but this had, the rage coming off him, in response to carpet he wasn't happy with.

'You need to calm youself down,' she said.

Clyde was still standing behind CJ, but he took a step forward when she spoke, as if he was about to enter the front room, and for the first time in the years they'd been together, she wondered if he was going to hit her.

'Calm down, Clyde,' Ellen said again, less confidently, unsure about how this moment had come about or what its basis was.

'Calm down?' Clyde asked, taking another step towards her.

CJ reached out, grabbed his father by the arm and stopped him. 'Mum's right,' he said, 'calm down, Dad.'

For a moment no one moved or spoke. CJ's words brought Clyde back to himself and the realisation of the extent of his overreaction, but it was a situation he had little experience of and so didn't know what he was supposed to do or how exactly to put it right.

'I'm gonna go in the kitchen and take off my shoes and socks,' CJ said. 'Okay, Mum?'

Ellen felt embarrassed. She didn't answer her son, just gave a flick of a nod in his direction and he turned around and carefully made his way to the kitchen. She felt like crying but she had never cried in front of Clyde before and was determined this would not be the day she did. The effort to hold herself together was fierce.

'You want some tea?' she asked Clyde, not because she had any real interest in making or drinking tea, but because it was something normal and familiar to fill the gap in the strange space she'd found herself in.

'No,' he said. 'Just stopped by for CJ to wash and change.' He felt like something more was required from him. He sidestepped it by adding, 'We going Wimpy.'

Sensing the change in his demeanour and realising she had the upper hand, and feeling angry with Clyde for bringing them so close to whatever that had been, angry he had raised up their thirteen-year-old son over her, that CJ now had greater authority and influence over his father than she as his wife did, Ellen's response was angry.

'You know it's two sons you have?' she asked Clyde, and the instant she said those words, regretted them. The words were incendiary.

But Clyde had calmed down. He knew he'd over-reacted. He was glad CJ had stopped him from doing something unforgivable, though he found it difficult not to believe he'd imagined the scene and none of it had happened at all. He realised his state of mind was even worse than he'd thought. He didn't just need to calm down, he needed to properly sort himself out.

'I was already gonna take him,' he said.

'Good,' Ellen said, then made her way towards the front room door, unsurprised to discover bits of mud on different parts of her glorious and newly carpeted floor. Had she not already said too much she would have had plenty to say about it. Instead, she checked herself then turned the corner and headed in the direction of the kitchen.

*

Clyde had been working at the sorting office for over ten years. When they'd arrived in England, Ellen had encouraged him to apply to the big companies for work: the Post Office, Ford, Matchbox, British Telecom, London Transport and the likes, instead of the hospitals, which were one of the largest employers campaigning hardest to workers in the Caribbean. Her mother had worked in hospitals and discovered that in the main the positions available for coloured people in them consisted of the hard and unsavoury jobs English people preferred not to dirty their hands with. She had wanted more than that for Clyde. He'd applied to the Post Office three times without success, so when he applied for a fourth time and was offered a position on the sorting room floor, he'd been so excited he made the mistake of telling Ellen exactly what he would be earning. A few weeks later he discovered his earnings divvied up by Ellen into portions for food, bills and savings, with a paltry amount allocated to him to do with as he pleased, except it wasn't really quite enough to do that with. From then on, he played down any wage increases and did everything he could to conceal any overtime, so that over the years, he'd reached the point where almost a quarter of his earnings had become invisible. He'd been so worried about what to do about Francesca and the baby he'd completely forgotten this till CJ had asked him whether he had any money Ellen didn't know about.

The plan they'd come up with was that Clyde would go and visit Francesca that afternoon. He would offer to give her money towards the child on a weekly basis.

He would see the child when he came by to drop off the money. She would not tell anyone he was the father. Unfortunately, this would mean that the child could not come to his home, but it was the best route to go down because if Ellen found out about it she would almost certainly divorce him, and as she already had four children with him and a house that still had a mortgage on it, it was very likely that if she was able to show the court he'd had a child out of doors, she would end up remaining in the home with the kids and not only might he find himself homeless while having to pay her child support, he would have to come up with maintenance payments as well, leaving him with barely enough to support himself, never mind Francesca and the baby. One of the fellows Clyde worked with at the sorting office was in that exact position and it had reduced him from being what he had himself described as a Jack the Lad to the pitiful and broken shell of a formerly care-free man, so in actual fact, he wasn't even lying; it was a scenario that could genuinely happen. The important thing was he would be supporting Francesca and his child. That was what he had to sell to Francesca. Ellen never needed to find out and nobody needed to die. That was the plan.

'I'm actually starving,' CJ said as he opened the car door and sat in the front passenger seat.

Clyde held open the back door for Clay to get in, and he climbed into the middle of the back seat, effectively the centre of the car, the seat he always sat in, where he had a good view out the front windscreen and could see and talk to whoever was sitting in the front seats – usually Clyde and Ellen or Clyde and CJ – and could also be in the centre of any back seat conversations going on – usually between his sisters.

'I've just got a stop to make,' Clyde said as he got into the driver's seat, giving CJ a wink.

CJ rolled his eyes. 'Can't we stop after we've eaten?'

'I'll be quick,' Clyde said.

He'd decided he would go to Francesca's first, and then the stomach he had discharged at home, no longer churning but still a little delicate, could begin to settle down, and perhaps he could get himself something to eat too and relax and enjoy eating it. It was already part of the plan that CJ would stay in the car outside Francesca's house, parked so that if she looked out the window or front door to see if Clyde was telling the truth when he told her he really couldn't stay long because his son was in the car waiting for him, she would be able to see CJ sitting in the passenger seat. As far as Clyde was concerned, having Clay in the back was a handy bonus that added even more urgency to his need to give Francesca the speech, hand over the money and make his speedy getaway.

Although Clyde was playing music on the tape cassette player inside the car which usually made him feel relaxed, he could feel himself becoming irritable, with CJ, yes, but mainly with Clay, who was as irritating as Cassius had been when they were younger: very touchy-feely, always up under their mother's skirt, hogging the attention that should have been shared equally between them both as brothers and which had already been weighted in Cassius's favour on account of him being their mother's firstborn son. His own sons were playing a game that involved Clay putting his hand on CJ's shoulder, and CJ trying to slap his hand before Clay could anticipate it and pull his hand away. To be fair to Clay, he was quite good at the game, unless, which was possible, CJ was holding back a bit in order to ensure his brother regularly won. What was stretching Clyde's nerves was the fact that every time CJ tried to strike, whether he missed or not, Clay shrieked, and whenever CJ successfully slapped his fingers, the shriek was even louder and more prolonged. Finally, he could take it no more, and in response to another successful strike from CJ, followed by screams and laughter from Clay, Clyde whirled around in his seat and shouted at Clay.

'Bwoi sit down and rest up youself!'

After that, the three of them drove in silence, and though Clyde felt bad about shouting at the boy, he was also glad to have the head-space to think. It was his brother that he thought about. Their mother had gone off to work in Curaçao when Clyde had been seven and Cassius twelve, had left them with her mother, their grandmother, who had brought them up for good when their mother never returned; no one knew why. There were rumours she'd gone to South America with some guy she met, that someone who knew her had seen her begging in Puerto Rico; also rumours she'd died. Another rumour said she'd lost her mind and gone into a mental institute. In summary, no one knew anything for sure apart from the fact she didn't come back. Clyde always felt jealous that Cassius, in addition to being his mother's favourite, had memories of her while he himself had none, not even one, not even a vague recollection of what she looked like, and there was no photograph of her. Even now as a big man, sometimes he dreamt of her and in his dreams, she always had her back to him and wouldn't turn around.

He passed the house Francesca lived in, drove down to the end of the road and did a three-point turn, then drove back and parked the car outside her house, so that the passenger seat was on the kerbside and the right side for Francesca to be able to see CJ easily if she tried. He turned off the car engine and stepped out.

'I won't be long,' he said.

The boys watched as he walked up to the house and knocked, as the front door was opened by a young woman who Clyde spoke to as she looked beyond him to the two boys sitting inside his parked car. As the two of them went inside, closing the door after them, Clay placed his hand on CJ's shoulder, who immediately successfully slapped it.

Ellen felt very tense. She was on her knees beside a basin half filled with warm water, into which she'd dashed a little washing up liquid, wringing out the cloth she'd been using to wipe out the mud stains CJ had left on her beloved carpet. She was stressed that the mud was on the carpet and that she was having to scrub it out. She was also realising for the first time the amount of work that was likely going to be involved in maintaining the new carpet she had believed she'd loved with all her heart, and it was nothing to do with her being a workshy person, because she was not. Had she been a workshy person, she would never have been able to survive her childhood, survive living with Mrs Skerrit. That woman had her up every morning from cock crow; working, cleaning, cooking, fetching water from river, all before she'd even begun getting ready for school, before she'd washed and dressed herself and had her breakfast and set out on the long walk to get to school. *That* had been hard work. By comparison, keeping her glorious shag-pile clean was a breeze, a wing on a long-legged fly, even less than nothing. She wasn't daunted by the amount of work involved. What did concern her was the bad feeling the additional work already had and might continue to create. On a daily basis, because she was busy taking care of the kids and the house and the shopping and cleaning and cooking and her husband, all the washing and ironing and tidying of his clothing as well as the household's, all in addition to holding down a full-time job – like Clyde himself was doing – it was so much work that naturally she'd had to delegate tasks out to other able-bodied people in the house. She and the girls worked very hard as a team to keep the house spotless and no one who'd ever visited them could say they'd met the place dirty. But whereas, normally, no one really dared challenge her authority, there was a great wave of anti-white-carpet sentiment rising, a mutiny. Clyde hadn't seen why the once-a-week hoovering routine he shared with CJ needed to be increased to daily hoovering when frankly he hated the white carpet and could see no reason for a busy household to have such a thing on its floors. He'd argued that when he came into the home he lived in, he wanted to relax, not to start worrying about whether he was going to make a mess, not for him and CJ to be dragging the hoover out every time anyone ate a biscuit and hoovering the whole ground floor, all because of her hard-headedness which meant that despite the fact no one else in the house wanted white carpet, she'd gone and bought the blasted thing anyway. Now with his crazy behaviour earlier, Ellen was questioning herself.

The cleanliness of her home was something she took great pride in. She'd been raised by Mrs Skerrit, who'd been houseproud, then worked hard by her mother who'd been houseproud. In Ellen's mind, being houseproud had become virtually synonymous with being female and having a home. So when she saw the white shagpile strip stretched across the window of the flooring shop, she felt she had seen the carpet that had been put on earth for her home, so much so that even the price tag hadn't phased her, shocking as it might have been attached to any other carpet she'd had an interest in. She'd thought there could be no greater demonstration of how clean her home was and how well she performed as a wife than having spotless white carpet in the hallway, up the stairs and in the front room, but while focusing on the amount of happiness it would bring to her, she hadn't given any weight to the unhappiness it would bring to everyone else in the house.

That was one of the trains of thought she was

ruminating over while hand-cleaning the carpet, but it wasn't the source of her tension.

Her tension stemmed from the fact she felt she had put her mouth on herself and challenged providence during her angry exchange with Clyde, and that had made her fearful. She wasn't a religious woman, but she was a superstitious one. She'd never opened a bottle of alcohol without shaking a little off the top of the bottle for the jumbies, had never cut any of the children's hair before they could speak or eaten meat on Good Friday, and if any child bent over and looked back at her between their legs she immediately topped up Clyde's supply of French letters and stopped allowing him to go bareback even for *just a bit* no matter how hard he pleaded. She feared one spirit especially and she respected the rest and the ancestors, those ghosts of her people past whose lives had been both good and terrible and whose mischief reflected that, whose attention in general it was best to avoid through words and deeds and who should never be provoked or challenged or given reason to pay her special notice. Yet that was exactly what she felt she'd done. She focused intently on not thinking about her mother, whose passing had been so hard, filled with so much anger and resentment, and whose spirit she had changed her name back to evade.

She dropped the cloth into the basin and stood up, clumsily, the heel of one foot coming down close enough to the basin that it tipped and almost spilt its sludgy brown contents over the carpet. The fright was a powerful jolt in Ellen's chest and she bent down like lightning, catching the edge of the basin, righting it, preventing the spill, feeling like she had successfully averted disaster. She hoped she had, and all of it, that the consequences of the mischief had been stopped, maybe even nullified. She picked up the bowl before it found another opportunity to put her theory to the test, carried it straight to the bathroom and poured the contents down the toilet then flushed it. She watched the water swirling, getting lighter, leaving the bowl clean. She turned the basin upside down in the bathtub to drain, then washed her hands. Maybe it would all be okay. There was reason to be hopeful. As she dried her hands, she felt the tension return and continue to build.

Clyde's walk back down the path towards the car was buoyant. He opened the driver's side door, smiled at the boys and said, 'Ready to eat?'

He jumped into the car and put the key into the ignition and turned it. Clay sat quietly in the middle of the back seat, aware he'd made his dad angry enough to shout at him twice in one day, determined not to provoke him into doing it a third time. He felt funny when his dad shouted at him, like he wasn't loved, even though he knew it was silly because mums and dads loved their children, even when two of their children were boys and they had already loved the first one for a long time before the next one had been born. He knew his mum loved him the same as his sisters and brother and sometimes he thought she loved him even more because she was kinder to him than she was to the others and hardly ever told him off. But he also knew CJ was his dad's favourite. Everyone knew CJ was his father's favourite because they were always talking together and laughing together and his dad never shouted at his brother, ever. He understood why everyone loved CJ, because he also loved his brother, who was smart and funny and fast and always played with him and hardly ever got bored and never ever shouted at him and because of that Clay loved his brother very much. It wasn't that he wanted his dad to love CJ less, he just wanted his dad to love him as much.

His dad's Cortina drove through the streets as smoothly as the wheels turned on the Matchbox car he'd taken out of his pocket, the top of which he held with the fingers and thumb of one hand while he held the other hand up as straight as the zebra-crossing lady's hand that stopped the cars so he could cross the road safely to get to the school gates, and he was sliding that palm down along the base of the car so the wheels spun as fast as his dad's Cortina but he stopped because he realised his dad and CJ were having a conversation and they were deliberately whispering so he couldn't hear what they were saying. He pulled himself forward so that his bum was perched on the edge of the seat, his head virtually between them both, but then his dad noticed him and stopped speaking.

Clyde's mood was jubilant. His brief meeting had gone very well, with Francesca accepting all his terms and just looking relieved that he had come round and brought some money, and that he intended to continue doing that so she wouldn't have to manage on her own. Without the stress of wondering what the hell he was going to do about her having his child, he was able to be a bit more relaxed with her and he couldn't help noticing how attractive she was. It occurred to him that visiting her on a regular basis in the future could turn out to be quite a pleasure. Ahead of Clyde, the traffic lights at the junction were green and his side of the road was clear, so he put his foot down, anticipating he could beat any change of the lights from the distance he was away from the junction. The boys were starving, and when he thought about the morning he had had, he felt bad he'd spent so much of it preoccupied by his own problems: missing CJ's goal, acting like a crazy madman with Ellen, shouting at Clay and stalling lunch till everyone was ravenous, including himself. He needed to make it up to everyone. The traffic lights changed to amber and he increased the weight of his foot on the accelerator, still confident he could clear the junction before they turned red.

He felt a tapping on his shoulder and turned his head. Clay was holding his Porsche out to Clyde and had he not already shouted at the boy, he would have shouted at him then. Instead, his earlier behaviour made him indecisive. He glanced from the Matchbox car to Clay's face in confusion.

'Dad! Look out!' CJ shouted.

Clyde jerked his head around in time to see that a van that had been headed in his direction on the opposite side of the road – and which had not been indicating, so should in theory have been travelling straight ahead – had already started turning right at the junction and was almost completely side on to his vehicle, which was travelling over sixty miles per hour; and although he knew instantly, instinctively, that he would not be able to avoid crashing into it, he slammed down hard on the brakes and heard the screams of locked tyre against tar combine with those of his boys as the Ford Cortina came to a violent stop in an explosion of crushing, grinding metal and shattering glass, plunging into the side of the van with such force he felt the rising of the back of the car, then the hard bounce as it forcefully dropped back down onto the ground, the impact of which sent him up into the air as effectively as an ejector seat. He felt the whack of the top of his head against the ceiling of the car and then nothing.

A cool breeze made him aware there was something wet on his face and he opened his eyes. He looked over at CJ who was unconscious, on his knees in the footwell, his body slumped over the seat. He reminded Clyde of the ragdoll Ellen had bought CJ in Montserrat just before they'd left to come to England. It had been made of calico, smartly dressed in a snazzy blue jacket with yellow waistcoat and bow tie. Its mouth was a semicircle crimson strip. Its surprised eyes were made from large white buttons with smaller black buttons sewn on top. Ellen had bought it at the general store in town, the only shop there that sold toys, because there was little call for toys to purchase when almost all the working adult population had had to leave the island and their kids behind in search of making enough money for their families to live on. The ragdoll had been stuffed with paper or straw or some such and nothing rigid inside that could support it to stand, so was floppy as anything. Clyde turned his head, aware that someone was banging on his window, and he found himself facing a shouting man whose words he could not hear, though he observed the man was fighting with the door to open it and it appeared to be stuck.

Clyde knew he was forgetting something, but for the life of him he couldn't remember what that was till another man climbed onto the bonnet of his car reaching towards some clothing strewn messily across it. The windscreen was so clear it was as if he wasn't looking through glass at all but out from inside the car without any kind of filter. He watched as the man put his hand onto the clothes then turned around and shook his head at another person just out of Clyde's line of vision. He saw a mother on the pavement, her hands on the handles of a pram, standing still, looking at the vehicles, crying. The man on the bonnet got off, bent down and picked up a small green car, and Clyde realised what he'd thought had been a pile of clothes was more than that, much much more, and though he still couldn't hear anything, including himself as he began to speak, he began to call out over and over again, 'Cassius!'

Birth Day

May 1972

(Six years earlier)

Although Ellen pressed her lips together as hard as she could, her contraction was so intense she couldn't stop herself moaning with the wave as it grew, only becoming quieter the moment its peak began to wane, immediately consoled and grateful again that the worst of another one was over.

'Deep breaths,' said Sister Hardy, 'You know the drill.'

Sister Hardy was an ancient-looking woman who Ellen assumed was younger than she appeared. Her midwifery uniform and cap made her look like a nun, though she was nothing like the stereotype of a sweet and kindly nun at all. She'd been with Ellen for the past three hours and despite Ellen's initial impression, she was now of the opinion that Sister Hardy was particularly lacking in warmth. She was the reason Ellen had been fighting to deliver her baby as quietly as possible, even though such a thing was impossible in her mind, because although the sister hadn't said anything explicit, she'd left Ellen with the distinct impression she thought she was exaggerating about how painful her contractions were. When they'd met, Sister Hardy had boasted she'd delivered hundreds of babies, and despite the coldness of her manner even then, it had comforted Ellen knowing she had the help of someone with so much experience when she felt so vulnerable, her backside out of doors in the flimsy hospital gown with its thin strings tied loosely at the top of her spine, and wearing no underwear of course, because the last item of clothing you needed to have on when you were giving birth was your drawers. She was lying on her back on a bed, the upper half of which was elevated just enough to allow her a clear view of the stirrups either side of its base, and despite her skill at ignoring issues she did not wish to explore, they were a stern and constant reminder that at some point her legs were going to be expected to mount them.

This was her fourth experience of being in labour, yet it was and had been so different from the other three that Ellen felt as bewildered as if it was her first time, like nothing of her previous experiences could be salvaged to ease her fear and uncertainty. For the first thing, she had been perfectly heathy and well throughout her first three pregnancies, but this time around she'd developed hypertension and because of that, the doctors had decided she should be induced as it was safer for both her and the baby if she gave birth at thirty-eight weeks instead of the normal full-term forty weeks around which all her previous labours had started of their own accord. Secondly, each time previously she'd laboured then given birth at home, but this time she'd been admitted onto the ward two days before being induced, which they had said was to give her an opportunity to relax before the labour began, but had in fact given her ample time to worry about what was going to happen, which was surely part of the reason her blood pressure had not gone down. Despite all the tablets and constant monitoring, it had remained at a level that was high enough to be of concern.

Her first three babies had been delivered at home by young Mary Sweeny, who had trained at the Kingston Public Hospital in Jamaica. When Ellen thought about it, the weather had made such a difference, all that hot bright sunshine in Montserrat that she had taken for granted while she'd been living there, that no one ever spoke about, which was so consistent every day that if you'd been walking around talking about it constantly people would've thought you had a screw loose or if, like her, you were a returnee from England and so had lost your status as a fully indigenous Montserratian, would have said you had snow on the brain. She had laboured with all three of her previous pregnancies under roaring sun. Sister Mary had encouraged her to move around, to go outdoors where the blue of the sky was so intense and the green of the tops of the coconut and palm trees and the wild bamboo were crisply defined against it. The breeze whipped the treetops as the lush foliage about her whispered and crackled. There was something very natural about being outside trying to manage her labour pains, feeling the sun beating down, warming her, experiencing the cooling western breezes as she paced and tried to massage her lower back with her fingertips splayed over the base of her spine; while the birds sang and crickets chirped and mountain chickens croaked and the mouthy cockerel crowed intermittently as he went about his business. There, the sounds of her moans and cries had been a part of those other natural sounds and she could walk or sit or move around as she liked. Though there had been a bed in the bedroom on which she could have delivered her babies, it was the sideboard she had used, placing her palms onto it as she leaned into the strength of her arms to spread the weight of her pain, or resting her bottom on the edge of it while waiting for a contraction to pass or a baby to come, so different to her current experience of being forced down on her back on a bed like a beetle staring up at the stark electric strip that cut across the centre of the ceiling, or at the tops of the heads then the faces of the medical staff as they raised their eyes from the activity between her legs. Yes, this was very different indeed. And much harder.

 Then she wondered whether the difference in country, temperature and midwife was all that was to blame. Her awareness of this pregnancy had landed upon her out of the blue like a rock. She hadn't actually realised she was pregnant till it had been pointed out to her two days before they were due to collect the girls from Tilbury Docks, by which time she was already five months pregnant, so hadn't visited her doctor in that time to tell him, nor had she let Clyde or anyone else know she was expecting – including herself – and it was the last thing on her mind when Wilhelmina passed by and casually asked, teacup halfway to her lips, 'So when's it due?'

Wilhelmina's forthrightness had not shocked her. She'd always known her friend spoke her mind and didn't fancify her words, ever since the time years back when Wilhelmina was renting a room in their home and had told Ellen Clyde had been having an affair with another woman. She'd told Ellen that in life there were some men who were habitual liars and her husband Clyde was one of them, so it didn't surprise Ellen that when Wilhelmina noticed her protruding stomach she'd come directly to the point and asked about it. What had shocked Ellen was the power of her own mind to block out anything she didn't want to think about.

Of course she'd noticed she'd had no period but she hadn't worried because her periods had stopped before, in the six months before her mother had died, after she'd been diagnosed with the sickle cell, back in the days when it was so rare and unknown a condition in England that her mother was little more than a guinea pig to the doctors treating her illness, a subject for experiments into pain tolerance and management. Like Sister Hardy, for some completely unfounded reason, the doctors were united in their belief she was exaggerating the amount of pain she was in and also about how ineffective the pain medication was. Once, during her mother's last winter, Ellen had been present at a shift handover a few days after her mother had been admitted onto the hospital ward and overheard the matron explaining to the team who were taking over that what the coloured patient was after was the stronger and more potent medicines, which could not be prescribed on account of the newcomers from the Caribbean being more susceptible to addiction. This meant her mother had been in unbearable pain in the months leading up to her death, excruciating, discharged from the hospital to manage as best she could at home – which she couldn't – and as a consequence was always angry and in agony and Ellen was the only person around to take it out on. During that time her periods had stopped, so when her periods had stopped this time, she assumed it was because she was stressed out. It had been an intense and terrible two years.

It all began in 1970 when they received that awful phone call. They'd arrived in England in 1967 so had been there for three years by then, both of them in theory working towards sending for the girls, but the truth was sending for the girls was not Clyde's number-one priority. They were living with Gran-gran, his grandmother, their great-grandmother. (Gran-gran would have preferred to have CJ, as her spirit took more to the boys than the girls, but Ellen had fought to leave the girls instead.) In Clyde's mind, they were being taken care of just as well as if they were in England being taken care of by him, so he didn't see the issue of them being sent for as a matter of any real urgency. When Ellen's mind ran on the matter, she realised he'd never spent the time with them that she had. She'd been on her own for the bulk of those three years she lived with her children, her babies all the time about her; in arms, on lap and back, sitting beside her, asleep against her, crawling over her. She missed waking to them smiling down at her, dribbling on her, breathing their laughter into her face. She had enjoyed taking care of her brood, loved that time, missed the girls.

Clyde was working in the building trade as a labourer – hard, dirty, heavy work, with his hands and feet so frozen inside his boots and gloves that he could hardly feel or move them. The work wasn't guaranteed, which meant his pay wasn't either, leaving them scraping by some weeks and broke others. The remainder of the small inheritance Ellen had come into after her mother died was just about enough to be able to put down a small deposit on a house, but they needed a steady and reliable income in order to get a mortgage to cover the rest, which they didn't have. Predicting how much money they would have week to week was one problem. The other problem was that left to his own devices, Clyde would merrily spend every penny he earned on himself: on horses, drink and weed, going out, living the high life, buying himself ridiculously expensive clothes that she had to admit he looked sweet in, but he was looking sweet while they were living in a rented room in a house where they were sharing the toilet with eleven other people and having to queue up to cook on the stove which had been set up on the landing. While Clyde was bussing style, they were having to argue with the facety man in the room next door to theirs who somehow always knew when they had topped up the gas meter and managed to get into the bathroom ahead of them and use up the hot water they'd just paid for.

While her husband was content to live like that indefinitely, seemed used to it in fact, Ellen wasn't, and it was she who kept her ear to the ground and sent Clyde out to apply everywhere for proper full-time work with decent pay whenever she heard of a vacancy, including at the sorting office, again and again till finally, eighteen months after their arrival in England, Clyde got a job there. One year later they moved into their very own property, a dilapidated three-bedroomed house so run down they'd had to rent its rooms out to raise the money to do it up, bit by bit; sort out the damp and the mould and drafty windows, fix the roof and decorate the place, which was in such a state of disrepair it swallowed up every penny of the income from their lodgers as soon as they received it. Then finally, as the house became liveable and financially things began to calm down, just when Ellen thought she might be able to relax from what had been years of relentless financial stress, Cassius rang Clyde and told him Junior was missing.

Ellen had been enjoying the unaccustomed luxury of a leisurely bath when the call came through. She was sure she'd heard Clyde come in from work but the phone continued to ring so she had been on the verge of getting out of the bath when Clyde finally answered it. Then as she'd been about to sit back down, she picked up on the shock and disbelief in Clyde's voice, so she got out of the bath anyway and dried herself then went downstairs into the hall where she found out Junior had been missing since the day before, when he went to the shop to pick up some groceries and didn't come back. They'd spoken with his friends, retraced his steps, searched everywhere they could think of and notified the police. For months after that call, every time the phone rang she expected it to be further news, good or bad, but that just didn't happen, which was even worse.

As a mother, she could imagine nothing worse than not knowing where her children were, or that they were safe. Despite Clyde telling her that Junior had been living with his mother and father when he vanished, even though that was true, Ellen wanted her children close so she could *see* they were safe with her own eyes and keep them that way. In the period that followed Cassius's call, they had some of the worst arguments of their marriage about Clyde's earnings and how he was spending it, with him arguing to keep hold of the money he was working hard for and continue to give her housekeeping, while she'd insisted he hand all his pay over to her, and together with her wages from the Heights, they would work out the household expenses and how much was needed to cover that and also to save towards sending for the girls by the date they'd agreed, which Ellen decided would be a year later, in January 1971. Out of the small remainder of their joint pay, Ellen gave Clyde a weekly stipend for him to do with as he pleased, though in his view, it wasn't enough to do hardly anything he pleased. Nonetheless, reluctantly, Clyde surrendered his pay to Ellen, who took charge of the family finances, and they began to save in earnest.

*

As her contraction began, Ellen knew this one would be different, like waves rolling onto the beach one after the next, all pretty much the same size, the rhythm broken up every so often by a big one, and as the pressure to be silent overwhelmed her, her eyes filled with tears.

'Tears won't help you now,' said Sister Hardy, 'Deep breaths!'

'I'm in pain,' Ellen said and tried to say it without sounding as though she was blaming Sister Hardy, as she was hardly in a position to be getting into squabbles with the midwife who had the power to help or hinder the process. She wanted the midwife assisting her to be on her side, not against her.

'Of course you're in pain; you're in labour.'

'Please, give me something,' Ellen said, 'Help me.'

Sister Hardy handed her the mouthpiece for what she had called *the laughing gas* when she'd given it to Ellen earlier, when her contractions had been less severe and the gaps between each one wider, and though Ellen hadn't cracked even the weakest smile after inhaling it then, she grabbed ahold of it and sucked at the mouthpiece like a drowning woman, hoovering the laughing gas down till the contraction peaked and she noticed how hoarse and sore her throat was becoming and stopped. As she pulled the mouthpiece away from her face, she realised a round middle-aged woman had entered the room, parked her tea trolly near the door and was now approaching with a cup of tea and two biscuits on the edge of the saucer, and though the contraction had not yet entirely ended, Ellen couldn't help noticing she'd not just left the delivery room door ajar behind her, she'd left it tear-back.

'Hallo sunshine,' said the tea lady, smiling at Ellen. 'Just leave this here for you.' She put the beverage down on the unit beside the bed. 'Your first?'

'You'd think so. It's her fourth,' Sister Hardy said to the tea lady.

The tea lady slowed then stopped near the end of the bed, making little effort to conceal the fact she was trying to peer between Ellen's legs.

'May I ask what you're doing?' Sister Hardy asked.

'Just looking.'

'For what?'

'The tail.'

'Sorry?'

'You know. The tail the coloureds have.'

'You may go now,' Sister Hardy said.

'Only wannid to see what it looks like,' the tea lady said, blushing as she stomped back towards her trolley, pushing it towards the door.

'Silly woman,' said Sister Hardy under her breath. Then she turned to Ellen, who hadn't realised her tears were rolling down her face, and said, 'Cry all you want, missy. You know how you got here.'

Ellen couldn't recall ever feeling so wretched in her life. About everything. Being in labour when she'd already decided six years ago that her family was complete and she didn't want any more children. About having to give birth in hospital. About the completely unsympathetic midwife who was experienced and efficient but not in the slightest bit human. She was crying because she was suffering and in pain and Sister Hardy thought she was deliberately making a fuss over nothing, the midwife who'd boasted she'd birthed many hundreds of babies; how was it possible she didn't know giving birth was painful, apart from when you were asking her for pain relief? At which point she used the fact it was supposed to be painful to justify not helping you. Of course Ellen knew giving birth was painful, but that didn't mean the midwife was exempted from providing anything, including patience and kindness, which at that moment would go a long way. She was crying because people were walking past the door the tea lady hadn't closed on her way out and could see her in a state of undress and indignity and, if their eyesight was especially good, would also be able to see the finished result of the close shave the auxiliary nurse had given her when she'd been admitted to the delivery suite. But most of all she was crying because Sister Hardy was right, she knew exactly how she'd got here.

Once the matter of Clyde's earnings and their savings had been resolved, Ellen and Clyde got into the stride of their new financial plan. Clyde's overtime at the sorting office paid handsomely, but unfortunately there was hardly any overtime available and when there was a system of management favouritism prevailed which meant it was only handed out to a select few people. It wasn't fair, Clyde had said to Ellen, then added with a shrug, 'But I can't do nothing about it.'

This meant that the person who'd had to do the overtime – and as much of it as possible – was Ellen, and at the Heights there was as much overtime available as Ellen wanted. However, because of CJ, she only took extra shifts at the weekends when Clyde would be able to look after him; night shifts, because they were longer than day shifts – twelve hours – and the hourly rate was a bit higher because of the unsociable hours. It was particularly hard because she was still holding down her full-time job during the week and, although Clyde picked CJ up from school each day, it was Ellen who was still responsible for the cooking and the laundry and, apart from the hoovering, the rest of the housekeeping, so her enduring memory of that time was one of tiredness, though she didn't complain and nor did she balk at working seven days a week, reminding herself every time she was exhausted enough to cry that every hour of the work she was doing brought them closer to her goal of getting the girls back, counting down the days till January 1971 when they would finally have enough saved to be able to send for them.

It was during that period that Ellen noticed a fundamental difference between herself and Clyde. She was sad most of the time. Her sadness was the by-product of her empathy for her in-laws and Junior, who continued to be missing, and the ongoing separation from her daughters, which was further heightened once a week when the two families spoke on the phone and there was no new information, no leads being followed up, just a deeper sense of foreboding and heavier pain. It was rare that she managed to shake the heartache off completely even when she was at work, no reprieve when she was with CJ. In fact being with CJ reminded her terribly of the girls' absence and of Cassius and Shola's devastating loss. Clyde, however, was only melancholy in the run-up to those weekly calls, while they were on the calls, or during moments when Junior's disappearance was brought up, usually by friends asking for updates. Outside of that, he functioned quite normally, drinking, smoking, making merry, joking, laughing, trying to cheer Ellen up, making her laugh despite her feelings. It wasn't that Clyde wasn't impacted – she believed in the authenticity of the unhappiness he did experience, could see it clearly on his face – it was more that somehow he seemed able to compartmentalise those feelings, something she was unable to do.

Her constant underlying sadness resulted in her being entirely financially disciplined, and their savings had been on course up until they received an overseas call from a devastated Cassius in November 1970 letting them know his wife, Shola, had passed away following a heart attack. Ellen packed their bags and bought their tickets and along with CJ, the family had flown out to Mississippi to give support to Cassius and to help him organise the funeral. It had been the right thing to do and Ellen would never suggest otherwise, but that trip wiped out their savings which meant bringing the girls over the following January was impossible. After months of hard grafting, financially, they were right back at square one and as there had been no change with overtime at the sorting office, Ellen rolled her sleeves up and began to take as much overtime at the Heights as she could physically endure.

That period in Ellen's life had been the only time her wages outstripped Clyde's. She worked every Friday and Saturday night and would stay on after her regular shifts during the week whenever she could get the hours. She was grateful Clyde was able to pick CJ up from school when she was working, but the issue of the same people getting overtime at the sorting office persisted. Wilhelmina had moved out by then but was only living down the road. Though she was working full time herself, she still stopped by regularly during the week to put on the food that Ellen had seasoned and prepared the night before, so that Clyde and CJ were able to have a proper homemade dinner served to them at a decent time, and it was also Wilhelmina who had been the biggest help in stripping down then decorating the bedroom that had been hers, which Ellen had decided to prepare for the three children to share once the girls arrived. That time had been the busiest and most stressful period of her life on the work front; and on the marriage front, the period during which she came to accept that Clyde would be Clyde and there was nothing she could do to change him.

When Ellen came to, another contraction had begun to build and she was astonished to realise she had managed to fall asleep in the middle of labour – or passed out perhaps? – that possibly the 'laughing gas' had been of some benefit after all. Sister Hardy was standing at the bottom of the bed next to a mobile caddy that had been in the corner of the room earlier and now had on top of it a shiny collection of what looked like instruments of torture, and she was speaking to a white-gowned doctor, the two of them so engrossed in the details in Ellen's medical file they hadn't noticed she was awake. The conversation was whispered, which, combined with the gleaming array of polished metal on the caddy, filled her with fear. She sat up. Immediately the sister walked over and put her palms flat against the tops of Ellen's breasts, pushing her back down into a lying position on the bed.

'You'll be up after you've delivered this baby, my girl,' Sister Hardy said.

'Mrs Fenton,' the doctor said, flicking through the pages in Ellen's file without looking at her, 'Sister Hardy has informed me you are not being very cooperative.'

The sister stared accusingly at Ellen as she said, 'This has been going on for the last five hours. She's holding the baby in. I've seen it before.'

As Ellen panted through the contraction's peak, the doctor peered at her over the frame of his glasses. 'The longer this goes on, the greater the danger to your baby,' he said, then added slowly, 'Do. You. Understand?'

Ellen nodded, and though she was trying not to cry, she could still feel the tears running down her cheeks, and with hardly a pause between this new one and the last, another contraction began to build. 'I'm trying my hardest,' she said.

The doctor lifted the forceps and held them up for

Ellen to see. 'If you don't make some progress soon, we'll be forced to use these. I'd rather we didn't have to, but it's our duty to protect your baby,' he said.

'Doctor, please,' Ellen said, 'Let me get up.'

She'd been mobile during her three labours back home. Each time she'd been the only heavily pregnant woman outside walking up and down, but other folk had passed by, including other women, and it had been nice, reassuring, more like what was happening was a regular part of life and less a surgical procedure or something that needed to be done away from the rest of the population, behind doors closed so firmly even Clyde could not be admitted – unless of course he'd wandered along by chance while the door to the room of her confinement had been left tear-back by the tea lady who'd been so desperate to spot Ellen's tail. When she was in labour with Claudette, the woman who lived above her place came down, probably because she knew it was Ellen's first time and that apart from the fact she'd have a baby at the end of it, she really had no idea what to expect. Mrs Molyneux had come down with some food she'd cooked for Ellen so she didn't have to worry about sorting food out later. Ellen had been outside, scared because young Mary Sweeny hadn't yet arrived, wondering if she would have to give birth to her baby on her own, hands pressed against the trunk of a palm, her weight on her arms while she waited for the contraction to wane, and Mrs Molyneux put her dishes onto a ledge cut into a rock beside her, placed one of her hands onto the small of Ellen's back and said, 'Don't fight it. Let it pass.' As the contraction built, she began to gently massage that spot, and she massaged that spot for Ellen during three labours, and it truly felt as though Mrs Molyneux had been blessed with healing hands which had made her labour more tolerable.

For years afterwards, just thinking about that moment was enough to bring Ellen to tears. It wasn't that Mrs Skerritt had been cruel to her when she was a child. Ellen's upbringing wasn't dissimilar to that of most of the children she knew. Most of those kids were in the same boat, parents off somewhere else in the world trying to earn enough money to make ends meet, being looked after by family or friends, some of them in a better position than hers, some worse. Only a few of the children she went to school with were privileged enough to have one or – even rarer – both their parents raising them, but for the most part, even those children had not been spoilt and when she used the word *spoilt*, she didn't mean facety, as back home children generally knew their place and there was every chance that rudeness might have got you a beating from the person you were rude to, followed by another beating when whoever was looking after you inevitably found out about it. When she used the word *spoilt*, she meant they hadn't been tossed in the air like Clyde had done with the girls when they disembarked at Tilbury Docks. They hadn't been massaged and caressed, and it wasn't because of a lack of love, because they were loved. It was more to do with the fact of being raised by adults who themselves hadn't been tossed in the air or massaged or caressed by their parents, and nor had their parents' parents, or those forefathers and mothers who were their ancestors, which meant that, generations on, they were still learning how to be soft and easy, gentle with each other and on themselves, all things that were so much harder to focus on when money was tight and you and everyone around you was doing little more than keeping themselves afloat. Mrs Skerritt hadn't touched her like that, and her mother hadn't touched her like that. The only person who had touched her like that was Clyde and she hadn't seen him since.

That hand on the back had reached out to her when she needed it most and she was convinced she wouldn't have made it through her first labour without it. Mrs Molyneux; Claudette. Sweet woman. Old. Very old. She'd taken newborn baby Claudette to visit her the next morning and then passed part of every day with her for six months before Mrs Molyneux died. By then she was already pregnant with Joycelyn and during that labour, it felt like Mrs Molyneux had been with her, and then, a year later, like she had helped Ellen through her labour with CJ. But she was definitely not with her now. Perhaps her spirit had been confined to the emerald island she'd lived and died on.

It was because of Mrs Molyneux that she had initially misjudged Sister Hardy when she met her, because she was also old and short, about the same height as Mrs Molyneux, and that had wrong-footed Ellen into thinking they might have had even more in common and that it might not be too bad, this experience of giving birth in a new hospital in a different country where you could go through days made bright by light without feeling any warmth from the sun for months.

As Sister Hardy restrained Ellen the doctor said, 'I'm afraid that's not how we do things in this country.' He scribbled something into Ellen's file and handed it to Sister Hardy. 'Let me know if there are any changes. Otherwise, I'll return after rounds,' he said. 'Hopefully there'll have been some progress by then.'

'Thank you, doctor,' the sister said, then as the doctor made his way to the door, she lifted the forceps he had shown Ellen and began slowly polishing them on her apron. She gave Ellen what felt like a very hard stare as she carefully put them back down. 'We'll have no more messing around from you, my girl. One way or another, we're delivering that baby today.'

Clyde's admission into hospital, into this exact hospital, nine months ago, had happened slap bang in the middle of that incredibly stressful time when it felt like she'd been working every hour of the day and night. Clyde had been admitted because his appendix had burst, but because the man was a habitual liar, when he started groaning and complaining about the pain he was in Ellen had simply assumed he was lying. Retrospectively, she blamed her disbelief on bad timing.

Wilhelmina had phoned her at work to say she'd just seen Clyde walking down the road in the direction of home with a woman who had her arm through his in a way that seemed *very friendly*. The woman was wearing the same sorting office uniform that Clyde wore, which led Wilhelmina to believe it could have been a friend from work and that the whole thing was completely innocent, just that it surprised her he would be inviting friends around in the daytime when he knew the house was empty, and not in the evening when he would be able to introduce his friend properly to all the family. In response, Ellen had told her manager she had a family emergency and needed to leave. As she had hurried home as quickly as she could, what had upset her the most was that over the last year she had been working like a dog. Every extra hour God sent that she could manage to work she did, every single one, and the point of it was to get the girls over here to England, living with her and Clyde and CJ so that none of them needed to worry themselves day to day not just whether the girls were okay but whether they were alive. She had never complained to Clyde that maybe he too could probably find a little extra work, maybe a bit of cabbing in the evenings in the great Cortina Mark 3 that he so worshipped and hoovered and polished and drove around in like it was his religion, had never said to him that instead of bigging himself up and living large, perhaps he could find a little job to help bring in a few extra shekels so that once in a while she could take an evening off to rest; nor had she asked him to do more in the house, to help out with the cleaning or shopping or cooking. No she had not. It was a matter of pride to her that although she was working every hour she could, she had still managed to ensure that neither Clyde nor CJ had ever had to prepare a meal in her kitchen, nor wash a cup, because if there was one thing she knew, no woman would be taking her husband or son and putting them to work in the kitchen while she sat around with her foot raised high taking the piss out of them. That was her decision, and she accepted that.

Nonetheless, she really did have some minimum expectations of the man that she thought weren't too unreasonable, like for example, to not be bringing home any dirty women to soil up the bedsheets she had to struggle to find the time to wash and dry and iron and remake the bed with, to not be doing any kind of nastiness on them so that when she finished her hard day with all its long extra hours and came home too tired to even eat before collapsing into her bed she didn't have to sleep in some other woman's filth. She accepted that even the world's strongest braces could not keep Clyde's trousers up, but she drew a line at him bringing his woman-friends into her home, into her bed. It was the single expectation she had of him.

Normally, she entered her home just like any other ordinary person who hadn't had to rush back from work to check whether their husband had brought another woman into their marital bed, which meant not having to worry about the sound of the key in the lock, then opening the door, stepping through it and swinging it closed behind her so that the noise of it shutting might serve as notice to everybody else in the house she was back. Unfortunately, having Clyde as a husband was not conducive to having a normal life, so on this occasion she slipped the key into the lock as silently as Clyde attempted to when he returned home just before dawn, on the occasions he was merely tipsy so still had sufficient wherewithal to try and quietly sneak in. Then she stepped inside the house, gently closed the door behind her, and, without taking a step away from the front door, took off her shoes. Usually, when Clyde came home from work, he removed his work jacket straightaway and hung it on the first coat hook behind the front door. When Ellen looked up at the coat hooks however his jacket wasn't there, and for a moment she tutted and sighed deeply, annoyed with Wilhelmina for wasting so much of her day. But as she bent down to retrieve her shoes, she heard the unmistakeable sound of a woman's voice laughing, and stopped dead. Angling her head like a meerkat, she realised it was coming from upstairs and not downstairs in the living room or kitchen which were the obvious places a married man might entertain a female guest in his home. The audacity made Ellen shake her head.

She went into the cupboard under the staircase and took out the mop and bucket and leaned the mop up against the cupboard door out of the way. She carried the bucket into the kitchen and opened the chest freezer, then quietly emptied out the bag of ice and pressed out all the frozen cubes in the icetrays into the bucket. She put it under the cold tap in the sink and let it fill slowly so the pipes wouldn't start groaning loudly and alert Clyde to the fact someone else was also home. As it filled, she took out the wooden spoon she normally used for baking, and slowly stirred.

Ellen would never forget the sight of that woman on top of her husband, riding him like a jockey, or the look on her face when Ellen flung the freezing contents of the bucket directly over her, or the scream, louder than any sound Ellen had made throughout her current labour, or the expression of astonishment on Clyde's face as he stared at her, mouth agape in shock, unable to find even a single word to say in his own defence, because for the most part his way consisted of lying to her even when he knew she knew he was lying. This time, he'd been caught red-handed so cleanly no lie could possibly suffice and, consequently, he'd been rendered momentarily speechless. He remained that way as Ellen chucked down the bucket and grabbed the pile of the woman's clothing that had been discarded on the bedroom floor beside the bed, including a grey and very unsexy pair of washed-out drawers, then took them to the window, tore it back and tossed them out with all her might, in the hope they would clear the front garden wall and the nasty woman wouldn't have to hang around the premises retrieving them.

'Ma cloves!' the woman cried.

'Stappit Ellen!' Clyde shouted, though it was already too late.

'Somebody better go fetch,' Ellen said.

'Well go on,' the woman snapped at Clyde. 'S'ma fuckin' uniform.'

Clyde jumped up, grabbed a towel off the back of the door, wrapped it around his waist and ran out of the bedroom, as the woman – Ellen found out later her name was Irene – stood up and pulled the top sheet from the bed, wrapping it around herself. Ellen grabbed the other end of the sheet and began to pull it away from Irene.

'You teef enough for one day a'ready,' she said.

Irene began to howl loudly, released the sheet and jumped onto, then over, the bed, running towards the bedroom door and through it. 'Clyde, help me! Clyde,' she shouted.

The long and short of it all was that once Clyde had given Irene her clothes and she'd got dressed and left and everything had calmed down, Clyde was still holding the towel around him with one hand, but the palm of the other, which had previously been flat against the side of his head in dismay, had moved to the part of his stomach just below his belly button, his face a picture of pain.

The kissing of Ellen's teeth was possibly the longest and loudest she'd ever achieved. 'You must really tek me fe a donkey,' she said, then watched him hobble out of the room, amazed at the breadth of her husband's capacity not only to lie but to make himself the victim of any circumstance; the wotless, shameless barefacedness of the man. If she'd had even a drop less sense, it would have been her comforting *him* after his traumatic experience of being caught by his wife with another woman in his marital bed.

Instead of fixing himself up and coming good, by the time Ellen had collected CJ from school and returned home Clyde was covered in sweat, and his face was flushed as red as if he'd had a skinful. Though he said he was dying she continued to ignore what felt like a very conveniently timed belief till Wilhelmina showed up, hours later, shocked at Clyde's appearance and insistent that an ambulance be called straightaway.

Even when the surgeon shouted at her for not calling the ambulance sooner and told her Clyde needed an emergency operation and it was possible he would die, some part of her still believed her husband was pulling the wool over everyone's eyes in order to avoid taking responsibility for his actions. That was what living with a habitual liar had done to her: stripped her ability to instinctively recognise what was true and what was lies. She waited alone outside the operating theatre, expecting the surgeon to come out and tell her they'd opened him up and, to their astonishment, discovered nothing was wrong with him, that the whole thing was a great hoax, like her marriage vows, like everything Clyde said to her and did, and perhaps because she was in that frame of mind, even when she discovered there really had been a medical problem and that he really nearly had died, her only thought was *good, serves him right*. Now, because of her own hospital experience, which was resulting in her feeling sorrier for herself than she could recall feeling ever, she felt badly about the way she'd treated him while he'd been suffering here – or more accurately, the way she hadn't treated him, seeing as she refused to visit him even once – aggravated as she'd been by what she knew would be the level of his neediness which never translated to faithfulness, his total dependence on her to restore his spirits and optimism when it felt like he was the person putting in the most work to destroy hers.

That's what she found herself thinking about during the hours she sat on her own in the sterile corridor outside the operating theatre, the fact that Clyde had never been faithful to her. Ever. To be fair, she had never asked him to be, but she had harboured some hope that maybe he would reduce the frequency with which he slept around; after all, he had all the nookie a man could want on tap at home. If the excess and easy availability hadn't eroded his energy and the motivation to seek more elsewhere, sheer exhaustion should've stopped him, yet that hadn't happened. He'd never paused or slowed in his cheating on her – though she didn't like to use the word cheating; it made her feel like a victim, and she wasn't a victim, never had been, never would be. It wasn't him sleeping with other women that was the problem, it was his lack of awareness that even though that was what he did and she never really got in his way, she still had feelings and deserved a bit of consideration; deserved not to be a running joke amongst his friends or an object of the pity of the women who knew her, needed him to know there were some boundary lines that should never be crossed, and one of those was sleeping with other women in her bed. But he was who he was. It was impossible to change him, and though this realisation was not new, following on the heels of his terrible act, it made her want to hurt him, string him up and kill him, and at the same time he was possibly dying. Never had she needed to be there for him or hated him more than on that day.

It was during the hours she'd waited on her own for his operation to end that Ellen phoned Cassius to let him know, which she regretted as soon as she heard the elevated panic in his voice and was unable to dissuade him from flying over straight away. When finally the surgeon came out to update her, he said it had been a fight to save Clyde's life. Because of her delay calling the ambulance, his appendix had burst, so they'd also had to treat him for sepsis in the stomach. He said Clyde had been sedated and wouldn't wake for some time, at which point they would have a clearer idea of his prognosis. The surgeon advised her to go home, get some sleep and come back in the morning. When Ellen arrived back home it was almost one in the morning and Wilhelmina was there, still up and sitting at the kitchen table, waiting for the news about Clyde. As Ellen repeated what the surgeon had told her, Wilhelmina made her a gin and tonic that was very heavy on the gin and Ellen had only taken two mouthfuls when she began to cry.

'It's a'right,' Wilhelmina said. 'Mark my words. He's gonna be fine.'

'I don't care about him,' Ellen said.

'Of course you do.'

'He's never gonna change.'

'What's new? You never know who you married to?'

'I don't wanna do this any more.'

'You prefer bring up three kids by youself instead?'

Ellen hadn't thought about the kids. She had only thought about herself and Clyde and his behaviour and how she felt.

'Then stop talking stupidness,' Wilhelmina said.

Ellen didn't say anything else. She put her damp mattress back onto the bedframe, wettest side down, put a layer of bath towels on top of it and beneath the bedsheet, then made back up her bed. She took CJ up from off the settee and put him into it. Then Wilhelmina helped her to prepare one of the beds in the room they had been sorting out for when the girls arrived. Cassius arrived hours later, jetlagged, red-eyed and full of anxiety. Later that morning she took CJ to school, and though she took Cassius to the hospital she didn't go inside to see Clyde on that day or any other time during the following week of his hospital stay.

Perhaps she had been less kind to him than she could have been. To be fair to herself, she'd had little idea what kind of experience he might have had during his stay, whether the tea lady on her rounds might have taken a sneaky peak and mistaken his willy for a tail, no idea what kind of ignorance he might have come up against during his admission, or the degree to which it might have made staying in such an awful place even more traumatic. What's more, she never found out because after he was discharged they never spoke about it. She hadn't given a single thought to his trauma till now, in labour for the fourth time and traumatised herself. And man, was she traumatised. Contraction after contraction and yet her cervix remained only six centimetres dilated. Contraction after contraction and she was no closer to giving birth.

When the doctor returned from his rounds and they hoisted her legs up and over the stirrups so he could do an internal examination himself, the only positive she could take from the indignity of the experience was that the doctor would be able to let the hospital staff know irrefutably that coloured people did not have tails, as there was no doubt whatsoever that had she had one, without even a single remaining pubic hair to provide a wisp of cover, it would have been impossible to conceal. The doctor listened to the baby's heartbeat and confirmed it was not *yet* in distress, so, along with Sister Hardy, they agreed a time for the doctor to return and if she had still made no progress they would begin helping the baby along. In the meantime, Sister Hardy was to have her tea break. Before she left, she insisted again she had seen mothers in labour keep the baby in and she was certain that was happening here and once again Ellen thought it was one of the most ridiculous things she had ever heard, as though babies coming into the world was mind over matter and not a natural process that was as much an unstoppable force of nature as an erupting volcano. She also wondered what the sister could see in her that made her think she, a married woman and mother of three, would want to keep a baby inside herself – if such a thing were possible – and could come up with no answer she felt easy with. Alone, she felt panicked about the possibility of stirrups, episiotomies, forceps and violence, and she wished she had been allowed to have someone with her – not Clyde, who was more likely to faint and need her help than be of use, which is why she'd left him with the kids, though she had little doubt that by now he was probably down the boozer and Wilhelmina was probably babysitting in his absence. No, not Clyde, Wilhelmina maybe, who would have had her back and found words of encouragement to buoy her and who, after she'd given the tea lady a piece of her mind for leaving the room door tear-back, would have greatly reduced the chances of the tea lady feeling she could be so brazen as to search for Ellen's tail. But Wilhelmina wasn't here, and Ellen had never felt so alone. This fourth baby had already been harder to birth than any of the other three and it wasn't yet close to being over. As another contraction began to build, Ellen looked around and grabbed hold of the laughing-gas mouthpiece. It had been ten years since the last time she'd set foot inside a church, but as she gobbled the air down her sore throat with all her might, she began to pray.

'He was sitting up today,' Cassius said.
'I'm happy for him.'
'And askin' 'bout you.'
They were sitting at the kitchen table having lunch, eating the leftover soup from dinner the day before. Cassius was looking at her but Ellen wasn't looking back because she felt too emotional. It wasn't that she hated Clyde – well, actually she really did hate him, but that didn't mean she didn't want him to get better, though she did still want him dead. For the first time in her life she felt something strong that wasn't primarily about someone else, wasn't about Clyde or about the kids or her mother's voice always in her head, reminding her that though a man *had* married her, she could never expect more from him, never expect he would do anything to protect her feelings or prevent her hurt and maybe he had married her because he wanted all that free sex she

made available on tap, maybe that was all he saw in her, all he had ever seen. Leaving him felt like a decision she had made for her own good, not as a wife or mother or daughter but as a woman, for herself, that was what *she* wanted. She still hadn't figured out how she would manage on her own with CJ or ever be able to afford to send for the girls, she only knew what he had done to her was wrong and he had finally crossed a line, even if it was one she hadn't known existed.

'Shame he never thought about me before.'

'My brother's a damn fool.'

'One of us is,' Ellen said. She looked up at Cassius. He looked so much like Clyde, or rather Clyde looked like him, and would look like Cassius looked now in maybe another ten years. First his son and then his wife, the grief was turning his hair near white. He was thirty-four, almost thirty-five, but already looked much older. Then she realised that although she'd thought the eyes of the two brothers were identical before, there was a significant difference, in that there was nothing sexual behind Cassius's, no raking of her body or her breasts as a routine part of taking her in, and she wondered what it would be like to be with someone like that, someone you could trust, a man capable of going out and coming back without even thinking about sleeping with someone else – what that would feel like? Shola had died ten months ago and he wasn't seeing anyone, and as far as she knew, hadn't been with anyone else. Having said that, they did live on opposite sides of the world. How would she know if he did? For all she knew, maybe he'd slept with a different woman every night since. She searched his eyes again and was confident he had not.

Ellen stood up and reached for his bowl. 'You finished?'

'Sure am,' he said, handing it to her.

Ellen took their bowls to the sink, where she put them into the washing-up bowl, turned the tap on, and stood there, her hands sunk into the water as it rose, wondering if she was about to cry, whether she could stop herself.

'That was good. Reminds me of the soup Gran-gran cooked back home when we was boys,' Cassius said. 'Same thing Clyde said. Thought he'd never stop licking that spoon.'

'Don't.'

'S'the truth.'

'I can't do this any more,' she said and, despite her strongest will, she could hear the shaky confirmation in her voice that she was crying.

'He's your husband.'

'Did you tell him that?' A future life with Clyde played out before her eyes, decades spent with the two of them together, filled with happiness of every variety for him and pain and hurt for her. Minute oases of physical pleasure for her and the rest of it nothing but pain and hurt. She didn't hear him cross the room, but she felt his gentle hand as it rested on her shoulder. 'It's too much,' she said as she turned around. As they stood facing each other, Ellen saw understanding in his eyes, compassion. In that moment, it didn't feel like he was looking at her, but like finally, someone was seeing her.

Then Cassius grabbed her, held her and kissed her, and

she was powerless to resist his magnetism and submitted, kissing him back and allowing him to lead her to his room, the spare room where all her children would be sleeping soon and onto Wilhelmina's old bed, and somehow all her clothes were off and he was possessing her and she was mindless, going along with it, lost and overcome by hurt. That was how she'd tried her hardest to remember and frame it. But in reality it was she who had kissed him and he'd said, *no*. Then she'd kissed him again and he'd said *you're my brother's wife*. And she'd replied, *no, I am not*, then physically dragged him by the arm to the spare room where she closed the door and began to undress and he'd said, *you have to go back to him*. She'd answered, *after*, then began to undress him. Then he'd said, *I don't know if I can*, and she'd said, *we'll see about that*.

That was how she'd got here, stuck on her back like a beetle, confident the baby inside her was not her husband's and that the suffering she was experiencing during her labour would be nothing compared to the suffering she would experience till she had suffered enough to put this matter right, not to her satisfaction, but to the satisfaction of the jumbies, the spirits and the ancestors. She was already suffering, already in hell. She deserved to be in labour with contraction after contraction coming without getting any closer to giving birth. She deserved to have Sister Hardy and the nameless doctor torment her, but even if she did deserve it, was she going to wait on her back for them to return and begin to enact the violence upon her they seemed a hundred times more keen on than any form of pain relief? She needed to know if she'd given up entirely.

As another contraction ended, she pulled herself up into a sitting position, turned to the side and dangled her legs over the edge of the bed. She gently lowered herself till her warm feet were on the chilly floor, keeping both hands on the edge of the bed, braced to endure her weight. She felt the baby move, a big movement, like the ones she'd been feeling inside her stomach over the last two months, from the inside out; the baby's head and feet and bum creating mounds and hollows like shifting dunes in sand on the surface of her rounded belly. She was sure it was getting itself ready, must have known, as she did, what they were up against, that their window of opportunity was as small as it took for a cold and unfeeling professional to have a hot cup of tea and maybe a couple of biscuits followed by a trip to the toilet, before returning to recommence indifference in this space into which Ellen was aiming to bring new life. As the contraction grew, she moaned aloud as much as she felt necessary and, ridiculously, laughed. Then she laughed again as the contraction grew, at her little private joke to herself that it wasn't laughing gas she'd needed, it was for Sister Hardy to get out. The urge to push became primeval. For a moment she was transported back to her first labour, wondering if young Mary Sweeny would arrive in time. She was afraid of giving birth alone, which she hadn't had to do during any of her previous pregnancies because Mary Sweeny had always arrived in time and been with Ellen at this point, guiding, encouraging, supporting her. Then she remembered that it wasn't Mary Sweeny who would be returning from her break and picking up those forceps and she began to push. As she did so, she cried out aloud and could swear she felt fingers splayed over the base of her spine massaging her there and a voice saying, *it will pass, let it pass*, and she realised that, at long last, Mrs Molyneux had arrived. On the next contraction, she felt the crowning and when she put her hand down between her legs, she could feel the warm curly hair on her baby's slick head. As she took a deep breath for the push that would deliver it, Sister Hardy entered the room, dropped the cup of tea she was carrying onto the floor, shouted for help and got to Ellen just in time for Clay to be delivered into her hands.

'Good God!' said Sister Hardy, passing the baby to Ellen before rushing around the bed to her collection of tools of torture, returning with a pair of scissors and what looked like misshapen pliers. As she clamped and cut the umbilical cord, Ellen gazed down into her tiny new son's face. He was the image of Clyde. He was the image of his father. Her eyes filled with tears as she hugged him close and said a silent thank you for all his fingers and toes and perfection. She'd been terrified this innocent baby would be made to pay for her transgressions, and the fact he hadn't filled her with a fearful joy. She knew she would have to atone one day, but it would be her who did the atoning, not him. For now, it was over. She wouldn't think about it. Her baby opened his unfocused eyes and she gently kissed his head.

Epilogue

CJ walked up the path past the people gathered in the garden and towards the front door. On the invitations, the family had asked everyone attending to wear something green, and the request had been embraced to such an extent that, at a quick glance, it was difficult for him to distinguish the mourners from the foliage around them.

'The hearse is here,' he said loudly, as he entered the hallway and walked towards Leah, who was standing with Candice and Shani, beside Wilhelmina who was dressed in green from her headscarf down to the New Balance trainers on her feet, and was dabbing her eyes with an emerald handkerchief. CC, on his mother's hip, looked at his dad and began to wriggle.

'You want Daddy?' Shani asked as CC stretched his arms out and CJ smoothly transferred him from her hip to his. He hadn't been sure about inviting Wilhelmina till Shani asked him why she was being held to a higher standard than the man who'd actually been married to his mother, a question which up to now he hadn't answered or recovered from.

'You're in the third car, Mrs W, with Leah and Shani,' he said.

'Thank you,' said Wilhelmina, as she firmly grabbed hold of CJ's hand. 'She would've been proud of you all today.'

CJ embraced her, crushing CC between them both, bewildered by an intensifying aroma of rosewater till he heard the chatter of other people lining the hallway and turned his head to see Linus walking towards him carrying a crate filled with roses of different colours, a pair of secateurs held between the crate and his right hand.

'That smell is crazy,' CJ said.

'Even her plants know,' Linus said, shaking his head. 'Those bushes are loaded, man. Could've easily filled two more crates.'

CJ heard the emotion in his nephew's voice and gently put his hand on his shoulder. 'Leave 'em in the boot for now. We ain't gonna need 'em till the graveside.' He handed his car key to Linus who nodded, took it.

'Where's your mum?' he asked Leah.

'In the kitchen.'

'Can you tell her the hearse is here? And Dumpling. She's probably still outside.'

'Sure.'

Leah walked towards the kitchen which she'd purposely been avoiding because her mum and aunt were in hostess overdrive. She got that it was related to the day, but her own grief was still raw which had left her feeling far too easily triggered. She found them wiping down the already clean surfaces around the biscuits, johnny-cakes and cocktail patties set out in meticulous lines on Granny's best plates.

'Mrs W's here,' Leah said.

'So I heard,' her mum replied.

'Looking like a sprout.'

'Stop it, Auntie.'

'A barefaced Brussels sprout,' said her mum.

'She's Granny's friend!'

'*Was*,' her mum said.

Joycelyn added, 'Till she broke Mummy and Daddy up.'

'Grandad did that,' Leah said. 'And while he was doing it, she still made everyone welcome.'

'This is different,' said her mum.

Though she'd sworn when she woke up she wouldn't argue with them today, she couldn't stop herself. 'No it's not!'

'Mummy's not here to decide,' said her aunt.

'She's still here,' Leah said fiercely, placing her closed fist over her aunt's heart. 'And here,' placing her fist over her mother's. 'And here.' She thumped it hard over her own. It was because of the silence that Leah knew her words had hit home and she noticed again a tiny yet meteoric shift in her relationship with her mother and her aunt that had occurred since her grandmother had passed; occasionally, they seemed able to hear her. She wasn't used enough yet to this new ground to know how to wind the moment back or down, how to smooth things over, make them okay, so she said, 'The hearse has arrived. It's outside.'

'Okay,' said Joycelyn.

'Did you tell Mrs W she's in the car with you?' asked her mum.

'Uncle CJ's told her.'

'Good.'

'I need to let Auntie Dumpling know.'

'Tell her to come here,' said her mum.

'She should be with us,' Joycelyn said.

Dumpling was sitting on Ellen's bench in the back garden staring at what remained of the rose bushes, breastfeeding the new baby. She'd only discovered what Ellen had seen in the garden after she'd died and it was one of the many things she'd had to add to the lengthy list of things she felt guilty about. She'd been switched off, thinking about her biological mother all those years Ellen had loved her, been there for her. She didn't notice Leah's approach till she sat down next to her, leaned against her and put her arm around Dumpling's back so she was cuddling her side-on.

'She was so good to me,' Dumpling said. 'And I never thanked her.'

She felt Leah move so that her head was resting on Dumpling's shoulder. Comforting. The two women remained like that till Dumpling felt the baby unlatch and she began to adjust her clothing.

'Let me take her,' Leah said. She gently separated the baby and her blanket from her aunt, rearranged them to keep her tiny cousin warm and snug. She stood and lifted the baby to her shoulder, gently patting her back. 'The hearse is here. Mummy and Auntie are waiting in the kitchen for you,' she said.

Dumpling hugged her niece, then turned around, walked towards the back door, went inside.

Leah took a step closer to the rose bushes, inhaled deeply, closed her eyes a moment then opened them again when she heard the sound of a burp. She shifted the baby from her shoulder and cradled her in her arms. The baby gazed up as Leah began to rock her.

'Hello, little Ellen,' she said.

Acknowledgements

Every reader who has bought or read or listened to my novels or borrowed them from libraries, thank you. I never take you for granted. You are the reason I write.

Thank you to everyone who has supported me and the writing with chats and discussions and interest and kindness. Also, everyone in the weird and wonderful world of writing who has been part of the ecosystem that keeps me buoyed, those writers I have shared time and space with, those organisations and people who have platformed and helped me in countless other ways, I see and appreciate everything you do. Thank you.

I would like to thank the diligent team at Greyhound Literary Agency, and my agent, Salma Begum, for her passion, vision and steadfastness, and for helping this novel find its way to the brilliant and insightful Anna Kelly and the dedicated team at Virago Press, all of whom have left me feeling like I have landed in my spiritual home.

Shona Abhyankar, thanks for so many unapologetic

too-late nights, the support, advice and laughter. Your friendship means everything. I would like to acknowledge my dear friend Olcay Aniker, valued early reader, for being present over the decades, sharing books and advice, support and allyship. Anni Domingo, you inspire me so much. Thank you for the friendship, for being an early reader, and for your invaluable feedback. I'd like to thank Bernardine Evaristo for being Bernardine Evaristo. Hermina Edwards, I'm so grateful for the time I have spent with you. Thank you for the chats and for being the best mother-in-law I could wish for. Joy Francis, thank you for your friendship and support in all its forms. Elizabeth Galloway, my mother. I could not have existed or been the person I am without you. Jaclyn Griffiths, world record holder for my longest friendship, most thoughtful and supportive writer's friend, and so large a part of everything that has shaped me: I thank you. Thank you, Antonia Hodgson, for your keen eye and efforts to straighten me out. Sally-Anne Lomas. It's no exaggeration to say this book could not exist in its current iteration without you. Thanks for being an early reader, for your friendship and support, for the gentle encouragement and tough love. Lauren Molyneux, thank you for being a valued early reader and for your helpful and constructive advice, superwoman. Irenosen Okojie, really value your friendship, the conferring, laughter and validation; thank you so much. Eva Verde, wonderful woman, thank you for your friendship and support. Much appreciated.

    Danielle, Ella and Hannah. I passed so many years

longing for sisters and now find myself in this era blessed with daughters. You are everything. From early readers to advisors, such great champions of me and what I do, deliverers, somehow, of everything I need. You are witches – no doubt! – my coven, and I love you deeply.

I would also like to acknowledge financial assistance in the form of grants from Arts Council England, the Drusilla Harvey Access Fund, the Royal Literary Fund and the Society of Authors, without which I would probably have given up writing years ago. So, thank you. Very much.